WITH THIS RING

IMP SERIES, BOOK 11

DEBRA DUNBAR

debra dunbar
FIENDISHLY FUN FICTION

I loaded more pancakes onto my plate, layered the top with some gloriously crispy bacon, then drenched the whole thing in syrup. One of the advantages of having Nyalla and Ahia on the Ruling Council was that we actually had decent food now. We'd gone from stale Danishes and the occasional tray of bacon to this lovely buffet of goodies.

Now if only they could provide a better quality of coffee than this watery crap. Hmm, I'd need Ahia to get on that. Once we were to the point of assigning duties in the meeting, I was totally adding that one to her list.

"Are you ready?" Gabriel glared at me. "Maybe we should just drag the buffet over here so you can eat directly from the trays."

The suggestion did have merit, but I wasn't sure about the physical logistics. Should the buffet be between me and the conference table? Beside me? Was my chair high enough to see over the trays? Or even reach them?

I threw a few more pieces of bacon on top of my syrup and headed back to my seat. As usual, I was the only angel with food. Well, aside from Ahia although I still had trouble thinking of her as an angel. She'd been raised among the humans and werewolves and was the most unangelic angel I'd ever met—besides me, that is. I sat and saw Rafael sneak a sausage patty off Ahia's plate, winking at me as he shoved the whole thing into his mouth.

Okay, Raphael was pretty unangelic too, come to think of it.

Gabriel's glare was now alternating between me and his younger brother. "The first agenda item concerns developing a purpose and long-term plan for angels living in this plane of existence since it seems highly unlikely that we will be able to return to Aaru in the next few million years or so."

Which was my fault. Normally I'd make some attempt to look ashamed, but I was done being dragged across the carpet for this one so I shrugged and dug into my breakfast. If I finished my food and they were still on this agenda item, I might get in a little Twitter trolling. It wasn't like I needed to have input on a project concerning angels and whatever goodly purpose the others on the Ruling Council came up with for them.

Uriel spoke up. "Those angels who fought by our side in Aaru are demanding to know when we are to return. Some wonder why they're receiving the same punishment as the rebels. Others are unsure of their purpose here and they have questions. Are they to bring the fight from Aaru to here and eradicate the rebels while they're in corporeal form? Are they to drive the rebels into Hel, and then be allowed to return to Aaru? They are also concerned as to as why we have allowed the demons to seize a portion of this continent."

Raphael sighed. "We need to put together some sort of official communication."

"To do that, we need to decide what we're supposedly

doing here, and whether to tell them the truth about the circumstances of our expulsion or not," Gabriel added.

"That's the primary issue to address," Gregory said. "I think it's time to tell them that there was an unfortunate event during the last battle that has made it so we are unable to return to Aaru."

I winced, knowing exactly how that was going to be received.

"Perhaps we should phrase it as if we are temporarily unable to return to Aaru," Asta said.

"They'll want to know *how* temporary," Uriel warned.

"They'll want to know how it happened," Gabriel drawled with a glance my way.

"I'd rather we not tell," Raphael said. "We'll just end up with our few allies deserting us for our adversaries. I think it's better to keep quiet about that and instead come up with some reason we're all still here—some holy mission regarding the humans."

"In other words, lie." Gabriel sneered.

Uriel sighed. "It *is* the lesser of the evils."

"We can't keep it from them forever," Gregory said. "I think it's best that we tell the other angels that they will not be returning to Aaru, and that we are putting programs in place to allow them to exist peacefully here among the humans."

Asta grimaced. "Some of us are perfectly happy here among the humans, and the rebels must know that they will not be returning to Aaru, but the others? I fear their reaction if they are told they will never go home."

"They'll feel as if they've been unjustly punished," Rafi agreed. "They'll be angry and hurt. They'll want to blame someone."

"And that someone will be me," I said.

"Us as well," Gregory informed me. "They fought by our

sides. We are the heads of their choirs. They will blame us for this as well."

"Not when you're banished too," I pointed out.

"We should put this to a vote." Gabriel shuffled his papers and looked around at each of us in turn.

Ahia lifted her hands. "I know I'm an angel, but I feel unqualified to vote on matters concerning your people. As an outsider though, I agree with Rafi. Let's give everyone some busy work to keep them occupied until you all can find a way to get back into Aaru."

"Busy work that potentially lasts millions of years?" Gabriel scoffed.

"We're angels," Uri said. "Millions of years isn't a terribly long time. And we *have* screwed things up concerning the evolution of the humans. We've got a responsibility to fix that, and, no offense to my older brother, how we've been handling it in the last ten thousand years since the fiasco with the tenth choir hasn't exactly produced the results we wanted."

Rafi nodded. "It's not a good time to have angels fretting over never being able to see Aaru again. Although I agree with Micha that we do eventually need to tell them, now is not that time."

"All those in favor of *not* telling the angelic host about our expulsion?" Gabriel asked.

My hand shot up, because I really didn't want to deal with having every fucking angel on this planet gunning for me. So did Rafi, Uri, and Asta's.

"And for informing them?"

Gabriel and Gregory raised their hands.

Gregory glanced at the two who had not weighed in. "Nyalla and Ahia. Are you abstaining from this vote?"

Ahia squirmed. "As I said, I really don't feel qualified to vote on this matter."

The archangel turned to Nyalla.

"As I'm not truly a member of the Council and only here to represent human interests, I'm abstaining," she told him. "Humans have other concerns right now, and I don't see this as having a major impact on them."

Gregory nodded. "Then let the record reflect the vote. We will not tell the angelic host about the expulsion at this time. At our next meeting, I expect everyone to have at least two ideas as to what holy purpose the angels are here to accomplish. Nyalla, as our representative for the humans, your opinions on these ideas will be especially important. We'll spend the majority of that meeting going over these ideas and in a mind-tsunami session."

"Brainstorming," I corrected, pushing my empty plate away and pulling Twitter up on my phone. Gregory turned his attention to Asta and Nyalla and their state-of-the-human-union reports while I started a rumor about the elves being carriers of an insidious virus that was the root cause of erectile disfunction among Caucasian males ages thirty to sixty. Then I went to various political hashtags and wrote a few incendiary comments. I was just creating a new username to announce the resurrection of Hitler when I heard Gregory assigning some shit to me.

"Can't. Too busy," I told him.

"We are *all* busy," Gregory snapped.

That got my attention. He might lose his temper with me in private, but in Ruling Council meetings, he usually treated me with the respect due my position. I wondered what was going on for him to lose control in a meeting like this. What hadn't he told us? What hadn't he told me?

"Okay, okay. Settle down, asshole. Whatever it is you just told me to do, I'll put it somewhere on my agenda." Which might be in a century or so, but he didn't need to know that.

Gabriel smirked and handed me a paper with a bunch of

names and dates and times on it. "These are the meetings. Make sure you're on time, because I've learned that humans despise tardiness."

He'd probably learned that from Nyalla, because in my experience most humans didn't give two shits about being on time to anything.

The others went on to discuss elves and their complaints about the jobs they were being assigned, the never ending issue with the wild gates, and something about an upcoming human holiday while I continued to spread chaos on the internet. I was in the middle of an incredible argument concerning alleged bigfoot sightings in Upper Manhattan when I realized everyone was staring at me expectantly.

"Huh?"

"You're on a committee with me to negotiate a universal labor agreement between the elves and the humans," Asta informed me.

I laughed. "A labor agreement? Me? You're fucking joking. The elves can work at the jobs they're assigned, and get paid whatever the humans want to pay them, or they can go back to Hel. There. No negotiation necessary."

"This will be the template for labor law between human businesses and non-human employees," Asta explained. I got the impression she'd explained this before, when I'd been busy on Twitter.

"There's nothing to negotiate," I insisted.

Asta began to check items off on her fingers. "Minimum wage. Minimum employment age. Mandatory benefits. Working hours. Breaks. Overtime pay eligibility. Workplace safety. Humans feel they should have a separate set of laws for non-humans. We need to make sure these laws are fair for the companies as well as for elves, goblins, trolls, dwarves, *and* demons who are employed there."

"Who the fuck would hire a troll?"

Asta ground her teeth. "That's not the point."

"The point is that you are on this committee with Asta," Gregory informed me in a voice that made it clear I wasn't getting out of that one.

"Fine." I picked up my phone again, only to realize that everyone was still staring at me. "What now?"

Gabriel let out a dramatic sigh. "We need your report on matters in Hel and New Hell, as well as any issues regarding the demons that are now residing here."

Shit. Was I supposed to prepare something for this meeting? I hoped they weren't expecting handouts or a PowerPoint presentation. Actually, I hoped they weren't expecting much in the way of a report because…well, because I wasn't prepared at all.

"Um…things in Hel are fine," I scrambled for something to announce. "The human settlement there is now receiving regular deliveries of groceries and Amazon Prime. They've put up solar panels."

Amber had relayed all that. She'd made quite a few friends in Hel during the last year and had worked hard with Kirby to make sure they had more than just the bare necessities.

"And?" Gregory prompted.

"Demons are doing good?" I didn't know what else to say. Hel was hell. Over half the Ancients were summering in Aaru, even though they still couldn't find a way to shed their corporeal forms there. The rest of the demons had either decided to remain in Hel, or had crossed the gates to try their luck living among the humans.

"What about the situation in New Hell?" Gabriel demanded.

New Hell was what the humans had called the area we'd designated as belonging to the demons after the Infernal War —which was another title bestowed by the humans. The area encompassed the coastal states in the western part of the United States as well as about half of the western edge of both Mexico and Canada. It wasn't *totally* run by demons. The humans still had some sort of government there. I remember someone saying it was similar to the wild west of lore. Basically outside of some overworked law enforcement professionals, any human with money and a weapon ruled, as well as any demon.

Although given the general affection for sloth, the demons did very little ruling unless they felt particularly motivated to do so. We were all about sensation, pleasure and pain, interesting experiences. Budgets for street repairs and police departments? That wasn't our jam.

"Things in New Hell are fine," I announced.

"The human government is unhappy with the situation," Nyalla told me.

I frowned, vaguely remembering that she'd told me this before. Last week, maybe?

"The US has lost states that contributed significantly toward their economy," she continued. "Also, many of them fled those states during the war, and it was difficult for them to absorb the refugees. They're asking for policy regarding immigration from the area, as well as compensation for the loss of revenue."

Ugh. "Fine. On it."

I so wasn't on it.

"And demons living outside of Hel and New Hell?" Gregory prompted.

How the fuck was I supposed to know what they were doing? If someone brought an infraction to my attention, I teleported there, smacked the demon around, then returned him to Hel with a stern warning. Other than that, I tried to ignore anything my brethren might be doing this side of the gates.

"Good?"

"Your brother has taken over the city of Chicago," Gabriel snapped. "How could you possibly consider that 'good'?"

Dar had taken over Chicago? That fucking rocked. I glanced over at Asta and saw she was studying her manicure. Why was I getting yelled at for Dar's political ambitions when his angel was sitting *right here* at the table with us?

"I'll go talk to him." That I might actually do. I liked Chicago and Lux enjoyed playing with Karrae. Dar and I could go out for some beer and pit beef while Asta, or their dwarven nanny, hung out with the little angels.

"The humans are worried about demons in their nations," Nyalla said.

She was so not helping here. I sighed and put my phone down. That bigfoot discussion was going to have to go on without me.

"All the demons have been told what they can and can't do while here. They know if they break the rules, then an angel can dust them, or worse I'll come and beat the everloving shit out of them and make them clean toilets in Hel or something."

"Humans have to have passports and even visas to travel between countries," Nyalla countered. "They're not comfortable that demons can come and go without any approval. They want a way to control what demons are allowed into their countries."

"Are the angels going to be held to these same standards?" I argued. "Because this is total bullshit. Angels get to go anywhere they want, but demons have to fill out papers and wait for approval?"

I knew how well that was going to go over with the denizens of Hel. No one was going to abide by geographic limits on where they could and couldn't go. And paperwork? Right.

"Actually, the humans feel the same way about the angels," Nyalla said with an apologetic glance toward the others.

Gabriel puffed up in indignation. "We're *angels*. We gave the gifts of Aaru to the humans. We're helping them achieve positive evolution. We're exempt from these travel restrictions."

"The humans don't see it that way," Nyalla replied. "They have sovereignty over their nations. Either the angels abide by their travel policies and procedures, or they'll be seen as hostile invaders."

Now this was a much better topic than the earlier ones. I leaned back in my chair and watched as Gabriel turned various shades of purple. He wouldn't dare get nasty with Nyalla like he would if anyone else delivered that message

"It's going to be rather hard to enforce that when angels can teleport," Rafi pointed out.

Ancients could teleport as well, and so could a few of the higher-level demons. I wasn't about to bring that up though.

Nyalla sighed. "I know. The humans still say they want an approval process and passports for any angel or demon entering their countries. The ones who currently reside there also need to have identification, and they would apply for residency following the same process humans do."

"Everyone should address these matters when they meet with the leaders of the countries on their lists. We'll discuss this in our next meeting as well." Gregory shrugged. "If it makes the humans feel better, we can come up with some identification paperwork, but in reality it won't actually restrict angels, or demons, from coming and going as they please."

Gabriel nodded, then turned to Ahia. "And the werewolves?"

"Although werewolves make up our majority, it's been decided that going forth we are to be called shifters. The new term is inclusive toward those of us whose animal forms are not wolves, as well as the Nephilim who have the ability to take multiple forms and have added abilities."

Gabriel rolled his eyes. "Noted. Anything else to report concerning the shifters?"

"We're meeting with federal, state, and local governments ourselves to propose anti-discrimination laws and other protections. We're pushing back against special identification as many of our kind are not public about the fact that they aren't human. There are fears of targeted violence, as well as both social and economic discrimination."

I yawned, wondering if the bigfoot discussion was still going on.

"Let us know if you need us to help in any way," Gregory told her.

I must have dozed off at that point, because before I knew it, Nyalla was shaking my shoulder. The room was empty. I wiped some drool off my chin and blinked up at her.

"Give me a lift?" she asked.

"Sure." I wondered why Gabe hadn't teleported her back home.

"I called Amber and told her we were done with the meeting. She's going to meet us at your house."

I stretched, not sure why Amber was coming to our house. She did stop by every now and then, especially when she was up visiting Wyatt, but this sounded ominously like there was a specific purpose for her being there.

"Is she staying for dinner?" That was the big question on my mind.

"We might be eating out," Nyalla commented mysteriously. "Now come on and hurry up. The shop closes at five and we need to get going.

CHAPTER 2

"*P*lease?"

Amber's words coiled around me like a warm scented spring breeze. She was good—not as good as her sire Leethu, but still good.

"What do I get out of this?" I grumbled. I had enough shit to do. It was bad enough that I was required to actually sit in a fucking church and attend this bullshit wedding. At least in the pews I could drink booze and torment whoever had the misfortune of sitting next to me. It still wouldn't be fun, but standing up front with Amber and her friends would be even less fun.

"I'll owe you a favor," she coaxed.

I was owed so many favors by this point I'd lost track of them all. I needed an Excel spreadsheet. And an assistant to keep it up to date.

"And?" I should just say "no", but I knew how this was all going to end and it was with me in some hideous fucking dress holding a bunch of flowers. Nyalla was standing next to Amber, staring at me with big reproachful eyes. I could never let my girl down. Her disappointment and disapproval was like a knife slicing through my spirit-self. She wanted me to be in this damned ceremony, so regardless of my protests and negotiations, that's what was going to happen.

Then there was Lux, beside me and holding my fingers in his chubby little hand. Amber had gone over my head to Gregory and our little angel was now the ringbearer—whatever the fuck that meant. Lux was inordinately excited about his role in this wedding. For days he'd been babbling about keeping rings safe and worrying about whether the ceremonial outfit would allow for him to have his wings displayed.

The kid had become obsessed with his wings. They were always revealed, and he'd taken to flapping them, shaking them, and other displays to draw attention to their creamy, iridescent beauty. They *were* pretty. I'll admit if I had wings like that I'd be shaking them in everyone's face too.

Wings weren't the only thing Lux liked to display. He liked being naked. And he'd become as enamored of the dangly bits between his legs as his wings. Gregory had tried to convince him that Angels of Order did not need to manifest sexual organs, but to my delight, Lux disagreed.

He was totally my kid, Order or not.

"A favor, and a standing invitation to stay with Irix and me in New Orleans any time you wish."

Whoa, she *was* desperate.

"It'll be fun, Sam," Nyalla told me. "We're going to have a bachelorette party, and we've got the bride's breakfast before the ceremony. We'll get our nails and hair done, and drink mimosas, then the limo will pick us up and take us to the church."

If this bachelorette party was anything like that horrible bridal shower, then I was going to be otherwise occupied. There was no way I was going to sit through hours of tiny sandwiches and non-alcoholic punch, watching Amber open gifts while her friends squealed in delight. No fucking way.

Lux tugged on my hand and a blur of angel-speech shot through my head. I didn't catch most of it, but I did get the part where he thought I'd be beautiful in a bridesmaid dress, and that he wanted me to be there with him when he performed his ringbearer duties.

I couldn't say no to Nyalla, and I definitely couldn't say no to Lux.

"All right. But the dress better not be ugly."

* * *

THE DRESS WAS UGLY. I had tugged and pulled on the puce satin fabric, but no matter what I did, I was still wearing a puffy, off-shoulder, asymmetrical hemmed monstrosity. I was so going to get drunk before the ceremony. Actually, I might be drunk off my ass from now up until the happy couple were on their honeymoon and I got to burn the expensive frock I was being forced to spend hundreds of dollars on.

And don't get me started on the matching shoes either.

Nyalla and Amber chatted excitedly while I stood on a narrow platform and had some woman stick pins in me for whatever alterations she was planning on doing. It wouldn't matter. There was no seamstress in the world that would make this dress remotely attractive.

We weren't done. After the fitting, we met with someone to discuss hairstyles, and what could be done with my straight, dark hair.

"You're not going to make me dye it, are you?" Amber and Nyalla were blondes and I wasn't sure about Amber's other bridesmaids. I *could* change my hair color myself, but I was oddly opposed to doing so. The soul I'd owned had been a brunette as a human. Yeah, I'd been blonde before and hadn't had any issue changing my shape, size, gender, or even species, but suddenly I felt like digging in my heels on this.

Black wings. Brown hair. I wasn't changing it. And I wasn't wearing a wig either. The fucking puce dress and shoes were enough of an embarrassment.

"Of course not." Amber smiled. "But those of us with long hair are planning on an updo. You can wear yours down if you want."

Huh. I *did* like mani-pedis. And although I occasionally put my hair up into a ponytail or a messy bun, the idea of a complex updo was intriguing. It reminded me of the hairstyles the elves always had.

"And here's our polish." Nyalla held out a bottle that matched the hideous dress and shoes.

Purple was so not my shade, but it was clear my opinion didn't have any weight here. I fidgeted while Nyalla and Amber finished talking to the stylist, relieved when we finally seemed to be leaving. For some reason Nyalla and I had needed to take a separate car. I found out why once we got to the parking lot.

"We've got one more stop before heading home," Nyalla told me once we waved goodbye to Amber.

A half hour later we were parking in front of a coffee shop. A young black woman waved at us from a table.

"Darcie, this is Sam," Nyalla introduced me. "Darcie is Amber's best friend from college and her Maid of Honor. She lives in New Orleans, but flew up to help Amber with wedding planning."

"And while Amber is off meeting Irix about the band for the reception, we're going to talk about the bachelorette party," Darcie added.

Both she and Nyalla squealed, while I wondered if this place had booze to go in the coffee. This wedding stuff was boring as shit. I was beginning to regret agreeing to even attend, let alone be *in* the damned thing.

I strolled up to get two extra-large mochas for me and Nyalla. When I returned, I caught the tail end of a conversation. Something to do with a penis cake.

Now I was interested. "I'm totally onboard for a penis cake," I told them. "I can handle that. Just let me know when and where to deliver it."

"Perfect." Darcie went to scribble my name next to the word cake on her list, and Nyalla shot out a hand to stop her.

"Um, Sam? It's a cake shaped like a penis, not a cake made with a bunch of dismembered male genitals."

Darci looked horrified.

"Well, fuck that," I grumbled. "Can I at least stick a real penis on top of it? For authenticity?

"No," both girls said in unison.

"Maybe I'll assign the cake to Harper," Darcie mused.

I handed Nyalla her drink and sat down. "So what is this bachelorette party really about?" I asked, worried that in spite of the penis cake, it would be just like the horrible bridal shower.

"It's a blast," Darcie told me. "The girls in the wedding party and some of Amber's friends have this big party. We all get drunk, give her inappropriate gifts, and watch a stripper. Sometimes it's at one place. Sometimes we get a limo and drive around to a bunch of bars. It's going to be all about dicks and vajayjays!"

This sounded a hell of a lot more fun than a bunch of us sitting around eating tiny sandwiches and drinking punch while Amber opened gift bags containing blenders, towels, and spatulas. I loved getting drunk. I loved dicks and vajay-jays. I loved inappropriate gifts. Wait…

"A stripper?" Now it was me who was squealing like a teenager.

"He has to be super hot," Darcie said. "What are the laws in Maryland concerning dancers? 'Cause I know someplaces they've got to keep the banana hammock on, and others they can let it all fly free."

I was beginning to really like this Darcie woman, even if she wasn't thrilled about a cake made out of actual penises.

I sipped my mocha and thought of any hot dudes I knew. Irix was smoking, but Amber had seen him naked a gazillion times already. Not Wyatt, because I knew Amber wouldn't dig having her brother as a stripper, and neither would Nyalla. Plus, I was pretty sure he wouldn't do it. Gregory would refuse, and half the time he didn't manifest sexual organs anyway. A stripper with an empty banana hammock wouldn't be any fun at all. Nobody wanted to see Gabriel naked except Nyalla. Rafi would be awesome, but I was pretty sure Ahia was going to be at this party and she wouldn't want her angel grinding on Amber. Uri? Leethu was open about that sort of thing, but I wasn't sure if Uriel would be. Besides, some of the female attendees might not get their rocks off on seeing another woman dance naked and at this time Uri was strictly female in her corporeal form.

"How about more than one stripper?" I asked. Although I was having a hard enough time thinking of even one dude who would fit the bill.

"You're in charge of strippers," Darcie told me. "At least one, but a few more would be awesome. Make sure they're gorgeous, and if the cops raid us, that they'll deny everything. Actually, I'll put you in charge of the venue and the logistics and party favors, since you're here and I'm in New Orleans. It'll be easier that way."

"Party Favors?" I asked.

Darcie grinned. "Fun themed stuff that each attendee can have. Sex toy stuff that you can buy in bulk."

Holy shit, this was going to be the most epic party ever. I couldn't wait. "Strippers. Venue. Food and drink, and party favors. Got it."

"We need a bunch of water guns filled with booze." Darcie tapped her lip with her pen. "I'm not much for straight alcohol, so maybe some sort of shooter?"

"I'll take care of that," Nyalla said. "I'll get some girls together and we'll spend an evening mixing drinks and filling squirt guns. It'll be fun."

"Penis squirt guns," I chimed in.

The girls squealed in excitement. What fun! I was completely revising my thoughts on this whole wedding thing.

"Good." Darcie made a note on her paper. "Sam will handle the location and the food, the strippers and the favors. Hunter will do the cake. Carla is going to do decorations. Heather is in charge of making bracelets for all of us so the bartenders know who is on the tab for our party. Sam will get the squirt guns and fill them with Nyalla and a few volunteers. I'll send out an email to everyone that the gift theme is sex toys—the weirder and kinkier the better. Let's make this wild and funny, girls."

Wild and funny. I grinned. Screw the actual wedding, this bachelorette thing was going to be the event of a lifetime.

CHAPTER 3

I dropped Nyalla off at Wyatt's and returned home to find a dead animal on my front porch. I'd been living among the humans long enough to know that the odds of something crawling up onto my porch and dying were reasonably slim. Besides, this thing looked like it had been dead a long time. Actually it looked like someone had dug it up out of the ground and left it like an offering on my doorstep.

"Boomer!" There was one being in my household that particularly liked dead stuff. My half-demon hellhound was a notorious grave robber, but he did occasionally snack on roadkill. He'd never offered to share before. I wasn't sure why he'd want to this time.

And what *was* this thing? Rat? Possum? It was so decayed and dirt-encrusted that I couldn't figure out what it had once been.

"Boomer! Get over here!"

The hound came loping around the side of the house. He came to an abrupt stop once he saw what I was pointing at, looking up at me with a surprised expression.

"Is this yours?" I demanded.

He shook his head. Walking up, he gave the animal a tentative sniff, then quickly backed up sneezing.

"Who put this on my porch, then?" I asked. "One of the Lows?"

Boomer did the doggy equivalent of a shrug. My Lows did have some odd hobbies, and food preferences. Maybe this was someone's idea of a gift? I wasn't going to wear it, and I certainly wasn't going to eat it.

"Can you get rid of it?"

Boomer shook his head, ears flapping with the motion.

I glared at him. "That wasn't supposed to be a question. Take this thing somewhere and bury it. Or ditch it on the side of the road. I don't want it on my porch."

Just then the dead thing moved. Boomer let out an unearthly howl and took off for the backyard, leaving me staring in astonishment at the twitching…rat? Yes, I think it had once been a really big rat.

Bending over, I tried to see if the thing was still alive. I didn't want to get too close, but I couldn't tell if the twitching was from insects that were feeding under the skin, or if it really wasn't dead. It certainly looked and smelled dead.

It twitched again. I jumped back, eyeing it. Yes, the abdomen had moved, but so had the front legs. Scooting closer, I stuck out my foot and nudged the rat. It twitched again.

Didn't matter if it was dead or alive, I needed to get this thing off my front porch. Unfortunately I didn't seem to have a shovel or a broom to move it with. I wasn't about to pick it up, so instead I stepped over it and went on inside. Hopefully it would wander off on its own. If not, I'd go out to the barn later, get a shovel, and toss it into the woods on the other side of my driveway.

"I'm back," I shouted to Lux as I threw my purse on the table.

I swear, having the responsibility of a baby angel had turned me into a total bore. No wonder demons in Hel dumped their offspring into the hands of dwarven foster homes the moment they were formed because parenting wasn't a demon thing. Thankfully Lux didn't require constant diaper changes or midnight feedings like human infants did. Lucky for me, angel babies were perfectly capable of raiding the fridge when they wanted to experience the sensory pleasure of eating food or drinking, and they didn't poop or pee.

Well, except for *my* kid who'd gone through a phase a few months back. Fortunately his fascination with human intestinal functions was short lived.

Lux said something in a rapid burst of angel-speech that I could never manage to keep up with. Something about working and responsibility and sacred duty. Fuck, had Gabriel been talking to him again? Damn it all, I hated that shithead. Last time he and Nyalla took Lux for a weekend, the kid tried to sneak kale into my coffee.

Let me tell you, kale flavored coffee is not pleasant.

"Sounds good." I went into the kitchen to get a beer, then headed into my living room to see what Lux's idea of sacred responsibility was. The baby angel was sitting on the floor surrounded by a pile of jewelry.

"Did you rob Tiffany's or something?" I asked, twisting the cap off my beer. "Anything cool in there for me?"

"Rings," he announced solemnly.

"I see that." I walked over and sat down beside him, running my fingers through what looked to be hundreds of diamond rings. Holy shit, some of these looked really expensive. I stuck one ring on each of my fingers and held them up, wiggling them at Lux.

"You've got some serious bling here."

He laughed and did the same. "Bling!"

They were pretty. Well, some of them. Although most of the rings were fairly run of the mill diamond solitaires, a few were more ornate, and some were engraved bands. Pulling the rings off my fingers, I inspected them and tossed them back into the pile. I held one up, wondering how many carats the diamond was.

"So what's up with all the jewelry? Did you make these?" Seemed kinda ambitious for an infant angel, but maybe not. Maybe these were the angel equivalents of macaroni necklaces. If so, this was a much better gift than the dead, or not dead, rat on my porch.

"No." A bunch of angel-speak followed.

"What sacred responsibility?" I was beginning to have a bad feeling about all this. "The rings are your sacred responsibility? What are you talking about?"

Lux stood and puffed out his little chest. Rings…something, something, something about taking his duties seriously just like his father had taught him.

"Wait…" Had Gregory told Lux to go buy a bunch of rings? "Exactly what is your duty, and what does it have to do with jewelry?"

Lux sighed, as if I were the most obtuse individual he'd ever met. "I am the keeper of rings. Sacred responsibility to keep the rings safe."

Keeper of the rings? "So you're a fucking hobbit now? Or that Gollum dude?" I asked.

Lux shuddered. He hadn't been a big fan of the movies. Seems there was a lot to frighten a little angel in *Lord of the Rings*.

"Who made you keeper of the rings?" I asked, wondering if this was something he'd picked up from the movie. If so, we were going to have an absolute blast tossing these things into an active volcano.

"Irix and Amber." He grinned. "Nyalla says I look cute in the tuxedo."

Fuck.

"Irix and Amber asked you to be the ring bearer for the wedding." It had been all the little angel could talk about for the last week.

Lux nodded.

"Did either Irix or Amber explain to you exactly what that job entailed?" Probably not. Amber hadn't been all that detailed in what my bridesmaid job entailed either.

Lux nodded again. "Keeper of the rings. Sacred responsibility to keep them safe."

I took a deep breath. "Um, Lux? Irix meant his and Amber's rings. Not every ring in the fucking universe. This is…this is too many rings. Where did you get them all?"

The little angel frowned. Then his bottom lip quivered. "Everywhere."

He was going to cry. He was going to cry and then I would break into a million pieces. If disappointing Nyalla was like being stabbed repeatedly in the gut, Lux crying was even worse.

"It's okay. It's okay. Don't cry." I looked around, frantically trying to figure out what to do. No one needed to know about this. That was the best thing about being a demon—we were good at covering shit up. All I needed to do was sweep this all under the rug, pretend it never happened, then Lux and I could go on our merry way.

Under the rug.

I lifted up the corner of the huge Oriental carpet and began to kick the rings under it. "We won't tell anyone, okay? You keep Irix and Amber's rings safe, and no one needs to know about all these. I'm sure there's insurance or something on them."

"Sam?"

I spun around, moving quickly to stand in front of the huge lump in the carpet. "Nyalla! Hi! How wonderful to see you!"

She shot me a quizzical look. "You dropped me off at Wyatt's fifteen minutes ago. I'm wondering why there's a dead rat on the porch out front."

Crap, I'd hoped the thing would have been gone by now. "I was just about to go out back and get a shovel to dispose of it."

"Did Boomer kill it?" She walked toward us.

"He says no. I think it just died there. Probably poison or something."

"Is Lux behind you?" She came closer, trying to peer around me.

"Yes, but he's busy. Let's go, uh, get coffee or something and catch up."

"We *just* got back from coffee." Nyalla frowned. "What's the big lump in the carpet?"

"Rings!" Lux shouted.

Traitor. Hadn't I just said we weren't going to tell anyone?

"Play rings," I said. "We're hiding them. Now, let's go get a beer. Or pizza. Or how about I buy you a new car?"

"Rings?" Nyalla scooted around me.

"Rings," Lux repeated, holding up a particularly gaudy one I'd somehow not managed to get under the carpet. "Lux is a bad angel. Not keeper of stolen rings. Hide them and not tell anyone."

Oh for fuck's sake, this angel couldn't keep his mouth shut if I duct taped it. We needed to have a serious talk about when to fess up—pretty much never—and when to pretend absolute and complete innocence of any wrongdoing.

Nyalla took the ring from Lux and gasped. "Where did you get this?"

"Hong Kong." His bottom lip trembled again. "If I hide the ring, I be good?"

"Oh, sweetie." Nyalla dropped the ring and scooped Lux up in her arms, cuddling him. The angel snuggled his face against her breasts and sighed happily. "You're always good," she crooned. "But even good angels do bad things sometimes. You have to make it right, to fix it. That's what good angels do."

"Which means hiding these rings and not telling anyone." I picked up the ring Nyalla had dropped and shoved it under the carpet with the others, trying to tamp down the lump with my feet.

"He has to give them back," Nyalla said, that stern gleam in her eye.

"Why are you looking at me like that? I'm not the one that stole hundreds of rings."

Nyalla frowned. "You're the one who's trying to hide them all under the carpet, though."

Damn it. First Lux was on the edge of tears, and now Nyalla was disappointed in me. There was no way I was getting out of this one alive.

"Look, it's ridiculous to insist Lux return all these rings. First, he probably doesn't even remember where he got them all."

"I remember!" the angel announced proudly.

Great. "Secondly, there's insurance for this kind of thing. Let those bastards pay out for once. People can go buy new rings, and everyone will be happy."

"What if they didn't have insurance?" Nyalla asked. "What if the ring was a family heirloom with sentimental value? What if it was a museum piece? Sam, he has to return them. If he were a human and he'd shoplifted a candy bar from the store, you'd make him take it back and apologize."

Like hell I would. "Are you kidding me? I'd eat the candy bar and tell the human kid to not let anyone know."

"Part of learning about right and wrong is putting in the effort to make things right when you've done wrong," Nyalla insisted.

I wasn't going to win this argument. I was never going to win this argument. Usually I'd agree with whatever Nyalla wanted, then just not do it, but I was feeling feisty.

"Okay. You win. If Lux steals a candy bar, I'll make him return it and apologize. But these rings"—I tapped the bulge in the carpet with my foot—"are staying right here. End of discussion."

* * *

"He's returning the rings." Gregory scowled.

So much for trying to hide them all under the rug. Gregory had seen right through my lies. Either that, or Lux had told him. Or maybe Nyalla had told him. Or Nyalla had told Gabe who told him. The end result was that he knew, and my happy family time and later sexy-times were in jeopardy over these damned things.

"Nobody wants these rings back. They're ugly." I held up a particularly hideous one. "See? People would rather have the insurance money than this stupid thing."

"That's not the point," Gregory said. "He has stolen, taken that which doesn't belong to him. As an Angel of Order, he must atone."

Fuck that.

"He's just a little guy," I argued. "He knows what he did was wrong. It wasn't like he was overcome with the sin of greed or anything, he only misunderstood his duties as ring-bearer in Irix and Amber's wedding."

"I'm not blaming him. It was an honest mistake, but an angel is never too young to learn that mistakes have consequences, and that it's his duty to mitigate the impact of his actions."

Like Gregory had done after the disaster with the mythical tenth choir. Although there was no putting *that* genie back in the bottle. Once the humans had been given the angelic gifts, they were off and running. And no archangel, no matter how powerful, could manage to guide these crazy humans onto the straight and narrow.

It's what I loved about humans. They were like us—full of chaos. And there was Gregory and his angels, trying to herd seven billion cats, with no awareness at all about the futility of their efforts.

"Fine." I knew I'd lost this battle. "But maybe he should only return the museum pieces and the family heirlooms? Because there are a lot of rings under my rug."

Gregory pulled back the rug and blinked. "That is…that is a lot of jewelry."

"Lux takes his duties very seriously." I bit back a laugh at the expression on my angel's face.

"I'm concerned that the owners of these rings might not understand Lux's innocent intentions," Gregory mused. "He is very young, and I don't want him to have to deal with physical or emotional attack by humans at his tender age."

"Good point." I tried to kick some of the rings further under the rug. "So he should only return the museum pieces."

"No, he needs to return them all, but perhaps you should accompany him."

I stopped kicking the rug. "Me?"

There were hundreds of these things. I had other shit to do besides zipping all over the world returning cheap diamond solitaires to Chad and Karen. And damnit, why was this sort of thing always *my* job? Yes, Lux was technically my responsibility, but Gregory had signed on for half this parenting-an-angel thing as well.

"If Lux needs someone to accompany him, it should be *you*," I told him. "The big archangel with all the calming blue shit who can make humans non-violent. Not me, who is liable to get shot, stabbed, or arrested."

Yeah, getting shot, stabbed, or arrested wasn't a big deal for me, but it didn't mean I enjoyed it. I expected an argument from Gregory, some bullshit about how he was busy and didn't have time for this. I hadn't expected him to look…tired.

"You're right." He knelt down and scooped up a handful of rings, picking through them as if he were looking for something.

"What's going on?" I suddenly felt worried. This wasn't like him at all. Where was my arrogant asshole of an angel? Where was the fiery-hot Gregory who would shove me against the wall and snarl at me? Who would demand I do this?

Whew. I got hot and bothered just thinking about it. I'd expected, maybe even wanted, an argument, not this easy capitulation and agreement.

He kept sorting through the rings. "Nothing is going on. I've realized that I've been relying on you to shoulder all the responsibility for when Lux does something…something impish."

"It's probably my fault that he's impish," I admitted. It was totally my fault. I was a terrible influence on a young Angel of Order.

Gregory smiled up at me, and my internal organs did a little jumpy thing. "A mere decade ago I would have found that a grave sin in an Angel of Order, but now I find it incredibly endearing when Lux does something that reminds me of you."

Yep. Internal organs jumping everywhere. "Oh." It was a stupid response, but all I could manage right now.

"He'll be a better angel because of you. He'll be more like we used to be, before the war, before we became so divided. It's important that he embraces the moments of chaos in his order, that he learns to appreciate and love that which is different."

"Oh." Yep. Still speechless.

"I'm a better angel because of you. You don't just point out my flaws, my sins, my hypocrisy, you smash them right in my face. You force me to see situations differently, to experience things that I've steadfastly refused to even consider doing for billions of years."

"And *that* makes you a better angel?" It didn't sound all that positive to me, but he was pretty fucking weird. All the angels were weird, but mine was the weirdest of all.

"Yes, it does. Life is unpredictable and terrifying with you, and I wouldn't have it any other way. You, my Cockroach, brought me back to life and gave me everything I never knew I needed."

"Does this mean I'm getting laid tonight? I mean, laid-laid. Dipping the wick? Hiding the sausage? Bumping uglies? Riding the flagpole? Because I love angel-sex, but whoo-boy, when you combine it with some balls-deep action, I'm pretty fucking close to worshiping your sexy ass."

His smile broadened and he extended a particularly garish ring toward me. "Beloved Cockroach, would you do me the honor of marrying me?"

I laughed, not sure where he was going with this. "With a stolen ring?"

"With a stolen ring. Which I will, of course, create a duplicate for the true owners," he said solemnly

"Of course." He couldn't be serious. Angels didn't do these human traditions. But he had been eating chips and drinking coffee. He occasionally manifested sexual organs. It wasn't too much of a stretch to think that he'd want to partake in certain human traditions especially since the angels were locked out of Aaru for the foreseeable future.

"Rings!" Lux squealed, his little wings flapping with excitement. "Love forever." He looked like one of those adorable cherubs on the Valentine's day cards. All he needed was a miniature archery set and he could be Cupid.

"You mean it?" I asked.

"I mean it." He was still kneeling, holding the ring out to me.

"Do we have to do the whole church thing?" I asked.

"Not if you don't want to. I have heard some humans exchange vows while outside in nature, or even at a city with the sins of gambling, excessive alcohol indulgence, and meaningless sexual contact."

"Vegas." I grinned. It was totally my style. "Yes, I want to get married in Vegas. Ooo, can I force my friends to wear ugly gowns in unflattering colors?"

"Absolutely."

"Can I have a bachelorette party with strippers and a cake made of actual penises? With gambling, excessive alcohol consumption, and meaningless sex?"

"I draw the line at meaningless sex, Cockroach."

That growly sound in his voice was making my insides all quivery again.

"Okay, I'll forego the meaningless sex, but our wedding needs to be officiated by Elvis."

He blinked. "Do you know of a necromancer who can perform the resurrection? Because I'm afraid that request is beyond my abilities."

Damn. "I'll settle for an Elvis impersonator then." I knelt

down in front of him. "I accept your proposal. Yes, I will marry you, Asshole."

He slid the ring onto the appropriate finger, shrinking it to fit. The band was some strange metal covered with engraving that had mostly worn off. Instead of a big-ass diamond, it had three gray-colored stones. I had no idea why Lux had decided this ring was worth stealing. I had no idea why Gregory had picked it out of the pile. It was the most hideously ugly thing I'd ever seen, which made it perfect.

I adored it. I adored him.

"Love!" Lux flung himself forward, smacking me in the face with a wing. Gregory's arms came around the pair of us, squashing us in a tight embrace.

"I'll help Lux return the rings," I said when he'd finally let go enough that I could breathe again. "You're in charge of the wedding stuff. Get Rafi to help you, because Gabe is gonna fuck it all up and I don't want a wedding with a two-hour monologue and kale."

"We have a deal." He kissed my forehead. "If you and Lux need help with the rings, let me know."

I nodded, but I wouldn't need help. It was a bunch of rings. What could go wrong?

"Oh, and Cockroach? There's a dead rat on your front porch."

Fuck.

CHAPTER 4

*A*fter popping open some celebratory champagne, the three of us talked wedding plans and decided what we were going to do for dinner tonight. That's when Gregory got a phone call which evidently was serious enough that he needed to run out to take care of emergency angel business. With dinner postponed and our champagne half-drunk, I figured it would be a good time to take care of the dead rat.

The sun was just starting to go down. I made sure the horses had hay in their feeder, checked the water trough, then poured some kibble in Boomer's bowl. The hellhound was perfectly able to scavenge his own dinner, but he still enjoyed regular dog food and I preferred that he didn't dig up half the cemeteries in the county looking for something to eat.

Then I grabbed a shovel and headed around to the front of my house. The rat was still on the porch, although it looked as if he'd dragged himself a foot closer to the door before dying. It was probably a good thing Boomer hadn't eaten him. The thing had probably gotten into poison and crawled here, taking an inordinately long time to die.

I scraped the carcass onto the shovel, walked over to the tree line on the other side of my driveway, and tossed it into the woods. That's when I noticed the other dead rat.

I was seriously going to have to have a talk with my neighbors. I didn't mind rodent control, but if all the poisoned animals were going to end up on my porch and driveway, then they were going to have to think of something else.

Just as I was about to scoop it onto the shovel, it jumped up and lunged toward me.

I screamed.

Yep. Me, an imp, a demon, an Angel of Chaos, the Iblis, screamed at an attacking rat. Then I jumped back, frantically trying to whack the thing with the shovel. It dodged my first few attempts before I finally managed to squash it. To ensure it was truly dead, I smacked it a few more times, then scooped it up and tossed it into the woods with its rodent brother.

Just in case there were any other dead rats laying around, I did a quick tour of my driveway, looped around my house, and walked around the patio by the pool. I didn't see anything, but wanting to be prepared, so I propped the shovel up by the front door then went inside to get Lux some dinner.

Gregory hadn't returned by the time I'd pulled the chicken nuggets and fries out of the oven, so Lux and I ate by ourselves, debating whether fries were best with ketchup, vinegar, or a combination of the two.

"Rings?" Lux asked, eyeing the lump in the carpet.

"That can wait for tomorrow," I assured him. Ugh, I was not looking forward to doing this. Accompanying Lux to hundreds of homes, museums, and jewelry stores so he could sneak in and deposit stolen jewelry back where it came from wasn't my idea of a good time.

It got me to thinking.

"Do you need me to go with you for every single ring return?" I asked. "I mean, you stole them all yourself, so some of them won't be too dangerous for you to take back, right?"

Lux nodded. "Some easy. Some scary. Some very scary."

Got it. Maybe I could just help with the scary and very scary and leave the rest to Lux.

"How many are easy?"

Lux motioned for me to sit down beside him, and I watched as he separated the rings into appropriate piles. The first were probably rings stolen from the bottom of dresser drawers, and safety deposit boxes—those that were seldom, if ever, worn and that probably hadn't even been missed. The second, scary pile included rings that most likely came from museums and those people who had definitely noticed the theft. The third, very scary pile, probably belonged to those who were liable to try to shoot us.

Thankfully the majority of the rings were in the easy pile. Still, I worried. He was young. It wasn't just that Lux was learning to be an angel, he was learning to live among humans with their rules, their laws, and their culture. He'd misunderstood his role as ringbearer. What if he misunderstood something else and ended up shot, or stabbed, or hauled off to a juvenile detention facility or worse, child protective services.

Could I lose custody of an angel because I let him break into people's houses and return stolen goods? I mean, I could easily break him out of the pokey and give the human government the middle finger, but after today's Ruling Council meeting, I got the feeling now wasn't the time to be making waves among the humans.

"Let's take one or two back and see how it goes," I told Lux. "Pick two from the easy pile that you felt might have been borderline scary, and we'll do those together."

Lux pawed through the pile and picked out a pretty white gold band with an emerald cut ruby, and a fat platinum band with round flush-set diamonds. Whatever Gregory was busy with, it clearly was taking a while. Just in case he got back before we did, I left him a quick note and took Lux's hand and told him to take us there.

Having a young angel teleport me was a lot like being stuffed into an industrial sized dryer and being tumbled at top heat and speed for thirty seconds. Normally the process was instantaneous and free of any side-effects beyond some vertigo and nausea. Unlike when *I* was first learning to teleport, Lux got us where he intended. It just took him an uncomfortably long time to get there.

We arrived in a dark room. I staggered backward, crashing into a piece of furniture that tipped over and landed me on my back staring up at a popcorn ceiling covered with yellow and brown water stains.

"Shhh!" Lux demanded.

I bit back a reply and got to my feet, righting the chair I'd knocked over. My eyes had adjusted and I saw that we were in a cluttered bedroom full of boxes and randomly stacked furniture. Even the bed was loaded with garbage bags and plastic bins.

Footsteps. Mumbled conversation. Light suddenly illuminating around the door.

I grabbed Lux and dragged him behind a bunch of cardboard boxes, squishing him against a bookshelf. The door opened. Light flooded the room with the click of a switch.

"One of the boxes probably fell over," a woman said. "We stacked them higher than we should."

"Beats paying a hundred a month for a storage unit,"

another woman replied. "Maybe we'll actually start going through her things this way."

"Did you ever find that ring?" the first woman asked. "The one Dad gave her on their thirtieth anniversary? The one with the ruby?"

Lux held the ring out and I clapped a hand over his mouth, holding him in place before he did something like jump out from behind these boxes to give them the ring.

"No, but it's got to be here somewhere. We'll find it eventually."

The light went off. I kept a tight grip on Lux. It wasn't until I'd heard the door close and the sound of footsteps receding down the hall that I let him go.

"Mom-ring," he whispered to me.

"Yeah, I heard." I stood, carefully making my way out from behind the boxes. Where was a good place to put this ring? I wanted it somewhere the women could easily find, but not in a place that might arouse suspicion.

"This?" Lux pointed to a plain white coffee mug that had half a dozen pens and pencils in it.

"Perfect." I took the ring from his hand, slipping it around one of the pens and angling the cup so it would be visible from the door. "Now let's get out of here before I knock something else over."

The second spot was another home and another bedroom. Thankfully it was daytime in this location, and I managed to steady myself against the doorway before I could stumble into any of the furniture.

The bedroom was decorated like it was photo-ready for a spread in Architectural Digest. Walking over to the window, I looked out at a beautiful view of an infinity pool and the ocean far below.

"Let me see that ring," I said to Lux. He put the platinum

band with the flush-set diamonds into my hand. I peered inside and saw engraving that said Cartier.

Too bad I couldn't keep this one. I handed the ring back to Lux and followed him into a walk-in closet that was the size of my living room. Moving a rack of ties aside, he dialed the combination to the safe, swung open the door, and placed the ring inside a little black velvet box.

In seconds we were done and back home in my living room.

It *had* been easy. And even if we'd gotten caught at the first house, I didn't believe Lux would have been in any danger. The two women probably would have been the ones needing an ambulance after seeing a winged, naked, golden-haired toddler in their spare bedroom.

"Do you think you can do this easy pile on your own?" I asked, still feeling guilty for letting my kid do this solo.

He sighed and looked at the huge pile. "Lots of rings."

I could have been snarky and informed him that he'd managed to steal those "lots" of rings on his own, but instead I decided to offer my help as a compromise.

"Why don't we divide and conquer? You do the rings you feel are the easiest and have the less risk of being caught. I'll do some of them on my own if you let me know where they need to go. And if you're worried about returning any of them on your own, I'll go with you."

He smiled up at me. "Deal."

I tucked a much less stressed angel into bed that night. Then I went downstairs, poured myself a glass of wine, and figured it was time to look at the list Gabriel had given me at the Ruling Council meeting.

I had a meeting tomorrow with the President of the United States along with a bunch of people I assumed were his advisors. The rest of my schedule for the week included

France, Canada, Australia, and Iceland. I winced at the latter, remembering that the elves had been welcomed there with open arms and were actually occupying key governmental positions. Not that I should point fingers since Dar was evidently now Mayor of Chicago.

I grabbed a pen and added Dar's name to my list. I did need to go see him, if only to warn him that his power grab had come to the attention of the Ruling Council and that not all were in favor of it.

Tossing the list aside I looked once more over at the piles of rings, not sure why I was having a weird sense of dread over the whole thing.

Getting up, I sifted through the third pile. Six rings. And only a dozen in the second pile. Between the two of us, we'd get through the first pile in the next week or so, then I'd go with Lux to return these—the scary pile, and the very scary pile.

Just touching a few of the third pile made my skin crawl. Something about these rings scared *me* as well as Lux. I could take a beating, but Lux was so young and he'd not come into his full powers for thousands of years at least. I didn't want him to be with me when I took this third pile back. I didn't want him to have anything to do with those rings. Hell, *I* didn't want anything to do with them.

But I wasn't going to worry about rings tonight. Tossing an afghan over the piles, I dug through my movie collection, deciding what I wanted to watch. I'd just settled onto my couch with a well-used copy of Jedi Orgy in the DVD player, when Gregory returned.

"Hey, babe. Grab some wine and come join me for some lightsaber-in-the-butt action," I said to the archangel. "Lux is asleep. It's time for porn."

"Are there chips?"

"Yep." Gregory had totally become addicted to chips, especially the ones with Old Bay seasoning on them.

The angel headed upstairs to see Lux while I grabbed the chips from the kitchen and poured him a glass of wine that I would most likely be drinking myself. Then I started the movie. Gregory came down before any serious boinking started, sitting beside me and putting his arm around my shoulder. I leaned against him, loving how his energy felt like the blast from an oven set on broil. His spirit-self reached out to caress mine, and I felt myself fall into him.

This was perfection. This was my idea of heaven. I loved when we angel fucked, when we joined our spirit-selves as one, but I also loved these moments when we were just together, touching physically as well as with our spirit beings.

"When are you scheduled to meet with the human leaders?" Gregory asked, totally disrupting my mood.

I handed him the schedule from off the coffee table. "First meeting is tomorrow."

He looked over the itinerary. "We need to obtain the humans' cooperation, Cockroach."

I turned on the sofa to face him. "And? Are you suggesting that I can't play nice in these meetings and come to a mutually beneficial agreement?" One of his eyebrows went up and I snickered. "Maybe you should give these to one of your siblings instead."

"It's true that the humans don't need any more chaos in their lives." He smiled and smoothed my hair back. "But there is a reason you've been assigned these particular meetings. The US President asked for you in particular as part of the negotiations include New Hell. The government in Iceland is run by elves, and they would rather meet with you than an angel. France preferred to meet with you. And Australia has become unwelcoming to angels in the last few weeks."

"And Canada?" I asked.

He shrugged. "Out of all the other countries, they're less likely to be offended with impish behavior."

"I still think you should let Gabe do these, just to be on the safe side," I teased.

"We're already doing the majority of the meetings. To ensure each human leader feels valued and important, we are personally soliciting input from every one of them. No country is too small for a member of the Ruling Council to visit."

Yikes. I guess I did get off light after all.

Gregory tossed the list on the coffee table, and pulled me closer. "That dead rat is still on your front porch."

Oh for fuck's sake. "I tossed it in the woods as well as the other one I found in the driveway. That one wasn't quite dead yet, so I had to smack it with my shovel a few times first."

"So this is a third rat?" Gregory's chest rumbled with a laugh. "All the rats are coming to die in front of your house?"

"It's my fucking neighbor," I huffed. "They're probably poisoning them and sending them over here to croak just to piss me off. They've hated me since I let those elves camp in my field."

"They hated you before that. And exactly how are they directing dying rats to your porch? I don't know much about human pest control products, but I assume they'd take effect quickly and the animal would die fairly close to the source of the poison."

"Some of those poisons take forever to kill." I went on to describe in detail all the gruesome particulars of what happened to the animal's body as well as how long it took until they breathed their last for the top four types of poison. It was just as exciting as the porno—well, except for the part where Leia was giving it to Han with the light-saber strap-on. *That* was pretty epic.

"I still don't understand how they could direct the animals to your house," Gregory replied. "Perhaps it isn't your neighbors."

"Oh, it is. If they're not sending them this way, then they're sneaking over and depositing the half-dead things on my porch. Tomorrow I'm going to head over there and have a little chat with them—right after I meet with the president. If they want to poison rats, then they should have to clean the carcasses up, not dump them in front of my door."

I was all fired up about this now, which Gregory seemed to find terribly amusing. He scooted me onto his lap, holding me tight in his arms. I teased him with the edges of my spirit-self, resting my head against his uncomfortably hard chest. It was like leaning against superheated granite and I loved it.

"Cockroach?"

His breath stirred across my hair and I smiled. "Hmm?"

"Why is that woman penetrating that man with her weapon?"

"Because swords are a symbol for dicks. Just about everything is a symbol for dicks. Humans are obsessed with sexual activity."

"Just like demons," he mused.

I squirmed on his lap, realizing that he was suddenly packing. Gregory didn't often manifest sexual organs. We didn't often have physical sex, since he preferred to fuck angel-style. I kinda preferred it too, but sometimes nothing beat a good banging in the sheets. Or on the couch. Hopefully that's where this was heading.

"Yes, just like demons." I kissed him, digging my hands into his chestnut curls. His hands caressed my back, his spirit-self teasing mine, but in spite of all that, something felt off.

I pulled back and looked into his dark eyes. "What's wrong."

He sighed, leaning his forehead against mine. "That phone call? Ten angels are dead about twenty miles outside of Dublin."

There had been a few angel deaths here and there since I'd banished them all from Aaru. Some angels hadn't been all that skilled in maintaining a corporeal form. Some had gotten flattened by trucks, or blown up, or stabbed in back alleyways and been too confused to form a new body in time. Quite a few had been slaughtered when fake-Samael had tried to take over the world. But lately the angel-deaths seemed to have lessened. Ten at one time seemed excessive.

"What happened?" I spun my new engagement ring around on my finger, dreading the answer.

"I'm not sure."

That hadn't been what I'd expected. "It's not demons?"

There wasn't any organized attempt at genocide, but there were plenty of Ancients as well as high-level demons who had a grudge against particular angels, or against them as a whole. I felt each and every one of my demons like they were stars at the end of gossamer threads, linked to my spirit-self, but that didn't mean I knew what each and every one of them was doing at a particular time. Keeping track of nearly a hundred thousand beings was way beyond my abilities.

"I honestly don't know, Cockroach." Gregory reached up to touch my cheek. "I want tonight to be free from these worries, to be only us celebrating our love."

I smiled. "But you have duties. I understand. So do I. Do you want to take me to where these angels died? Maybe together we can figure out what happened."

"No. I would rather experience carnal physical relations with you, then join our spirit-selves."

Me too, but I knew damned well that Gregory's focus would be elsewhere, and if he was going to be slamming into me, then I didn't want his attentions divided.

"Let's go." I kissed him. "We can fuck when we get back."

Suddenly I was no longer sitting on his lap on my couch in my living room. My ass was in a puddle of mud in the middle of a field with cold rain pouring out of a black sky. I assumed this was Ireland, about twenty miles outside of Dublin.

Gregory had created some sort of illusion to hide the dead, but with a flick of his hand the bodies appeared. My eyes adjusted to the darkness and I got to my feet, trying not to slip in the mud as I made my way to the nearest corpse.

I'd seen angels reduced to a pile of sand. I'd seen angels who'd had their spirit-selves ripped from their corporeal forms and devoured. I'd seen angels whose bodies had perished and whose spirit-selves had died along with their corporeal form. But I'd never seen a dead angel who looked like these ten.

They were chewed up, as if some animal had attacked them. And I didn't just mean their physical bodies either.

"Hellhounds?" Gregory asked.

"No fucking way." I knelt down beside one of the corpses. "Hellhounds prefer to feast on those who are already dead. They're definitely capable of attacking the living if they feel threatened, but I've never seen one go after an angel."

"But would they?" Gregory knelt down beside me. "Ten angels congregated here for a reason. Let's assume they knew of a hellhound nearby and had taken exception to its being here. If the hellhound was defending itself…"

"Then we'd be looking at a dead hellhound and a few injured angels."

I frowned, looking at the wounds that had clearly been inflicted by something with very large, very powerful fangs.

Beyond the physical damage, hellhounds *could* kill a being of spirit. I'd had Boomer for a very long time, and I knew more about him and his kind than probably anyone. Hellhounds were psychopomps. They had the ability to release the souls of the dead and send them to their afterlife. Releasing the souls of the dead was pretty much the same thing as separating a spirit-being from its corporeal form—basically killing it. In theory, a hellhound could kill an angel. In theory. In reality, it would take a fucking monster of a hellhound to take down an angel. Boomer might be able to do it if he were sufficiently enraged.

But ten angels at one time? Even Boomer couldn't do that. I didn't know any hybrid that could do that. Fuck, I didn't know many demons that could do that.

"Maybe it was a pack of hellhounds?" Gregory asked, as if reading my mind.

I didn't want to voice that this was more likely to be a group of demons targeting a group of angels. As for the bite wounds…well, some demons liked to fight with their teeth as well as their more traditional energy weapons.

Damn it. I didn't want demons attacking angels, or angels attacking demons. I wanted us to be in one giant lovefest. I wanted to get Infernal Mates going again with Rafi, to pair off demons and angels, to get everyone laid. I didn't want ten dead, chewed-up angel corpses out in a cold, soggy night in Ireland.

Wiping the rain away from my eyes, I took a breath and placed my palms on the dead angel. Then I pushed my spirit-self into the body and tried to discover what lay beneath the flesh. The second I touched the angel, I knew neither a demon nor a hellhound had caused this death. The angel's spirit-self had been mauled. Bits of it still remained in the corporeal form after death, chewed around the edges with an energy pattern I didn't recognize at all.

I pulled my hands away and shook them to rid my fingers of the sensation. A hellhound would have torn the angel's spirit-self cleanly from the physical body. A demon would have left a different energy signature than this. Even a devouring being wouldn't have left bits behind with strange bite marks.

"I don't know what did this, but whatever it is, it isn't from Hel." I looked over at Gregory. "I'm sorry."

"Do you think the humans…?" His voice trailed off, then he shook his head. "No. I've seen what they're capable of during my time here with them, and this isn't it."

He stood and held out his hand, helping me to rise. I went to check the other nine bodies, hoping there would be something there that would give me a clue as to what happened. At the end, I was just as perplexed as Gregory.

"There's nothing more to do here. Let's go home." He walked over to me and wrapped an arm around my shoulders. Suddenly the rain slanted around me, and my body warmed with the heat of his energy. I glanced over at the lights from some suburb in the distance, then frowned.

One of those lights wasn't like the others.

"Do you see that?" I asked Gregory before I realized that of course he couldn't see it.

"See what?"

That confirmed my suspicions. With considerable regret, I shrugged out from under his arm and shivered as the rain hit me once more. Sloshing through the mud, I approached the light. It spread wide, welcoming me as I came near.

"A wild gate?"

I smiled, thrilled at how in tune our thoughts had become. "Yeah."

The angels wouldn't have been able to sense it, so I assumed it was a horrible twist of fate that brought them to congregate right next to a rift that led to some other world.

Reaching out a hand, I touched the gate, wondering what had come through here that was powerful enough to kill ten angels. Hopefully whatever the fuck it was, it had gone back home after its murderous rampage.

Gregory scowled. "We need to close it. I'll assign three of my best hunters to this area, just in case whatever killed these angels is still on this side of the gate."

Yep, it was as if we thought as one. I traced the outlines of the gate with my hands, then reached out to Gregory with my spirit-self, showing him the gate through my sight.

His eyes narrowed, then energy poured off him in hot waves, turning the rain to steam before it even hit my skin. The edges of the gate glowed, and it narrowed, pulsing with a gold and silver light. The light shrank to a dot, then vanished. Gregory sighed and stepped back, dusting his hands against his jeans.

"These wild gates are continuing to be a problem, Cockroach. I know the issues with angels and humans are a priority, but we cannot allow the prevalence of these anomalies to slip from our notice."

At one time we'd been devoting substantial effort to closing these rifts, but then other more pressing matters had commanded the attention of the Ruling Council. Maybe instead of my negotiating overtime pay for elves, I should be focusing on this instead. But in spite of there being two Angels of Chaos on the Ruling Council, it was still a governing board with a majority of members who relished being bogged down in paperwork and committees. I hated to think of it, but perhaps if another ten angels died, the others might decide this was more important than worrying about Dar being the mayor of Chicago or legislation about shifter employment discrimination.

Once more Gregory put his arm around me, and the rain

slanted away from my skin. He pulled me into his arms to teleport, as he always did. And just before we left, I could have sworn I saw a blink of light growing and stretching right where the wild gate we'd just closed had been.

CHAPTER 5

Gregory spent the night and woke me up at an obscene hour of the morning. Neither of us mentioned the ten dead angels, but I could tell it weighed on his mind as he made pancakes shaped like stars for our breakfast. Lux was also an early riser and stood on a chair by the stove, guessing which stars the various pancakes were made to represent. They all looked like blobs to me—delicious blobs about to be drenched in butter and syrup. I hated getting up early, but pancakes were a good reason to haul my ass out of bed. Plus, something delightfully warm and heavy settled in my chest as I watched the ancient archangel and the little one that looked up at him with such awe and adoration.

Uncomfortably aware that I probably had the same expression on my face as Lux, I left them discussing which galaxies they were going to visit after breakfast and went outside to shovel more half-dead animals off my porch. This time it wasn't just rats. There was a mangled possum right outside the door, four rats at the bottom of the steps, and two groundhogs over by my SUV. None of them were dead yet, although they certainly looked like they should have been. Every single one of them attacked me, which meant I spent a good bit of my morning hopping around the driveway in my pajamas, beating dying animals with a shovel.

After I'd tossed the bodies into the woods, I went inside, cursing my shitty neighbors. That pile of dead animals was probably getting big enough to stink. I'd need to go shovel some dirt over them, maybe pick up a bag of lime at the hardware store to keep the stench down. It was ridiculous how humanlike my life was getting. I enjoyed living in the human world, and having an angel make pancakes for breakfast was pretty epic, but I could do without early morning dead animal clean up.

Lux was at the table, already eating his pancakes and drinking coffee. I ruffled his blond curls and went into the kitchen. Gregory had put on an apron that said Mr. Good Looking Is Cooking. I'd gotten it for him for Valentine's Day in hopes he'd expand his food preparation beyond coffee, and that horrible sandwich he'd once made me. It had worked, judging from the beautiful golden-brown pancakes stacked on a plate beside the stove.

"Where in the universe have you and Lux decided to go today?" I stole a pancake and bit into it. It was soft, buttery, and rich with little bit of crisp at the edges. The angel could really cook. Who would have thought?

"We are still undecided." There was melancholy behind his words.

I wrapped an arm around him and pressed my face into his back. "Are you worried about last night? The angels outside of Dublin?"

He sighed. "Yes. There were no human deaths in the area, so whatever killed them either returned directly after slaughtering ten angels, or it has had no reason to attack further."

I rubbed my cheek against the soft cotton of his polo shirt. "They were in the wrong place at the wrong time. Something came through the wild gate. They were startled and attacked it. It killed them in self-defense and either returned home through the gate, or is roaming the Irish countryside in peace."

It was wishful thinking on my part, because nothing I was involved with ever turned out to be this simple. Still, an imp could hope. This had all been a fluke. The toothy thing had returned through the gates and was no further threat. And the newly closed gate had *not* glimmered as we'd gone to leave. Nope. It had been an illusion of the rain and lights from the nearby town.

"I miss Aaru," Gregory said, out of the blue.

I knew he did. I also knew he tried not to talk about it too often since I couldn't help but feel guilty.

"I wish I could take Lux there," he added. "I fear that he'll never know our homeland, or that I'll never be able to experience it with him."

I needed to work harder at finding a way back in. If only all this other stupid shit didn't keep happening. Actually, it wasn't just the stupid shit. I'd tried everything to get in there. I'd tried my sword, I'd tried the wild gate, I'd tried shouting all sorts of profanity at the weird barrier that kept me and the other angels from entering Aaru. Nothing worked and I'd run out of ideas.

Samael might know how to undo the banishment, but if he did, he wasn't willing to tell me. Not that I blamed him. The Ancients had been banished for two and a half million years. Now they could enter Aaru, but they found themselves unable to shed their corporeal forms and live there as beings of spirit. They were trapped in a second sort of Hel where they continually needed to reform a physical body that always degraded. Fuck, I'd be bitter too.

The Angels of Order were dickheads, and they probably deserved the same punishment they'd dealt to the Angels of Chaos so long ago, but that wasn't what I wanted. I didn't want revenge. I wanted both to be able to live together in Aaru, or wherever they chose. Instead there was a group of Ancients stubbornly holding on to Aaru, a group still living in Hel, and a group who were making their homes here in the human world. Meanwhile, the Angels of Order were stumbling around among the humans, wondering what the fuck was going on. Aside from a few, they still hated the demons and the demons still hated them. And lately it seemed like the humans might be hating both angels and demons. The elves too.

All I could do was create more chaos, no matter how hard I tried. Was this the pendulum swinging too far to the left after millions of years of Order? When would we finally see balance?

Balance. Fuck, I was starting to sound like Gabe.

Gregory turned and handed me a plate of pancakes. "Stop blaming yourself. I love you, and I love our life together here with Lux. When I chose you, I knew I would have a life filled with chaos. The quantity of that chaos may still continue to surprise me, but I never regret my choice. Never."

"I love you too." I stood on tiptoe, but still could only manage to kiss his chin.

He grabbed his plate, and we went into the dining room to have breakfast with Lux. As a family. And weird as it was for angels and a kinda-angel/ still-a-demon to sit down and eat pancakes together, I loved it.

And I loved them.

* * *

I TRIED TELEPORTING DIRECTLY to the Oval Office, figuring

that's where today's meeting would take place, but instead I found myself in a tiny bowling alley. Not one to miss an opportunity, I tried my hand at the sport, then filled a glass with ice, rum, and Coke from a handy nearby bar. Figuring from the lack of security that my presence hadn't set off any alarms, my mixed drink and I started wandering around. The White House was much larger than it looked on postcards. It was also one of the most boring homes I'd ever seen. The rooms were bland with marble floors or carpeting, giant heavy furniture, and walls covered with pictures of old white men. I encountered no one until I turned a corner and saw one of those tour groups down the hall. Ducking under three red velvet ropes, I joined the group, sipping my drink as the guide talked about china patterns and place settings. Seeing a suited man who looked like he could possibly be security, I wandered up to him.

"Hey, think you can tell me where the head honcho is? Sorry I'm late, but I wound up in the bowling alley by mistake."

"This tour doesn't include a meet and greet with the president."

His tone of voice was rather snotty. Not that I blamed him. If this was my job, I'd be in a pissed off mood as well.

"Yeah. See, I'm not really with the tour." I took a swig of my drink and revealed my wings, knocking a vase from a table onto the floor where it smashed into big chunks of colorful porcelain.

The guide screamed. The tourists pivoted and began taking pictures of me. I was pretty sure I'd be trending on Twitter in about five seconds.

The guard had instinctively reached for his gun, but dropped it once he realized I wasn't attacking anything more than a poorly placed vase. "You're supposed to be in the Oval Office."

I shrugged. "Like I said, I ended up in the bowling alley. At least there was a bar down there. This place is like a fucking maze. Can you point me to the right spot?"

The guard stepped aside to talk into his headset. I posed for pictures with a few of the tourists, confirming that yes, I was Satan, and no, that I didn't have any immediate plans to unleash a demon army on the Capital.

"What are you going to do about California?" a blonde woman asked me. "Is my chardonnay going to go up in price? Will I even be able to get it anymore? And what about the fruit?"

Thankfully the guard waved for me to come with him, so I didn't respond. Waving to the tourists like I was a film star, I followed the guard around two velvet ropes, and down several halls that were lined with suited security. Just as I was beginning to wish I'd brought some breadcrumbs to mark my path, the guard opened a door and ushered me inside.

The Oval Office did look just like the postcards, only more spacious and more populated. The president was sitting in the big chair behind the big desk with a big pile of papers in front of him. On either side were big men with big guns. I was no expert in firearms, but I'd never seen ones with the muzzles painted white. Maybe they were Nerf guns? I would absolutely be on board for these meetings if we had Nerf battles.

"Iblis. Welcome, welcome." The president stood and extended his hand. Some humans just don't age well, and this guy was proof of that, even though he'd clearly made many desperate medical attempts to halt the impact of time on his face.

I shook his hand, sneaking a glance at the papers on his desk. They said something about increased military spending on a project called Woo-woo. "Where are the hamburgers?" I asked the president. "I thought this was a lunch thing."

He laughed. "I like you! When I met you at the photo shoot over Christmas, I wasn't sure, but any angel who likes burgers and booze is someone I can talk business with. Jones, run down to McDonald's and get some Quarter Pounders with cheese and bacon. Oh, and lots of fries. Perkins, freshen up the Iblis's drink. What do you have there?"

"Rum and Coke." I handed the empty glass off to Perkins and sat across from the president as he squeezed himself back into his giant wingback chair.

"Now, let's get down to business." The guy clapped his hands, then rubbed them together. I wasn't as enthusiastic about business, but if I was getting fast food and booze, he had my attention. Well, maybe had my attention. If this dude was about to go on a long speech like Gabriel did, then I was going to take a nap.

He pursed his lips and rubbed his hands once more. "Personally I don't have any problem with demons in our country. I've met that new mayor of Chicago and he's a great guy. A great guy. The best. Fan of mine, you know. Voted for me in the last election and said he one hundred percent supported my policies."

Dar. I stifled a grin, wondering how many people he'd said those exact same words to.

"Like I said, I'm in favor of demons living among us. I'm even going to give them a fast-track to citizenship and the vote. But those angels..." He wiggled a finger and sighed. "They're dangerous. They've got mind control powers. They secretly want to take over. And we're not going to stand for that."

Perkins shoved a drink in my hand. I took a sip and sat up in my chair. The president had my complete and full attention. No wonder all the demons wanted to Own this guy, he was cool as shit.

"Yes, those angels are very dangerous. So… I'm guessing you want to kick all of them out?"

He waved a stubby-fingered hand. "Let's not go quite that far. But any angel who didn't go through the appropriate process for legal entry into the United States needs to be sent home. I have no problem with legal angels, it's just the illegal ones I have a problem with."

I nodded. Of course, all the angels were illegal and they'd have no home to go to, so I wasn't sure where this guy thought he was going to send them. Probably Mexico or something.

Wait. Lux was an angel. And so was Gregory, although I couldn't see him, or any of the archangels, abiding by this guy's policy. Like Rafi had said in the Ruling Council meeting, if they got kicked out, they'd just teleport back in.

I found myself mimicking him with the hand-wave. "Just hypothetically here, what about angel-spouses of demons or human citizens? Or kids. I might have an adopted angel kid. What happens to him with this policy of yours?"

"We need to take a firm stance on angel chain migration." He puckered his lips, then spoke through them, as if he were kissing the words out. "But we would certainly make exceptions for our supporters, like that mayor of Chicago. I think his wife is an angel. His daughter too."

Huh. I really didn't want any of those other angels hanging around me anyway. Uri and Rafi and Gabe could fend for themselves. I was sure they could hire a lawyer to get them the angel equivalent of a green card. It wasn't my problem.

"Deal." I slugged down the rest of my drink and held it out to Perkins.

"Marvelous." The president smacked and rubbed his hands together again. "Now let's talk about our western states."

"Nyalla said something about reparations?" I took the refilled glass, wondering where the hamburgers were. Had Jones needed to drive to Virginia or something? Surely there was a McDonald's somewhere close to the White House?

He held up his hands. "Don't get me wrong, I have no love for the state of California. Or the state of Seattle. But there are some very good people in the western part of those states and they are upset."

"Got it. Maybe they can move to Idaho or Montana? Or Detroit? Aren't there a lot of vacant houses there?"

He looked down at his papers. "They don't want to move. They're staying, and I'm just warning you that they may not be willing to follow demon laws or pay your taxes."

Then they could duke it out with whoever Doriel had put in charge of laws and taxes, which was probably nobody. New Hell was pretty close to an anarchy. These people were probably going to be less pissed off than the president thought they'd be.

"Our biggest points of discussion today need to be lost revenue, trade, and immigration." He was waving that finger again. It was beginning to annoy me.

"So what do you want? Lay it on the table because the hamburgers are probably going to be here soon, and I'm not going to want to discuss this shit when there's food to be eaten."

He roared out a laugh and slapped the table. "I like you. You know that? I like you. So here's the deal, Iblis. We want first rights to the licenses to any technology coming out of New Hell."

"Sure." That would probably be nothing. Like demons were going to be creating new cell phones or something. Idiot.

"We also want first rights to any food products for sale at three percent of current wholesale market value."

I shrugged. "Okay."

"And no further humans can leave New Hell into the United States without appropriate immigration documentation."

"Whoa, whoa. We're not going to be responsible for humans trying to leave," I told him. "If you don't want them coming over here, then it's your problem, not ours—I mean, not New Hell's."

He nodded. "We'll take appropriate measures, although I'm going to announce that New Hell is paying for them."

"We're not paying for anything." Where the fuck were these damned burgers?

"I know that. You know that. No one else needs to know that." He chuckled. "Lastly, we would like to send certain humans into New Hell—those we feel might be better suited to that sort of government style."

I wasn't fucking born yesterday. "Convicts? You're going to use New Hell as a giant prison?"

He waved a hand, not meeting my eyes. "Weeeell, that's a rather harsh way of putting it. I just believe that convicted murderers, rapists, and other dangerous people would be better off there."

Hadn't Nyalla said incarceration cost eighty thousand dollars per inmate? Or was it forty thousand? I knew it was a fuckton of money, either way.

"We'll take your criminals, but you need to pay for each one that you're shoving into New Hell."

"How much?"

Damn, this guy was desperate. "Two hundred grand per person."

He made a choking noise. "Per year?"

"Nope. Flat fee." I watched him as he did the math. "That's saving you and your taxpayers big time. Anyone sentenced more than five years? Huge savings. And I assume you'll only be sending lifers and death penalty people our way?"

"Yes." He frowned. One of the men loitering around the room stepped forward and murmured something to him. "Okay. Deal."

I stood and shook his hand just as Jones walked back in, a dozen bags in his hands. The delicious aroma of beef and fries wafted through the air. This wasn't so bad. I was getting lunch and booze. New Hell was going to make money on this convict thing. We'd totally black-market tech and sell produce around the trade agreements I'd just made, *and* I'd just worked out some sweet immigration deals for demons while sticking it to the angels.

The whole thing was a win-win.

CHAPTER 6

J walked in on Lux and Samael sitting on my kitchen floor playing quarters, only with rings instead of coins. For a moment I stood, transfixed by the beauty of the original Satan. He was so breathtaking with his tanned skin, white-blond hair, and incredibly perfect physical form which, of course, was absolutely naked. Just as I was counting rippled abs that led to a truly impressive cock, the fallen angel bounced a ring off the floor. It chimed when it hit the wood, then made a splosh sound as it landed right into the plastic cup. Beer foamed up around it.

"Yay!" Lux raised his little fists in the air, then grabbed the cup and downed the contents. A beer-foam mustache framed his upper lip as he slammed the cup down.

Samael waved a finger and the cup refilled. Lux pulled the ring from his mouth and bounced it on the floor, landing it squarely in the fallen angel's cup.

"Nice! I'm impressed by your quick mastery of this game," Samael said.

Lux belched. I swear the house shook from the vibration.

I sat down beside him and picked up one of the empty beer cans.

"Natural Light? Are you fucking kidding me? If you're going to get my kid drunk playing quarters, at least use a decent brew—maybe a local brewpub IPA."

Samael made a gagging noise. "Pretentious shit. This is real beer. This is the stuff humans were making thousands of years ago so they didn't die because they drank water that every boar, deer, and wolf from a hundred miles around had shit in. This was what they drank so they could work all day and not be falling down drunk. *This*"—he held up the can —"this is real beer."

I snorted. "It's got corn syrup in it. Unless natives on this continent were making beer a thousand years ago, then this isn't what your peasants were drinking."

Not that I had room to talk. I'd drunk my fair share of light American beers with both corn and rice fermentation sugars.

"Natural Light is the elixir of the gods," Samael declared.

"Of the gods!" Lux lifted the red cup in the air then went to drink. I snatched it from his hands before he could take a sip and downed the whole thing.

Then *I* belched. Lux clapped his hands and cheered.

"Been to New Hell yet?" I asked Samael as I filled the cup and placed it back on the floor.

"A few times. Nice place. Course I'm not one to set down roots anywhere."

Of course not. "What have you been up to today, besides playing drinking games with your uncle?" I asked Lux.

"Rings," the little angel told me. "I taked back ten after I go to two galaxies then Uranus with Da."

Uranus. Hahaha.

"That's awesome." I ruffled his golden curls. "The easy pile, right? You didn't have any problems?"

The little angel gave me two thumbs up. "No problems. Sneak in. Sneak out. Just like you say."

"Bravo!" I grabbed a couple of cans and popped the tops, handing one to Lux. We clinked them and each took a sip.

"Should I take back more?" Lux asked.

I hesitated. This was the easy pile. There was no risk for him to do these by himself. The kid had managed to steal all these rings without any issue, he certainly could return some of them without incident. And less rings under my living room carpet would be a good thing.

"I've got a few things to do today," I told him. "Why don't you wait. I want to be nearby in case you need me."

"I'll go with him," Samael said, bouncing a ring into the other cup.

I gave the fallen angel some serious side-eye, not sure what had suddenly prompted his offer of assistance. He'd always been fond of Lux, but that fondness didn't seem to extend beyond the occasional visit or the delivery of a strange gift—like the goat out in the pasture with the horses, or the hot sauce of the month subscription. He was that whacky uncle, here one day and gone the next, but not the sort to offer to actually help when help was needed.

None of that mattered though, because I was taking him up on this before he changed his mind.

"Deal," I said, realizing I sounded a lot like the president. I'd wanted to take Lux with me to see Dar so he could hang with Karrae, so I'd push that off for tomorrow, and try to squeeze something else in today.

Fuck. When did I become so industrious? I looked down at the hideous ring on my finger and turned the band so the gray stones were more centered. I really hated all this work, but the sooner I got shit done, the sooner I could get back to relaxing in my house and spending time with those I loved.

I'd get through this. The meetings with national leaders.

The updates on Hel and New Hell. The fucking rings. Amber's equally fucking wedding. Yelling at the neighbors about all the dead shit out front of my house.

But there *was* the epic bachelorette party. Then *my* bachelorette party. And *my* wedding, which would be a huge fun party.

"You coming to the wedding?" I asked Samael as I twisted the ring around my finger.

"Amber and Irix? I'm not sure. I mean, I didn't get an invitation, which makes me particularly inclined to attend, but then again I'm not fond of churches, and weddings are boring as fucking hell."

"No, I mean *my* wedding."

Samael was mid-swallow on a beer when I'd said that. He made a horrible gurgling noise, and beer came out of both his mouth and nose. After a few minutes of coughing with Lux helpfully pounding him on the back, he managed to catch his breath.

"You...Michael..." he gasped.

"What? Is it so shocking that your eldest brother would decide to go through a human commitment ritual with me?"

"It's that my eldest brother would go through a commitment ritual with anyone. He's older than the fucking sun and he's never done more than some recreational joining with an angel here or there."

"You had to have known this was serious. I mean, I'm an imp for fuck's sake. The Archangel Michael starts fucking an imp, you know he's gone over to the dark side."

Samael laughed. "That's true. If he's fucking an imp and helping raise her adopted angel, then he's in it for the long haul."

He better be in it for the long haul, or I was going to shred his wings. Or maybe chain him in my basement with an elven collar on him so he'd never escape me, serial killer style. No way my asshole angel was ever walking away from me. Ever.

"I want you at the wedding. Seriously. You're whacky Uncle Samael to Lux. You pop in and out of my house all the time. I consider you sort-of a friend, sort-of a brother-in-law already. I mean, look what I'm marrying into here. I'm going to have to put up with Gabe for the rest of my fucking life. Uri and Rafi are pretty cool, but they're still Angels of Order. I need you bro. I totally need you."

"I'll think about it." He scowled, but I could tell he was flattered. Samael's sin was pride, and I knew how to stoke that fire.

"You can be my Maid of Honor," I told him. "You'd look incredible in an ugly turquoise dress. We're getting married in Vegas. There will be blackjack, drugs, booze, and hookers. It's gonna be awesome. Elvis is officiating."

Samael's eyebrows shot up. "You've got a necromancer who can bring him back?"

"Nah." I waved a hand. "But there are plenty of Elvis impersonators. I want you there. And I'm sure your brother wants you there, if he only had the guts to admit it."

"Who's his best man?"

There was a tinge of bitterness in Samael's voice that made my chest hurt.

"I don't know. We haven't really sat down and planned much or even thought of dates." I resisted the urge to reach out to him, instinctively knowing that Samael wouldn't appreciate my sympathy over his sibling issues.

We drank beer in quiet for a while. Even Lux was silent. Finally Samael sighed, draining the his beer and tossing the can into the trash.

"Okay. I'll be your Maid of Honor. But the dress needs to be really ugly and I want one of those corsages on my wrist like girls wore to high school dances back in the '80s."

I did a fist pump then leaned over to hug the fallen angel. "Perfect! Lux, you hang with Uncle Samael for the rest of today. Return as many rings as you can. I'll order dinner, then I need to run out. I'll be back late, but I'll check in on you if you're asleep. Okay?"

Lux gave me a wide grin. "Okay. Love you."

Again, my insides twisted into a heap. "I love you, too."

* * *

I LEFT Samael and Lux playing quarters, and headed out to work.

First stop was my neighbor's house where I argued with them about the dead shit on my porch. They swore on every relative they'd ever known that they weren't poisoning rats and other animals and sending them my way. In fact, they were claiming they'd become vegan and didn't even wear leather anymore, let alone set out poison. After listening to them lecture me about the evils of horse and goat captivity, and how Boomer would be better off turned loose in the wild, I finally left.

Boomer loose in the wild would be a fucking nightmare. No cemetery would be safe. He'd be digging up and eating corpses the night after their interment. And Diablo? Nobody wanted a demon horse terrorizing the neighborhood. The horses were all happy, eating grass and hay, lounging in my pasture and occasionally being ridden. And the goat too, although I hadn't figured out how to ride it yet.

But if my neighbors weren't poisoning these animals, then who was? It certainly wasn't Wyatt. He ignored any insects or wildlife that came into his house, too occupied with gaming and his internet security business to bother with pest control. Hell, his fridge still had that door that nearly fell off every time someone opened it. But Wyatt and those asshole neighbors were the only ones within half a mile of my house. No poisoned animal would be able to travel that sort of distance to die on my front porch.

Maybe it wasn't poison. Magic? A curse? I thought about what I'd learned of elven magic and the human offshoot. A curse seemed reasonable. There was a list longer than my driveway of those who might be pissed off enough to curse me, but dead animals? That seemed a bit lame for a curse. In my experience, curses tended to be things like wasting disease, daily vehicular breakdowns, incurable diarrhea—that sort of thing. Not dying animals on the porch.

On my way back, I stopped by my guest house to see if the Lows had any idea about what might be causing my dead animal issue. They seemed surprised, and went on to suggest all sorts of things, including that I might be attracting dead things because of my titular role as leader of Hel.

I was the Iblis, not the fucking grim reaper.

Deciding the dead animal problem was a mystery which had hopefully ended since I hadn't seen any more since this morning, I decided to forget about it and head off for an errand that wasn't on my to-do list.

The sun was setting in Ireland, but it had stopped raining, and even with the gray cloudy skies I could see a hell of a lot more than I could last night. The fields were a vibrant green, the mud from last night's downpour lined the shoulders of the two-lane road. The bodies of the angels had been removed instead of just hidden from view, and there, smack in the middle of a cow pasture was a wild gate—*the* wild gate. It was the same wild gate Gregory had closed last night.

The rain had washed away prints, but I could see from the churned-up mud and grass that a struggle had definitely taken place. I was no expert, but as I walked around to the various spots where the dead angels had been, I began to suspect something. It wasn't one monster that had killed these angels, it was a several. And that was a good thing because the thought of one monster powerful enough to kill ten angels was disturbing. Four, five, or ten monsters? That was a whole lot less scary. Although that meant there could possibly be four, five, or ten things roaming around Ireland right now.

Walking over to the gate I reached out and touched its energy, confirming that it was the same gate we'd closed last night. If I'd been with any other angel, I would have suspected they'd screwed up, but Gregory didn't screw up. This gate had been completely closed, then reopened—which made me think it wasn't actually one of the wild gates that were randomly popping up here and there around the world.

Gregory had said he'd send his enforcers to look for whatever might have come through the gate and stayed, but if the gate kept reopening, then we were going to have a problem with shit coming and even going. But if the oldest of the archangels couldn't close this thing, who could?

As an experiment, I tossed a clod of dirt through. Nothing came back out, so I took a deep breath, pulled my spirit-self away from my arm, and shoved the limb through the gate. The other side felt cold, and when I pulled my arm back, I saw it was pale with frostbite. Recreating the limb, I left my spirit-self in the cells and tried again. Although my flesh seemed ill equipped for whatever was on the other side, my spirit-self wasn't affected, so I decided to do something incredibly stupid and shove my head through to take a look around.

It was so cold that my breath frosted in the air and my inhalation stung my lungs, but the other side of this gate was unexpectedly full of color and light. I reached out with my spirit-self and touched a wall of ice and glass. It was like someone had taken a mirrored funhouse and stuck it at the South Pole. Reluctant to do more than just stick my head and arm through, I looked around and saw nothing but glass and ice. Whatever had come through and killed the angels, it was nowhere to be seen.

Pulling back, I recreated my frozen flesh, glad to be in the relative warmth of Ireland once more. There were no hideous creatures on the other side waiting to rip my head off. Whatever had come through before was probably unlikely to come through again. Other than the occasional cow wandering into the gate and dying of frostbite on the other side, I couldn't see any immediate danger. It had to have been a complete fluke what had happened to those angels—and that was a relief.

What the fuck should I do about this stupid gate, though? If cows started vanishing, some farmer was going to check, and then people would start vanishing too. Maybe I could surround the thing with orange cones and caution tape as if it were a sinkhole? Although that might just make the humans more curious to examine what was beyond the tape.

No, I'd need to let Gregory know the gate had reopened and we needed a different solution—perhaps some sort of force field around it like he'd done with the gates to Hel so people and animals wouldn't accidently stumble through.

Jamming a few sticks in the ground to mark the spot for Gregory, I sent a text to him outlining the problem, then headed off to what I hoped would be my last errand for the day.

* * *

HEL HADN'T CHANGED MUCH since I'd been a young demon. The swamps were the same, the arid deserts were the same. The only things that had changed were in the places that had once been the Elven kingdoms. They'd been lush forests when I was young, but with the elven exodus, their lands had been slowly changing. Deciduous trees were wilting and drying away. Half a mile into the former elven territories the land was quickly reverting to desert. There were still elves in Hel, but they weren't the elves who were skilled in environmental management. They were the left behind ones, the ones who'd been deemed not critical to the plans to take over the human lands. I felt for them, but they still had choices. They could remain here and live in the environment that Hel provided, or they could walk through the gates and deal with what the humans demanded—and the angels demanded.

I headed for Dis, going straight to Gareth's shop. The last time I'd been there the building had been surrounded by several layers of tight spells to keep thieves and intruders from getting within fifty feet of the door. Not only were those wards gone, but the shop was closed.

This wasn't the "be back after lunch" sort of closed either. It looked like the place had gone out of business. Plywood covered the windows, and the locked door had lumber in an X nailed across it. There was no way a skilled sorcerer would have gone out of business in Dis, so I peeked through cracks in the plywood to see inside, wondering if this was some new security system.

Inside the store was empty. Even the cabinets and shelves were gone. It was just a building, without so much as a sprig of herbs to indicate what had previously been sold here.

Had Gareth died? What the hell had happened? I left the store and went over to my home, hoping someone in my household would know.

The freaky horror show of a house that had once belonged to Ahriman had a few new skulls decorating the porch along with a blackened section of the stone from an explosion, but was otherwise the same as I'd last seen it. Ahriman may have been a psychotic asswipe, but the guy knew how to build a sturdy house. If it could stand up to the antics of my Lows, it could stand up to anything.

Inside a dozen of my household were doing keg stands, taking bets on how much they could imbibe before they puked or their stomachs exploded. The Lows popped back and forth between Hel and my home in the human world regularly, so I was never really sure who would be here and who wouldn't. Recognizing Snip, I was just about to ask him where they'd gotten the keg when I read the tag on the tap.

Natural Light. I was really going to have to do something about that guy's beer preferences.

"Iblis!" Snip shrieked. I was instantly mobbed by a dozen Lows who tried to pull my wings, and claw my skin in an affectionate greeting. One of the Lows vomited, thankfully missing me and spraying two of his buddies instead.

I held up my hands, trying to push the crowd back a bit. "Sorry I can't stay and do keg stands. No, I didn't bring a beer funnel. Yes, you guys can break into that case of pork rinds in the kitchen."

Finally they went back to their beer games, leaving me with only a few rips in my clothing and some splatter on my pants leg that I hoped was drool.

"Did you need our assistance, Mistress?" Snip asked. "Are we going to kill more angels? Let the air out of police car tires? Set all the animals loose from the pound?"

I sighed, remembering those antics. Good times. "Sadly, my duties right now are terribly boring. I wouldn't torture you all by making you sit through meetings with foreign leaders."

Snip patted my arm with a tentacle. He'd modified his demon form a bit, and I admired the lovely peach shade of the suckers.

"I actually came to Dis to see Gareth. Did he die or something? His shop looks like it's been shut down for a while."

"It has been, Mistress," Snip replied. "He started spending the occasional time across the gates about a year ago, and moved permanently a few months back."

Of all the humans I'd expected to leave Hel, Gareth hadn't been one. He was a changeling child, brought to Hel as a baby. He'd spent his whole life being trained by the elves in the magical arts. After fleeing slavery, he'd made quite a good living among the demons. I couldn't imagine why he'd give that up for a life in a human realm where he didn't even know any of their languages.

Well, I could imagine, but it still seemed a bit farfetched for him to pull up stakes and move.

"Do you know if Kirby is still around?" *He* was the one I figured might decide to return to the human realm, although his primary loyalty had always seemed to be with the human settlement in Hel named Libertytown.

"I think so, Mistress. The humans don't always let me inside the gates of their city, so I'm not sure. I did hear Bleek say she saw him a few weeks back when he was out gathering river stones."

I thanked Snip and watched my Lows get drunk and puke for a while, just to be polite, then I headed to the human settlement, the home they'd carved out of Hel at the edge of the elven lands.

The last time I'd seen Libertytown it was a stone-walled village with rustic houses and cobblestone streets. A lot had clearly changed in such a short time, because I barely recognized the town before me. The streets were asphalt. The houses were gorgeous structures with solar panels and electric power lines. As I walked through the gates, a delivery truck appeared from nowhere, cruising down the street to halt before a house. A man got out and began hauling grocery sacks full of vegetables and fruits from the truck.

Amber had totally made good on her deal with both me

and Kirby as far as food delivery went, but the rest was a huge surprise. I made my way through the town, noting the window air conditioning units, and a Segway parked outside one of the brick homes. People peeked out at me through windows, and suddenly decided they needed to sweep their porches. Kirby's shop and residence was near the center of town, and by the time I opened the door of the magic shop, I'd acquired quite a group of followers.

A bell on the door rang merrily. A blonde woman looked up with a smile on her face, saw my wings, then called for Kirby.

The mage came out of a back room, a bundle of lavender in his hands.

"Iblis!" He set down the flowers and came to shake my hand—which was a whole lot less painful than the Low's greeting. "Have you come to check up on us?"

"I actually came to ask Gareth a few questions, but it seems he's moved?"

Kirby nodded. "He's living in Florida now."

Okaaaay. Moving to Florida was definitely what elderly humans seemed to do, but Gareth was a sorcerer and had never stepped foot over the gates since he'd been stolen from his crib.

"Do you know why?"

Kirby's face turned pink. The dude was a horrible liar. He obviously realized this, and decided to just come out with the truth. He looked up at me and shrugged.

"Remember the business venture to sell magical items to humans? Amulets, and wards, and spells that could be used to protect against demons, angels, shifters, and elves?"

I did remember. "Yeah. Hunter's been selling them for you off a website."

"It's been very successful, and I got the idea that we could do more than just magical home security and personal protection. I went to Gareth with the idea, and he agreed to go into a partnership with me."

"And this business is based in Florida? Where Gareth is now living?"

He nodded. "Blue Fire. We intended to produce scaled-up magical items for businesses and law enforcement. We figured it would make a bit more money than the personal protection stuff, but the whole thing went crazy when the demons stormed across the gates. I mean *crazy*. Gareth and I needed an investor who knew more about how finances and contracts work in the human world. We had to hire anyone we could find with magical skills to keep up with demand, including a few elves—and the irony of that doesn't escape me. It grew overnight. I can't be there full time with my commitments here, so Gareth took over. He's learning English, and one of the other mages translates for him."

"And this business is supplying magical items to humans," I said, just to confirm. "Items they can use to defend themselves against angels and demons."

"Yes, but it's not just weapons," he protested. "One of our first products was amulets so that elves don't kill themselves with all the iron around them. Nearly every elf needs one to function in a human world. But yes, it seems security systems and weaponry are going to be our main products."

"Weaponry like guns?"

He nodded. "We've got different options for firearms, wands and amulets, specialized wards and defensive perimeters—that sort of thing."

"Project Woo-woo," I mused.

Kirby's eyebrows shot up. "You know about that?"

"A certain first world leader had some documents clearly visible on his desk. I made a wild guess that you or Gareth have something to do with it."

"We do. It's our biggest contract. Military grade stuff. I'm a little nervous about it, but Gareth says he can make it happen."

I thought back on this afternoon's conversation at the White House. The money saved on prisons was most likely going for defense spending—to support project Woo-woo. Had the president lied about welcoming demons and providing them with citizenship? Probably not. I could see him wanting to secure the votes, plus he seemed quite enamored of Dar. But the weaponry *would* be a wise precaution if we demons did what we always did. It would also be useful against angels, and even the shifter population.

All the government needed to do was stoke their constituents' fear. Powerful supernatural beings were poised to take over. The demons had already seized the western states. There were still a significant number of people who believed those doctored videos of werewolves and bear shifters slaughtering humans. And the angels...suddenly they were everywhere, all powerful, and *not* the benevolent messengers humans had always assumed they'd be.

I had one more question for Kirby, though.

"Who is your financial backer? The one who is helping you with contracts and that kind of thing?"

"A demon. He's got money, connections, and clout. We cut a deal where he owns thirty-four percent of the company in exchange for the money we needed and his leverage on government deals."

I nodded. "And this demon's name is...?"

Kirby winced. "Dar."

CHAPTER 7

No one was home when I returned, and thankfully there were no dying animals in front of my house. I was still stuffed from gorging myself on hamburgers, fries, and rum and cokes earlier in the day, so I took a quick power nap, then decided to keep my promise to Lux and return a few rings.

He'd selected five rings and written down addresses on printouts of Google Maps pictures. There were detailed instructions about where each ring was to go, and a few notes about possible hazards, like barking dogs or squeaky floors.

Two I ruled out because the time of day wasn't optimal. I didn't want to show up in the middle of a mall jewelry store during business hours. Same with the bank safety deposit box. I did a quick eenie-meenie-miney-moe with the remaining three and decided I'd take back a diamond solitaire from Phoenix. If I hurried, they'd still be at work, and I'd be in and out before rush hour even started. Thinking I'd try to get the other two rings in before nightfall, I shoved them in my pocket along with Lux's print outs and notes, and headed out.

Phoenix was hotter than Hel. Literally. The pavement shimmered with the heat. The bottom of my sneakers started to melt as I crossed the street and eyed the house I was about to break into.

It was really pretty, and just what I'd envisioned from Lux's description. At the edge of a preserve with the blue shadows of mountains in the distance, the house had amazing views. It was a reddish gold adobe with terra cotta tile roofing. I meandered up the driveway toward the three-car garage and what I'd assumed was the front door. It wasn't. The doorway had an iron gate and led to a central paved courtyard with huge potted plants and citrus trees as well as a southwestern themed fountain. Toward the back was the main door, but a French door off to the side led to what looked to be a bedroom from my view between the slats of the shades.

Inside the house was starkly contemporary with wide open spaces and white everything except for the dark walnut flooring. The living room was open past the second floor and filled with huge picture windows and doors to the loggia and the pool. I looked out back and saw in addition to a pool, they had a sunken spa, and a built-in barbeque grill—all in matching stone.

I wandered around taking in the library, the formal dining room, the theater, the huge kitchen with granite countertops and a butler's pantry. Everything was white, white, white, and walnut wood. It was a gorgeous house, but I was itching for some color.

The stairs were carpeted—in white, of course—and the balusters were wrought iron. Upstairs, the first bedroom had gray drapes and pillow shams to accent the walnut and white. I checked out the funky mid-century bedside table lights, then the equally monochromatic private bathroom.

Perusing three more bedrooms and a few hallway bathrooms, I finally found the master. The walk-in closets—yes, there were *two*—had an insane amount of clothing and shoes. The master bath had a spa tub and a shower so big it could have easily hosed off an elephant. All white and walnut, with none of the daring gray of that first bedroom.

It was pretty and I loved the view, but I preferred the other house with the infinity pool. Even if I went to town on this place with some paint, and gaudy upholstery and rugs, it still seemed rather sterile.

Deciding I'd taken long enough on my tour, I headed back downstairs to where Lux had said I was supposed to put the ring. Evidently he'd swiped it from a ring holder beside the kitchen sink. I'm sure the owner had missed it, and would be perplexed to find it back on the holder, but that wasn't my problem. I'd be long gone by the time they got home, and they'd never suspect an imp had been prowling around their home, criticizing their decorating choices.

I'd just left the bedroom when I heard a noise in the living room below. Shit! Were the owners home early? I froze, listening carefully for another noise. Maybe I could just ditch the ring on a bedside table and get the heck out of here.

There was another sound—a click noise. And it sounded like it came from down the hall. Had I been so busy checking out the ginormous walk in closets that I hadn't heard the owners coming home and walking up the stairs?

Holding my breath, I turned around, thankful that the upstairs was carpeted. Before I could step back into the bedroom, a figure came around the corner and shot me.

Fucker. I recognized the uniform and knew instantly it was a cop. Lux hadn't said anything about a security alarm, and I hadn't seen one when I came in, but that was the only explanation for why a cop would be roaming around this house. And why he'd be shooting me. Unless the owner was a cop and he'd just gotten off work. Or the cop was here robbing the place. Honestly the first was probably the most likely explanation, though.

All this ran through my mind in a split second, along with outrage that I'd been shot without even a warning to put my hands up or something. Was this the way police in Arizona did things?

"On the floor. Hands on your head."

Oh, *now* the cop was giving me instructions. *After* he'd shot me. It was a good thing I was a demon, or I'd have been bleeding all over the white carpet. Actually I should have been bleeding, even as a demon. I looked down to see a blue splat on my shirt, as if I'd been shot by a paintball gun.

"I said on the floor! Hands on your head!" The cop moved closer, still holding the gun in one hand, and reaching for something else with the other. That blue paint better come out in the wash, because I liked this shirt.

"Fuck you," I told the cop, then teleported out of the house and back home.

Only I didn't teleport anywhere. I tried again. Nothing happened. That's when I ran.

Normally I'm pretty damned fast, but for some reason I felt like I was slogging through quicksand as I ran down the stairs. The cop was on me before I reached the front door, shoving me against the wall, then shooting me with his Taser.

The electrodes dug into my skin and I felt a zap of pain. None of my muscles worked anymore and I crashed to the floor. The asshole was sadistic about it, keeping his finger on the button for what felt like a fucking half hour. When he finally let up, I could do nothing but twitch and try to breathe.

Before I knew it I was on my back with my hands cuffed behind me. A second cop had arrived, and he searched me, finding not only the ring I was intending on returning here, but the other two as well as Lux's notes and the maps.

I was patted down with a thoroughness that would have turned me on if I hadn't been in so much pain. Everything hurt. I'd never hurt like this before. Ever. Is this what it felt like to be human? If so, it really fucking sucked. How did humans deal with this on a day-to-day basis? I needed an aspirin. I needed morphine. Fuck, I hurt.

The two cops hauled me up and dragged me out of the house, stuffing me into the back of a police car without any respect or care whatsoever. They didn't even seatbelt me in, and I think they were getting evil satisfaction in taking every corner as fast as they could just to hear me bounce around the back of the cruiser. Once we'd arrived at the station, they lugged me inside like I was a side of beef, printing me and taking a mug shot.

Then I got seriously searched. We're talking fingers in cavities searched. Traumatized as I was, I still managed to crack a few jokes about how foreplay would have been nice, or at least some damned lube.

They took all my clothes, my cell phone, and my wallet. I was given a scratchy orange jumpsuit to wear, then was put into a tiny cell with a crude toilet in the corner and a hard metal bench to sit on.

This was *not* the way arrests went on TV. Weren't they supposed to put me in an interview room with my own clothes still on? Weren't they supposed to question me? Get me nasty police station coffee and snacks from the vending machine? Let me have my one phone call? I didn't even remember them reading me my rights. Had those television shows been completely wrong? Was this how they conducted arrests in Arizona? I'd been hauled in a few times in my life, and never experienced anything like this before.

And then there was the paint ball gun, which obviously *wasn't* a paint ball gun. Was this the sort of weapon Kirby and Gareth were selling? I wasn't sure what I'd been envisioning, but it hadn't been spelled paint balls that kept me from using any of my demon abilities. This was horrible. It was as if I'd suddenly been turned into a human. How long was this supposed to last? Shit, I hoped the effect was temporary and not permanent.

The idea chilled me. No, it couldn't be permanent. Kirby wouldn't make something like that. Actually, I'm not sure either Kirby or Gareth *could* make something like that. I felt around my spirit-self, trying to gauge what had actually been done to me. It felt just like when I'd worn that elven collar, although this time there was no collar around my neck.

What the fuck had they done to me? And how long would it be until it wore off? Once again I pushed down a wave of panic, refusing to consider that it might not ever wear off. Would I still be the Iblis if I had no demon, or angel, abilities? Was I even a being of spirit anymore? What would my life be like as a human. In jail.

I took a deep breath and tried to calm myself. I was still the same imp even if I couldn't teleport, or fix my bruises, or run any faster than an incredibly out-of-shape couch potato. I could still beat the shit out of any inmate who tried to steal my pudding at lunch. I could still stir up chaos. Fate still had my back. I'd come out on top, even if I had to tunnel through a mountain of shit first.

But I didn't want to tunnel through shit. I didn't want to wear an orange jumpsuit for ten to twenty, fighting other women for pudding at lunch and sleeping on a hard, stainless steel bench. I wanted to be home with Lux and Gregory and Nyalla. I wanted to attend Amber's bachelorette party, to wear that hideous dress in her wedding. I wanted to marry my angel in Vegas with his prodigal brother by my side in a turquoise gown with a wrist corsage, with Elvis officiating the ceremony. I wanted to ride Diablo, visit with Little Red, kill the not-yet-dead rodents on my front porch. I wanted to eat hot wings and drink iced vodka—the good kind, not that cheap shit.

Did they serve hot wings in prison? If they didn't, that surely would be the definition of cruel and unusual punishment.

I waited in that nasty-ass cell, but no one came. Shouldn't someone have been telling me what I was charged with, even though I knew they'd arrested me for breaking and entering as well as theft. Fuck, I'd had those other rings with me too. No doubt they were checking burglary reports for the locations Lux had helpfully written down for me, matching the rings in my pocket to those descriptions, and preparing to charge me for those thefts as well. Great, my ten to twenty was probably looking like fifty to seventy. And I doubted an imp would be getting out early for good behavior either.

I tried to shake off my funk by standing and trying to see what was outside the bars of my cell. This was clearly a jail at a local station or county courthouse, because it was far too quiet to be an actual prison. I could see a short hallway, and what looked like another four to five cells to my left. Either the people in them were passed out drunk or comatose, or they were empty because I couldn't even hear footsteps or the sounds of someone peeing.

There was no way to tell the passage of time in here. No clock. No watch. No cell phone. The florescent lights were painfully bright, and buzzing with a constant noise that made me want to rip my ears off. Bored, frustrated, and feeling completely off-kilter, I curled up on the stainless steel bench and closed my eyes. I was pretty sure hours had passed before I'd finally fallen asleep.

* * *

I WOKE up to someone unlocking my cell door. It must have been morning because I was absolutely starving as well as dehydrated as fuck. I still had bruises and my back didn't want to bend properly, no doubt because I'd lain for hours on a cold metal bench.

The bailiff, or whoever the hell he was, hooked another set of cuffs on my ankles with a chain that led to the ones on my wrists they'd never removed from last night. I followed him out, taking fast tiny steps to try to keep up. As I passed the other cells, I glanced to see if I'd had any neighbors last night.

Nope. I'd been the only one privileged to be incarcerated here awaiting whatever I was heading toward right now. I assumed this would be my arraignment, as I'd learned from watching countless hours of *Law and Order*, but who knew what the fuck was going to happen.

Once I got inside the tiny courtroom, it became evident that no one knew what the fuck was going to happen. The judge and a woman I assumed was the prosecutor were having an interesting argument about whether I should be arraigned here or sent to ICE for deportation, as I was not truly a citizen.

Every time I'd been arrested before I'd been treated as a human, as a citizen, as Samantha Martin. ICE? Where the fuck were they going to deport me to? New Hell? Hel? I'd almost welcome that if they could give me my demon abilities back before they did.

Evidently federal immigration did not yet have the policies and procedures set up to deal with non-humans, which left me stuck with this judge who looked as if he really didn't want to be handling my case.

The woman read the charges of breaking and entering and theft, saying there were possibly pending charges in other states as well. Then she went on to say that because I was a demon, I was a flight risk and she was recommending bail be remanded.

I knew exactly what that meant from all those episodes of *Law and Order*. Frantically looking around, I wondered if anyone had assigned me an attorney or if I was supposed to be representing myself.

"Can I speak to that?" I asked.

"Go ahead," the judge told me.

"First, I didn't break anything, although I did enter. I also didn't steal anything. I was returning the ring that someone else stole. Same with the other two rings."

"You'll have time to put forth that defense during the trial," the judge said.

"I'm the Iblis. I'm on the Ruling Council. I've got important things I'm supposed to be doing."

"We're determining bail," the judge snapped. "You need to be telling me why you're not a flight risk."

"Maybe because I can't even fly right now," I snapped back. "That cop shot me without saying a word. I can't go anywhere unless I take a bus. I can't do anything. They took my clothes, my phone—"

"We were worried she'd call another demon to magic her out of the jail," the woman interrupted.

"They *shot* me. I didn't get to make a phone call. I didn't get questioned or read my rights. I got put in a cell overnight with my cuffs still on. I haven't had food or water since they arrested me. Where's my lawyer? I don't even get a lawyer or an opportunity to call one?" I held my hands up. "At least set bail so I can get a lawyer."

"I can't see denying bail on these charges," the judge told the woman. "B&E with no property damage. Possession of a ring valued at ten thousand that was reported stolen three days ago. I can't see anything that shows she's a danger to anyone. She didn't even resist arrest."

"Because the arresting officer shot her," the woman argued.

"And I have a problem with that." The judge scowled. "Even shot, she still could have hit, or kicked, or bit, or swore. She didn't do any of that. Is your only basis for requesting remand that she's a demon and might not show up for trial? Because we take that risk with pretty much everyone we set bail for."

"She's a demon…" the woman said.

"Who currently has no demon powers whatsoever," the judge interrupted. "Bail set at five thousand dollars, which is still uncharacteristically high for these charges."

The prosecutor woman clamped her mouth shut and glared over at me. I resisted the urge to stick my tongue out at her, or flip her the bird. The bailiff took me back to my cell, and an hour later I was dressed in my paint-stained clothes, putting my bail on my credit card, and calling for an Uber.

On my phone were a bunch of messages from Nyalla. In the first she wanted to know if I was coming back last night or not. It seemed Samael had dropped Lux off after their ring returning expedition, and she wasn't sure if we had plans or if she could take Lux to an arcade then to a sleepover with Austin.

There were another two messages, then one saying she was going ahead with her plans for Lux, and to let her know if I needed Lux back before tomorrow (today) at noon.

There was a message from Gregory about the wild gate near Dublin, then another annoyed that he'd had to drag

Snip there to show him the gate's exact location, then yet another message where he questioned the efficiency of this communication method when I clearly was refusing to return his calls or message him back.

Darci had left a message wanting to know if I'd picked the location for the bachelorette party. The dress store had called to let me know my alterations were done and my gown ready for pick up.

As the Uber driver took me to the airport, I tried to decide what I should do. Being without any demon abilities was frightening and embarrassing. I didn't want anyone to know, but I was pretty sure it would be obvious once I started driving and taking a plane everywhere instead of teleporting. Looking down at the blue stain on my shirt, I wondered once again when, or if, the effects were going to wear off. Was there a counter spell I'd get after my trial? Could I wait that long before I went crazy or someone killed me?

I'd purchased a ticket and was making my way through security when Nyalla called again.

"Oh good! Are you almost home? I'm on my way to pick up Lux from Harper's. And there's another dead rat on the front porch. At least I think it's another dead rat. I might be a small groundhog. I'm not sure."

"I'll take care of it as soon as I'm back," I told her. "I'll be home around…" I glanced at the ticket. "Five. I've got a few more things to do first. Lux should be fine on his own, but tell him to absolutely not return any more rings unless his father or one of his uncles or Aunt Uriel goes with him."

As frightened and powerless as I felt right now, I was more worried that Lux would have the same thing happen to him. I'd like to think that no human would shoot a winged, golden-haired, toddler, but I didn't want to risk it.

I chatted for a few moments with Nyalla, pretending like

everything was normal as my brain tried to process what the fuck had happened and what I was going to do about it. I'd need to tell Gregory, but if I called him now, he'd swoop in and zip me out of here and back home. It would have saved me a six-hundred-dollar flight, but for some reason I was reluctant to let him know. At least right now. I needed time to think, to process, and to plan before I told him.

I cleared security just as they were announcing boarding for my flight. Unusually subdued for an imp, I boarded, took my seat and stared out the window at the various workers loading luggage and checking whatever the hell they check before the plane takes off.

I would contact Kirby or Gareth and find out what the fuck that cop had shot me with and how to reverse it. Hopefully it was something they'd sold, because if it wasn't I was in a world of trouble. But getting an antidote or a cure wasn't the only thing on my mind. With these weapons widely available the balance of power would shift. What if humans refused to release the counter spell? What if they decided this sort of thing should be permanent? I needed to know exactly what the fuck this spell was, how it was structured, how it could be defeated without an antidote that might be withheld and used to control us.

I needed someone who had at least a layman's knowledge of magic. I needed someone who understood human politics, who understood demons and how magic worked on beings of spirit. Gregory was ancient enough that he probably knew more about elves than anyone, but his knowledge was from millions of years ago, and clearly times had changed. Plus, Gregory had this adorable obliviousness when it came to humans and their world. For a dude who'd been heading up the Grigori for ten thousand years, he really knew jack shit about the people he was supposedly guiding to enlightenment.

I needed someone with knowledge—knowledge that was untainted by any prejudice they might bring to the table. I needed someone who saw information as something sacred and pure, who I could count on to let me have the cold hard unvarnished truth.

I needed a Noodle.

CHAPTER 8

I had the Uber driver drop me at the end of the lane, too embarrassed to have him pull up to my house. Wyatt's and my houses were the only ones on the long narrow road because I'd bought up all the land that was supposed to be developed into six cookie-cutter houses with one acre lots. I'd eagerly awaited the moment when my asshole neighbors, whose field adjoined my pasture, put their place up for sale, but they never had. The only other nearby house was the one Wyatt lived in. I would have bought Wyatt's house when the elderly people living there left, or died, or something, but he outbid me. There was no way I was going to pay that much for a house in such disrepair, so I'd given up a slice of my privacy to the hot blond dude.

Honestly, the fact that he was a hot blond dude greatly outweighed my need for privacy.

I'd flirted shamelessly with him and we'd become friends, then more than friends for a short time. I still had a warm spot for him in my heart, and I suspect he felt the same for me. He'd been a major catalyst in my life. His friendship had sparked a change in me that I still wasn't all that sure that I liked. But change is what an Angel of Chaos is about, so like it or not, it was here to stay.

I eyed his little house as I walked past, irritated that with all the money Wyatt was now making, the place still looked like it should have condemned property tape stretched across the front door. The roof was covered in moss and sagging on the right side. It had to be leaking. Did he even notice the water dripping from his ceiling when it rained? Damn it, the fucking thing was going to come down around his head before he realized it was rotted. Even then he'd probably throw a tarp on the roof and just sweep the debris in a corner.

Fucking hell. I stopped in the middle of the lane and made a call to Michelle, my right-hand woman in my property rentals business.

"Hey, can you get a roofer out here sometime this week?" I said when she picked up the phone.

"Didn't you just have your roof replaced? After the dragon sat on it and nearly came through into your bedroom."

Little Red had gotten the hose for that one, me screaming the whole time for him to get off my fucking roof. That dragon hates the hose. All I have to do is wave it at him, and he takes off. Unfortunately, him taking off meant he took a chunk of my roof with him. I didn't bother explaining to the contractors exactly what had caused the damage. It was one of those don't ask, don't tell situations.

"Not my house, Wyatt's place. Tell them I want new underlayment as well. And check the roofing joists for any rot. Who knows how long it's been leaking."

To Michelle's credit, she didn't even question why I was having my neighbor's roof replaced. The woman got me. She always had, even before she'd known I was a demon.

"Should I call Wyatt and clue him in that he's about to have some construction?" she asked.

I snorted. "Don't bother. He won't notice. The Russians could drop a nuke on his house and he wouldn't even notice."

Actually no one would notice that sort of thing, because death happened pretty quick with nukes. An archangel would survive if he acted quickly, but pretty much everything else would be gone before an "oh shit" could even cross their mind.

I disconnected the call, knowing Michelle would have a new roof on Wyatt's house by the end of the week, and continued toward my home. I'd left the wooded properties along the lane untouched and they were overgrown with briars and poison ivy. My privacy may be long gone with all the Lows, demons, angels, and werewolves in and out of my house day and night, but I still loved the illusion the woods gave. Dark. Secret. The world would never know that something not human lived back here. Except now everyone knew.

Ah well. At least having Satan for a neighbor might make those assholes decide to finally move.

Nyalla's car was parked out front of my house. I picked up the pace, eager to see her and Lux, and almost stepped on a dead rat.

Holy fuck, they were everywhere. It was like a biblical plague of dead rats, except quite a few of them were twitching and crawling around on the ground. The place stank of dirt and rot and maggots. I gagged and tip-toed my way around the rat carcasses to my front door where the shovel was propped up against the trim. A few rats nipped at my feet along the way, and let me tell you it fucking hurt clear through my sneakers. With two of the rodents hanging off my pant legs and blood staining my shoes, I grabbed the shovel and started whacking.

The effort required a good bit of aerobic activity, and since the only thing I'd had to eat in nearly twenty-four hours was a packet of dry roasted peanuts on the plane, I was shaky and weak by the time I'd smashed all the rats. Deciding clean up would have to wait until after I got some food in me, I went inside.

"Ma!" Lux ran to hug my legs, wrinkling his nose once he got within sniffing distance. "You stink."

"I haven't had a shower, and I just sweated a gallon of vodka and old beer killing the rats out front." I scooped him up into my arms. "How are you? Did you have a good time with Austin?"

He grinned. "Austin is funny. He and Karrae are my best friends. Besides you, Ma."

Awww. "You didn't take back any more rings, did you?"

He shook his head. "No. Did you return the three you took?"

"Absolutely," I lied. It wasn't really a lie. The police would get the rings back to their rightful owners. I'd just need to deal with the legal repercussions. My sticky-fingered kid was causing me serious legal nightmares here.

"Thanks." He put his hands on my cheeks and gave me a sloppy kiss. "Missed you, Ma."

"I missed you too." I looked over his shoulder to see Nyalla. "Thanks for taking care of him. I got caught up in a few things and didn't have access to my phone."

Nyalla smiled. "I'm just glad you're back. I grilled up bratwurst and some corn. Are you hungry?" She headed to the French doors that led out to the back patio.

"Starving." I set Lux down. "Oh, and I'll clean up all the dead rats after dinner."

Nyalla stopped and looked over her shoulder. "Sam, there's something weird with those rats. At first I thought it was just animals poisoned by one of the neighbors, but there's so many of them. And they don't look like they were all that healthy before they were poisoned. One of them was nothing more than a skeleton. It tried to bite me."

I felt a flame of rage tear through me. Nyalla was *mine*. No one would hurt her and live. No one.

"I'll find out what's going on." I tried to keep my voice cool and composed as the fire tore through me. "In the meantime, you and Lux use the back door if you see any animals out front."

While Nyalla was finishing dinner, I sent Gregory a quick message letting him know I was home, then I walked over to visit the Lows. Thankfully Snip was there. I pulled him aside and asked him if he remembered Terrelle.

"Yep, although I haven't seen her since Aruba," he told me.

"Can you go get her? I need her to come to my house. I've got a job for her."

Snip shot me a puzzled frown. "I don't know where she is, Mistress."

Of course he didn't. I expanded my awareness, opened myself up to all the demons this side of the gates, then traced the energy signature I knew belonged to Terrelle. Thank the fuck at least this part of my abilities still worked. Still, the ability to sense other demons was so new to me, and it still felt very weird. How did Samael get used to sensing everyone in his choir? How did any of the archangels?

"Orando, Florida," I told Snip. "I'm not exactly sure where in Orlando, but I think she's near the penguins at Sea World. Tell her to pack because I'm not positive how long she'll be staying. Maybe a week. Maybe a month. Can you do that?"

The Low puffed his chest out. "Of course, Mistress. I'll get right on it. Will you teleport me there, or should I purchase a plane ticket?"

Ugh. I couldn't teleport—either me or anyone else. "Take a plane down. You and Terrelle will need to fly back too."

Snip headed off to the airport and I walked back to the house and began cleaning up the dead rats. Then I went inside to shower, coming down just in time to help Lux set the table. It was amazing to have a home cooked meal for once. Deciding I should do my part, I cleaned up the dishes after dinner while Nyalla read stories to Lux.

I was ready to take a food-coma nap on the sofa when Gregory appeared in my living room. He took one step toward me, and halted. He could tell. Just one look at his face and I knew he knew. And he was smart enough to not say a word.

"Did I miss dinner?" He smiled over at Nyalla as he picked up Lux and walked the rest of the way to where I sat on the couch.

"Leftovers are in the fridge," Nyalla told him. "I grilled. Sam called me to say she'd be late, and I knew Lux would be hungry. It was fun to cook for once."

"Well, thank you. And thank you for watching over Lux while we were occupied," Gregory told her

She blushed pink. "It was nothing. I love taking care of him. He's smart, and fun, and so sweet."

Nyalla went into the kitchen and warmed up a plate of food for Gregory, then scooted off to meet some friends. We both listened to Lux tell us about his day, holding off anything more serious until the little angel went up to bed.

After tucking Lux in for the night, Gregory and I came downstairs, but instead of sitting beside me on the sofa, he went into the kitchen. A few minutes later he returned with the bottle of Van Gogh Double Espresso Vodka from my freezer and two shot glasses.

Pouring us both a shot, he put a glass in my hand and sat down. "What happened to you?"

"First tell me what you see, or feel. What does this look like from the outside?"

He tilted his head, narrowing his eyes. "Like you're covered in thick clear plastic. I can see you, but everything about you that's an Angel of Chaos is under the plastic. I can't touch you. It's like you're in a giant cell where only your corporeal self is free to move about."

I let out a breath and downed the shot. It was icy cold and tasted like bitter coffee with an afterburn that scorched my throat. As it settled in my stomach, I felt the alcohol shoot right up to my brain, leaving me with a pleasant fuzziness. As much as I tried to experience every sensory pleasure and pain as a demon, somehow feeling it all as a human was... different. More, somehow. It gave me a new appreciation for these seven billion beings walking around each day.

"I was worried it was all gone," I confessed. "That all you'd see was a human me."

He sat his shot glass on the coffee table and pulled me into his arms. "You're still there. Whatever happened, it didn't destroy the demon part of you, leaving only a human shell. And even if it had, you'd still be my imp, my Cockroach."

My vision blurred with tears and I buried my face into the soft cotton of his shirt, letting all the fear leach out of me and into his strong arms. When I felt better, I wiped my nose on his shirt and sat back, giving him a watery smile.

"So, any idea how to break me out of this clear plastic prison?"

He reached forward to take a lock of my hair and rub it between his fingers. "I'd prefer to know what happened before I start attempting to smash my way through whatever it is imprisoning you."

"I think this all has to do with Project Woo-woo." I picked up his shot glass and drained it before settling back in his arms to tell him the whole story, from my meeting with the president, to my stint in jail.

"And this weapon was a gun? A human firearm that has been modified by sorcery to neutralize our abilities?"

I nodded. "From what you're describing, I'm thinking it acts like the elven nets and the elven collars did, except there's nothing to physically remove to undo the effect."

"Do you want me to pay a visit to this sorcerer Gareth?" Gregory's voice was dark and menacing. It totally turned me on.

"No, I'd rather do it myself. He knows me. We've done a lot of business together in the past. I know this doesn't sound very impish, but I think we're better off not sending in the big guns here—that's you, in case you didn't realize it. You're the biggest of the big guns."

"Are you referring to when I manifest human sexual organs?"

He was teasing. I felt lighter, as if a burden had been lifted from me. If Gregory was teasing, joking about sex, then this couldn't be too bad. He could still see me somewhere beneath this spell. It would all be okay.

And that realization allowed me to stuff the worry and fear under the rug with the rings and think strategically.

"That's the big gun's big gun," I teased back. "I do want to see if this is something you can break through. Snip is out finding Terrelle. She's an information demon, a Noodle. If anyone knows how this weapon works and if there any cracks in the system, she will. Worst case scenario, I'll wait until my trial. I'm assuming they'll reverse it then if I'm acquitted."

"Doesn't the human justice system take months, or sometimes years? Now is not the time for you to be powerless even for such a short time."

I agreed. "If you or Terrelle can't break it, I'll get Gareth to reverse it. I'm going to meet with him in a few days. But I don't like the idea of the humans holding the only cure on this type of weapon."

Gregory leaned forward and filled both shot glasses again. "I understand the humans want a way to fight back if an angel or a demon gets out of hand, but the potential for abuse here is substantial."

"True. But if we have a way of reversing it, then we can correct cases where an angel or demon has been unfairly shot. And if the shooting was justified, then they can just suffer through the human legal system."

"We wouldn't want the antidote to have widespread availability though," Gregory mused. "Let the humans have the comfort of some control, and let both angels and demons know that there will be serious consequences for their actions. We'll let the humans manage justice their way and only intervene in cases where the angel or demon is clearly in the right."

Like me. Or like Lux truly not understanding that what he was doing was wrong by human standards.

"So we'll need to keep quiet about any method we have of reversing the effect," I said. "Just keep it within the Ruling Council."

I liked this idea. Responsibility for policing demons breaking laws would no longer be on my plate. Let the humans deal with it. I'd laugh at those who got stuck in jail, and tell them that maybe next time they'd follow the rules, or just stay in Hel.

And as for the angels…well, I especially liked the idea of humans being able to plug those jerks in the ass and stick them in jail. Those stuffy pricks deserved to sleep on hard metal benches and get yelled at by human judges.

"Sounds like an optimal plan." Gregory handed me both shots of vodka. "Drink up."

He didn't have to tell *me* twice. I sucked down the

contents of both glasses, amazed at how incredibly drunk I was. Damn, I was a cheap date as a human. Four shots and I was practically under the table.

"Ready?" Gregory asked.

"Yessssh," I slurred. "Ready."

I stared at him. He stared at me.

"Are you doing anything?" I asked.

"Clearly not anything that's working," he drawled.

He pulled me onto his lap wrapping his arms around my waist. I rested my head on his shoulder and enjoyed the hug. Damn, I was drunk. If he kept this up, I was going to fall asleep here and now.

"I'm guessing that's not working either?" he asked.

"Nope," I murmured, snuggling my face against his neck.

"I'm going to try something else," he told me. "It might hurt."

"Mmmm." He was so warm, smelled so good. What did angels wash their clothes in? Did they even wash their clothes? His shirt smelled like sunshine.

Something deep inside me pinched. Tight. Hard. It was like a ghostly hand had grabbed my intestines with a vice grip and twisted. My hands fisted, my shoulders were rigid as I braced against the pain. There was a sharp tearing sensation and I gasped, trying to jerk away from Gregory.

He stopped whatever he was doing and held me tight, rubbing my back until I was able to breathe again.

"I punched through, but couldn't completely tear apart the barrier without possibly damaging you."

I laughed weakly. I'd been damaged before. I'd been so damaged that I'd needed to live in a bucket as slime mold for what felt like fucking forever. While I didn't want to go through that again, I didn't want to be trapped as a human until some asshole judge reversed the spell.

Gregory continued stroking my back and I remained

curled up in his arms for a while longer before sitting up and taking stock of my condition. The first thing I noticed was that I was sober. The second thing was that I felt…something.

Frowning, I tried to teleport to the kitchen. Nope. Then I tried to create electricity and nearly squealed when sparks jumped from one hand to the other. Desperate, I tried to reach out to Gregory's spirit-self with my own. Nope on that as well. It was like shoving my hand between the bars of a jail cell, straining to reach something across the room.

"Do it again," I urged him. "Try to make the hole bigger. Let's see if we can crack it open."

He reached up and touched my cheek. "I don't want to hurt you, Cockroach."

"Hurt me, baby." I turned my head and kissed his hand. "Do it. Just once more." I'd endured a fuckton of pain in my life. It would be totally worth it to see if he could undo whatever the cops in Phoenix had done to me.

He stared at me for a while, then nodded. "All right. I'm going to try something a bit different."

With no more warning than that, he dove into me. I felt the scorching heat of his spirit-self. My skin blistered, my clothing singeing. The torn edges of my magical prison twisted and melted, cracks spiraling outward. The heat radiated through the opening, searing my own spirit-self with an agonizing fire. I was burning. Inside and out, I was burning.

My physical body thrashed in flames. I tried to scream, the sound dying as my lungs charred. Through the agony, a part of me wondered if I'd be able to recreate my physical form. That thought would have terrified me years ago, but now I trusted Gregory to keep me safe. Even if my corporeal form died, even if I could not form so much as a microscopic body to live in, Gregory would hold me close inside his own form. He'd protect me. I trusted him more than I trusted anyone.

Suddenly the heat vanished, leaving me freezing cold, every nerve in my body screaming with pain. I looked down to see the blackened skin of my arm, a yellowish fluid oozing from the cracks.

Fix yourself. Recreate your form.

Gregory's words were unspoken. I sucked in a painful breath, realizing that I *heard* him. I heard the angel-speech. And I'd inhaled with lungs that should not have been able to function at all.

Concentrating, I slowly repaired nerves, muscles, blood vessels and skin. What should have been done in a blink of an eye took me about twenty minutes of focused effort. But I did it. Finally breathing easy, I sat up and unfurled my wings, knocking shot glasses and the half-empty bottle of vodka off my coffee table.

"Fuck, this feels good." I grinned at Gregory. "You are a damned god, Asshole. I don't care what anyone else says, you're a god."

"I am *not* a god." His smile faded. "Don't ask me to do that again, Cockroach. Don't ever ask me to do that again."

"Oh trust me, I don't want to ever go through that again. How the hell anyone survived going up against you in battle, I'll never know. Fuck, you're hot. I mean, you're hot as in sexy, but you're also hot as in hot. Like you could burn your way through a small planet hot."

"I believe I could incinerate a moderately sized solar system, although it would be taxing."

So modest. I rolled my eyes, remembering that Samael wasn't the only archangel who had the sin of pride. Though it probably wasn't pride if it was true, and I got the idea that Gregory was not exaggerating his powers in the least.

I reached out and touched his spirit-self, delighted that I

could still do so. But as thrilled as I was with my newly regained abilities, I was still very aware that some of my prison remained intact. There were jagged edges of it that still hindered me. I hoped they'd break free in time, but if they were still there in the next few days, I'd confess to Gareth what had happened and see if I could buy an antidote.

In the meantime, I was relatively free, and enormously grateful that I had this big jerk of an angel on my side. *Mine.* I snuggled against him, yawned, and this time I did fall asleep.

CHAPTER 9

I was up uncharacteristically early the next morning, testing to see what I could and couldn't do. Teleportation was still a no. I had wings, though and that was certainly a hell of a lot faster than most human modes of transportation. I could summon electricity, but not quite to the level of lightning. My energy attacks were sadly the equivalent of smacking someone with a broom. My sword did appear when I called it, but I couldn't get it to change shape or do anything beyond what a normal sword would do.

Basically I wasn't much of an angel or an imp right now, if I used those yardsticks to measure my abilities. What I did have was a shit-ton of energy still stored inside me. I could fix injuries, but couldn't manage to grab enough of the energy to recreate my entire form. Transmutation was the real magic of demons, and right now I sucked at it.

Devouring? I wondered if I still had that ability or not. I suspected I did, but wasn't willing to sacrifice someone to test it out.

"You'll recover."

I nearly had a heart attack at Gregory's voice behind me. Normally I could feel him just as I could my demons—more so, actually. But this morning I'd been focusing so hard on what I could and couldn't do I hadn't noticed the archangel coming down the stairs.

He wrapped his arms around me. "You are indestructible, my Cockroach. No matter what happens, you always recover."

"I just need to devour an entire archangel this time," I teased.

"No, you just need to do whatever your chaotic impish self feels like doing, and things will fall into place." He nuzzled my hair. "They always do with you, even if the journey is often incredibly painful."

I smiled and leaned back against him. "Is Lux up yet?"

"Sleeping as if he actually needed to do so." Gregory's spirit-self reached out to caress mine. "Thank you for texting me about that wild gate in Ireland, by the way. I don't know what intuition led you to check on it, but I'm glad you did. We put up a barrier around it to protect the humans and their livestock, and I assigned one of my angels to keep an eye on the area, just in case it reappears and something tries to come through again."

I turned in his arms to face him. "Did your guy ever find whatever things killed those ten angels?"

He shook his head. "The humans saw nothing. There were no deaths beyond those angels. Not even a cow was killed, and nothing has been out of place since that night— except for the reappearance of the wild gate, that is."

"Good. Maybe they were freaked out at coming through and having to defend themselves against a bunch of angels, so they went back home. It's not like I saw anything when I stuck my head through the gate either."

Gregory sucked in a breath. "You did *what?*"

"Stuck my head through." I patted him on the chest. "Don't worry, I put my arm through a few times first, just to check. And I made sure the majority of my body was on this side."

There was a rumbling noise in his chest. I wasn't sure if it was anger, disbelief, laughter, or a combination of the three. "Cockroach, your senseless disregard for your own safety will surely be the death of me one day—most likely after it has been the death of you."

"Probably," I agreed.

"Since it does no good to chastise you, go ahead and tell me what was on the other side of the gate."

"Cold." I shivered at the memory. "Like a carnival funhouse. It was all ice and glass and mirrors and lower spectrum colors. Everything was in constant, disorienting motion, but I sensed nothing alive—and definitely nothing sentient."

"Some gates are long," he reminded me. "The other side could be quite a journey away."

"If so, then I can't imagine how anyone could get through to either side. It was a maze. I got the impression that if I walked through, I'd never be able to find either exit."

"That changes things a bit," Gregory mused. "I had been envisioning a pack of powerful, unknown beings accidently falling through the wild gate on their side, and attacking the angels out of fear and confusion, then running back. But with the long gate you describe, I can't see how that would be possible. How did they manage to find their way through? And back again?"

Something clicked in my mind. "Perhaps the gate has always been there on their side. Maybe they travel by these long gateways and know how to navigate them. They thought they were going somewhere, and were alarmed to find themselves in a strange world with a bunch of angels attacking them."

"If that is true, then they are sentient as well as powerful," Gregory said.

Sentient. Powerful. And now they had an opening into our world that even the most powerful of the archangels could not close.

* * *

I WARMED up some leftover pizza for Lux to have for breakfast and he wandered off to the guest house to play with the Lows. The house was empty. Gregory had left after our conversation. Nyalla had either stayed with friends or was off with Gabe somewhere. My horses and the goat were grazing in the pasture. Boomer was sprawled out in the sun next to the pool, snoozing away.

I was fucking bored. A few years ago, this would have been an ideal day. I would have sunned by the pool and drunk beer, taking the occasional dip to cool off. I would have checked in with Michelle on my properties, pestered Wyatt into riding with me, and planned something impish. Now I was fretting over my hindered abilities, wondering how I was going to get to all these meetings without asking Gregory to zip me around. Yes I could fly, but taking five or six hours to get somewhere was a pain in the ass. I'd gotten used to teleportation, and I was damned pissed I no longer had that convenience.

And those fucking rings… I was tempted to throw them all in the trash and lie to Lux about returning them. The only thing stopping me was the worry that somehow the owners would find out and either Lux or I would have to face the human justice system. I already had one court date in my future—that was one court date too many. Plus some of those rings were really expensive. The sin of greed was an old friend of mine. If I wasn't forced to take those rings back, I'd keep them. No way would I be tossing them in the trash.

There was no sense in sitting around moping about things I couldn't change, so I went upstairs, put on my swimsuit, and decided I was going to make the best of the day old-Sam-style.

There was a little chill in the air still, but the sun was toasty warm. I filled a cooler with ice and beer, put on some music, and plopped myself down on a chaise lounge. Boomer came over to greet me, so I scratched his smelly head and got up to pour a bottle of beer in with his morning kibble.

I must have fallen asleep because suddenly the speakers were blaring out Ariana Grande and there was someone on the lounge next to me, singing along to "Be My Baby." I opened my eyes when my visitor hit a wrong note and turned to glare at Terrelle. The Noodle was wearing one of my favorite bikinis, oiled up like she was in an eighties porno. Her brown curls were pulled into a messy bun, her dark blue eyes hidden by a pair of Ray-Bans—*my* Ray-Bans.

"Want a beer?" She turned to pull two Bud Lights out of the cooler, popping the cap off one and handing it to me before I could answer. "I forgot what a sweet setup you've got here. Your kitchen completely rocks. And you must have twenty swimsuits in your room. Lots of other things in your room, too."

"Yeah, I know." I eyed the bikini, wondering what else she'd pilfered. Terrelle might be an information demon, but she was still a demon and evidently had some sticky fingers.

"I'll admit I was kind of worried when Snip told me I was supposed to come see you. I mean, you're scary for an imp, what with that sword and everything. The whole trip here I kept thinking about all the shit I'd done and wondering if you were going to dust me for something or another. But when I got here and saw there was leftover pizza, and beer, and catching rays ..." She leaned forward to clink her bottle against mine. "Girlfriend time. Besties in the sun. Pals by the pool. Where am I going to sleep? With the kid? With the human woman? With you?"

"In the guest house with the Lows," I told her the moment I could get a word in edgewise. "I need your help with something—actually I need information."

"Well, you have come to the right demon. I am the girl who delivers. I know everything, and if I don't know it, I can find it out. I've got books. I've got the internet. And I listen." She reached up to touch her hair. "Big ears. I hear everything. No one pays any attention to the nerdy girl at the bar, so I know who is sleeping with whom, who is padding their expense account, who ate that pasta salad at lunch that was *so* not Keto."

"Project Woo-woo. It's—"

"A government contract awarded to a company called Blue Fire which is co-owned by a sorcerer named Gareth, a mage named Kirby, and a demon named Dar." She shot me a sympathetic glance. "Who is your foster brother."

I resisted the urge to strangle her. "Yes, I know all that. Let me finish and I'll tell you exactly what I need you to find out."

Terrelle made a zipping-her-lips motion with her fingers and stared intently at me. Noodles were so fucking weird.

"I'm meeting with Dar and Gareth in a day or two. They're probably going to give me a bunch of bullshit half-truths. I need to know who their customers are and what they've bought. Receipts, girl. I need receipts. I also want to know what exactly is the spell, or amulet, or whatever to reverse what these weapons do, and who has that antidote. And—" I held up a finger to keep her from interrupting. "I also need to know if there is any way to reverse the weapon effects besides what Blue Fire is selling."

She frowned. "The last one is going to be hard. If the company isn't aware of an alternate antidote, then there might not be one. Or it might be something no one has discovered yet. Or I might need to talk to a whole lot of mages and elves, and that would take time."

"You can start with the Phoenix Police Department," I told her. "They shot me yesterday with something that stained my shirt blue and felt as if I'd had an elven collar slapped around my neck."

She lowered the sunglasses. Her eyes widened, then she looked at my neck. "They shot then collared you? How did you get it off? Did your human friend remove it?"

"It's not an actual collar. It's not a physical device with a spell attached. That's the problem. Whatever is in that bullet, it covers a demon's, or angel's, entire spirit being. It makes us human."

"That's…that's horrible," she whispered.

"Damn straight." I settled back in my lounge chair and took a sip of my beer. "I'm not going to go into how I managed to break it. Let's just say it was painful, and I don't think that's a method that's going to work reliably on others."

Terrelle let out a breath and shook her head. "Fuck. I knew about the weapons, but my information said they weren't supposed to be available for another week or two. And I'd heard from several sources that the effects wore off in anywhere from five minutes to a few hours based on how powerful the demon, or angel, was. I didn't hear anything about needing an antidote, or the effect being permanent."

"I can promise you this didn't wear off in a few hours. This is going to be an ongoing project, so I'll need you to stick around for the foreseeable future. Stay here in the guest house with the Lows until I no longer need your services," I ordered. "Call me, or come find me once you have any information at all."

She looked around. "Can I use the pool?"

"Sure." I let the Lows use it, as long as they cleaned up afterward.

"Food? Your kitchen?"

I scowled. "The guest house has a kitchen and food. Snip makes sure there are plenty of groceries, and there's pizza delivery every Tuesday and Thursday."

She looked down at the bathing suit. "And clothing?"

For fuck's sake. "I'll give you a hundred dollars for clothing. There's a Walmart ten miles west off Route 26."

"Travel and expenses?"

Maybe this hadn't been such a great idea after all. "I'll give you a credit card, but if there is so much as ten cents unaccounted for, I'm going to shoot you with one of those Blue Fire weapons myself."

"Deal." She stuck out her hand. "Oh, and there's a bunch of dying rats on your front porch. Thought you should know."

Fucking rats. I left Terrelle by the pool with my cooler full of beer and went around to the front of the house. Sure enough, there were over a dozen rats shambling around my porch and driveway. I dodged them, kicking a few to the side before they could bite me, and grabbed the shovel from its spot beside the door. This was getting old. This was getting real old. Who the fuck decided it would be fun to send a bunch of half-dead rodents to my house? Normally I'd think this sort of prank was hysterical, but I didn't want Nyalla or Lux getting bit.

I chopped the rats up with the shovel then threw them into the woods, then inspired by Nyalla's cooking the other night, I went inside and made pasta with a roasted garlic sauce for dinner. It was ready just as Gregory came through the door.

It was like a fifties television show. All I needed was a dress and a bouffant hairdo instead of my bikini and ponytail.

"Dinner smells wonderful." Gregory walked by the dining room table where I was setting out the plates.

"Please tell me there aren't any more half-dead rats out front. I just got done putting a bunch of them out of their misery. Who the fuck is doing this?"

"The Pied Piper of dead rats?" Gregory took the plates from my hand and began to put them on the table. "Maybe it's a necromancer. If it is, you should ask them if they can resurrect Elvis for our wedding."

Haha. "I haven't pissed off any necromancers."

"That you know of." He frowned down at the plates. "Four for dinner?"

"Terrelle is here. I'm sending her off to hang with the Lows, and felt I could at least give her a decent meal first. After tonight it's roast beaks and pizza delivery."

Gregory nodded. "I like Terrelle. She's helping you with the Blue Fire weaponry?"

"Yeah." I stopped putting the silverware down and faced him. "I spent the day hanging by the pool, disposing of the dying rats in front of my house, and having one of my bathing suits and a pair of sunglasses stolen by Terrelle. How was your day?"

He sighed. "Like a giant pile of fresh excrement. The rebels have quickly become accustom to being corporeal, and they do not take their expulsion from Aaru as losing the war. I've been dispatching my choir to locate and track them as they're coming together. I fear they are planning an attack."

I hesitated, a fork still in my hand. "Attacking who? The Ruling Council? You and your supporters?"

He ran a hand through his hair. "Yes, but not just us. Like the Angels of Chaos were before the first war, these rebels are unhappy with the human evolutionary project. They originally were in favor, but over the last hundreds of thousands of years they've begun to feel that we made an error in granting the gifts of Aaru to the humans. They feel that contact with humans is detrimental to angels. The fall of the tenth choir ten thousand years ago reinforced this. And now after being among the humans, they are convinced the whole thing was a terrible mistake on our part. They also strongly disagree with any angels resuming relations with the Fallen, which we've been supporting lately."

I winced. "Relations such as what you and I have."

A tired smile twisted his mouth. "Yes. You and I. Others as well. They are absolutely opposed to any demon/angel relations."

"I'm sure the existence of New Hell isn't helping, or that I got everyone banished from Aaru." I sighed.

"Only the Ruling Council knows about the extent of the banishment," he reminded me.

"But the rebels must know they're barred from Aaru permanently."

He nodded. "They do. And that means their choices for the future are either living in Hel, or living here."

"Or somewhere else." I lifted my hands. "You've been to how many solar systems? Planets? Universes? Angels can live in any form. Matter. Energy. Just because they're barred from Aaru doesn't mean they have to stay here or go hang with the demons in Hel."

"Not all demons have the ability to activate the gates, and many demons cannot survive outside the form of a higher being. Angels are the same. Few angels can travel to or live in the wide range of environments that the universe has to offer."

I stared at him. "Seriously?"

"I know prior to the past few years you haven't had contact with angels beyond escaping the occasional gate guardian. Angels are not the all-powerful beings you believe them to be, Cockroach. Even my siblings would struggle to survive more than a few centuries in the form of energy. Angels were meant to live as beings of spirit. Aaru is the only place that is possible. Life in corporeal form for any amount of time causes the degradation of our spirit-selves. Life in other forms will do the same—sometimes more quickly, sometimes more slowly."

And now I felt like even more of an asshole for the banishment. It was wrong two and a half million years ago when the Angels of Chaos had been banished, and it was wrong now. I'd do anything to reverse it, even if it meant the rebels still had access to Aaru.

But that was a problem for another time. Right now there were more urgent things for us to deal with.

"So the rebel angels feel they only have two choices left to them—here and Hel," Gregory added. "Hel belongs to the Fallen. There is no way they will ever go there. So that leaves here."

"With humans who cause angels to sin," I said. "So first they plan to kill the angels who fought against them and banished them from Aaru, then they kill all the humans?"

"That's what I'm worried about. At a bare minimum they'll be unconcerned about humans who die as they are fighting us."

Gregory had said we needed the good will of the humans to live in peace here among them. I agreed, and still agreed but for different reasons. With weapons like the one that had been used on me, the humans could be valuable allies. The rebel angels would discount them, would be vulnerable to attack from beings they felt nothing but disdain for. I knew what an advantage it was to be discounted. Partnering with humans would give us the element of surprise—at least for a very short time.

But weapons that could be used by humans against angels could also be used by angels against angels. Blue Fire and the weapons they were developing needed to be kept out of the hands of the rebels. And the humans needed to know about this division among the angelic host. They needed to know what was coming.

But first, *I* needed to know exactly what was coming.

CHAPTER 10

*L*ux had to give me a lift to Chicago because I still couldn't teleport. He promised not to tell anyone, but I felt completely embarrassed. It was one thing when Gregory hauled me around all over the place, but an infant angel? Ever since I'd acquired this skill, I'd gotten used to instantly appearing anywhere I needed to be, and I felt the loss acutely.

Karrae and Lux had been thrilled to see each other. They were both Angels of Order, and watching them together I realized how nice it was for Lux to have another young angel as a friend. He and Austin were close, but the other boy was a Nephilim living among a pack of shifters and one vampire. Karrae was facing the same challenges and experiences as Lux, living with an angel and a demon parent in a world filled with humans.

I wondered if Karrae ever misunderstood something and brought home a few hundred stolen rings. Probably not.

The pair grabbed juice boxes and a handful of fruit bars then went up to the rooftop to play while Dar and I stayed inside his and Asta's penthouse apartment.

"Where's Andor? Your dwarven nanny?"

"Day off." Dar rolled his eyes. "It's annoying that he can't work twenty-four/seven. Dwarven foster parents don't take time off in Hel."

Because shit would get real. You couldn't exactly leave a few hundred newly-created and juvenile demons unattended and expect any of them to be alive when you returned—or anything to be alive. There would be a big smoking crater and charred bodies everywhere. But Chicago wasn't Hel, and Dar was lucky to have a nanny at all.

"You don't like it, then you and Asta can move to Hel where you can get twenty-four/seven dwarven care," I pointed out.

"Right. Like Karrae would be happy in Hel surrounded by demons. Or Asta. And that's assuming I could get either of them across the gates. Have you ever tried to get an Angel of Order to do something they don't want to do? It's damned near impossible. Sometimes bribery works. Or sometimes if I look at Asta with big sappy eyes, I get my way. Like this." Dar's gaze softened, his brown eyes large and dewy as he looked at me with exaggerated adoration.

Which reminded me…. "Where *is* your angel?" I asked Dar, just to make sure she wasn't listening in from the kitchen or something. I might be a bit irked with my brother, but I didn't want to get him in trouble with Asta.

"Equal employment opportunity meeting. She says you need to stick around so the pair of you can go over proposed legislation on working conditions for non-humans."

I'd forgot about that, and I'd been hoping Asta would have as well. Normally I'd try to duck out before she got back, but I was relying on Lux to transport me and the little angel wouldn't want to cut his playtime with Karrae short.

"Okay, but if I'm going to have to deal with that shit, I'll need booze."

Dar snorted. "I'm with you on that. You should see all the meetings I have to attend for the city. Boring as fuck. No wonder I'm drunk all the time."

Which brought me to one other subject I needed to discuss with my brother. "I hear you're the mayor now?"

He grinned. "I am, and through a democratic voting process no less."

"How much election fraud did that take?"

Dar shrugged. "No more than any other election in this beautiful city. They even knew I was a demon. Can you believe it? If you'd told me two hundred years ago that we'd be living openly among the humans and that I'd be elected to public office, I would have thought you were fucking nuts."

"So what's your long term plan here?" I asked. "Is politics now your thing, or are you using this as a cover for something else you're doing."

"I always have a lot of irons in the fire, but I'm thinking politics is right up my alley. Mayor for now, then maybe I'll run for governor, or even a federal office." He looked a bit worried. "Except Asta doesn't want to leave the city. She loves it here, so I might end up mayor forever."

That was the only thing keeping Dar from becoming president, or emperor. Asta. He did love her, and while she seemed to be letting him run free on a pretty long leash, she was still an angel. Dar could talk his beloved into a lot of things, but world domination wouldn't be one of them. Plus, I knew she'd keep his sneaky, demonic tendencies in check. Asta actually cared about humans in a different way than most angels. Where the rest of them wanted to guide with a very firm hand, she loved watching them live their lives as they were, only course correcting if she saw one or two who were about to fall off the edge of a cliff or something.

"The president seems to like you. I spoke with him yesterday and he was singing your praises."

Dar preened. "What can I say, I'm a personable guy. He wants me to golf with him next week at that swanky country club of his. We've got some business in Florida, and he can't wait to show the place off. Steaks. Booze. Eighteen holes of golfing fun."

Terrelle had been right. Dar was in thick with the movers and shakers in the human world. I definitely needed to connect with him more often—and to remind him that he was still part of my household. I didn't give a flying fuck about him being mayor of Chicago, but I needed to be in the loop on these things.

"The steak and booze sounds good, but Dar, you don't golf," I reminded him.

"All the better. I hear he's horrible. I'll be worse and it'll make him feel like he's a total winner."

"And while he's feeling like a total winner, you'll raid the US Treasury for project Woo-woo."

Dar's nose twitched. "How do you know about that?"

"The big question is how did you find out about this opportunity to partner with Kirby and Gareth?"

"Are you kidding me? How could you not realize this sort of thing was going to happen? You used to be good at this business stuff, Mal. What happened to you?"

I'd wound up Iblis with a position on the Ruling Council, that's what had happened to me.

"So you're a majority shareholder in this company," I commented.

Dar nodded. "Yep. And we're going big. It's not just this DOD contract either. We've got countries all over the world wanting to buy our products. Countries. States. Cities. Even HOAs are throwing money at us. Everyone's scared, Mal—and fear makes for good business dealings."

I definitely knew that from past experience. "You're going to be selling into New Hell too?"

"Oh yeah. There are humans in those states with a significant financial stake. They're not moving, and in order to protect their assets, they need to have weaponry they can use against elves, werewolves, demons, and other humans. Blue Fire is the great equalizer."

Just like Smith and Wesson. And I was sure demons would be buying a few of these goodies as well, just to ensure the playing field wasn't *quite* equal.

"Does Asta know about this?"

Dar wiggled his hand back and forth. "She's supportive of humans being able to defend themselves, especially now that demons and rebel angels are roaming around the world."

Ah. Dar had framed this as a humanitarian effort. I was pretty sure Asta had seen through some of that bullshit, but even partnered with Dar, she was probably more pro-human than pro-demon.

"So, when did you start shipping the goods?"

"A few weeks back. Just the little stuff, though. The really big weaponry that falls under Woo-woo isn't ready yet and that absolutely pisses me off. We lose money and market advantage for every second we waste, but the fucking magic users are all about quality control and safety. It's bullshit, but I can't convince them to go any faster."

"What's little stuff and what's big weaponry? And what exactly falls under the Woo-woo contract?"

Dar shrugged. "I'm more of the big-picture guy. I don't know the details. All I know is that the stuff that goes to the military, the stuff where the big money is—that's not going out yet."

"So are you, or are you not selling guns to the Phoenix police department?"

"Fuck if I know. If they placed an order, then yeah." Dar's eyes narrowed to little dark slits. "Why?"

"They've got paintball guns. The paint balls are spelled

with something that takes away our powers, like an elven net or one of their collars."

He laughed. "Shit! Thanks for letting me know. I'll make a note not to do anything illegal in Phoenix—or at least not to get caught."

I punched Dar in the shoulder. "Fucker. I'm not joking. They don't warn you, they just shoot then haul your ass down to central booking."

He was laughing even harder. "This sounds like you've had some personal experience here, Mal. It can't have been too bad, or you'd still be in jail and not popping around meeting with world leaders and visiting me."

I wasn't about to admit to him what Gregory had to do to partially break through the spell, or that I still couldn't do half of what I should be able to do.

"I'm the Iblis. Anyone else would still be in jail. This is serious, Dar."

He waved the idea away. "It wears off. Gareth promised me the general stuff that gets sold to individuals and municipalities only lasts a few hours max. The military grade stuff lasts longer, but that's so expensive that no police department is going to be able to afford it."

"That shit the Phoenix police had didn't wear off in a few hours," I told him. "It didn't wear off at all. Like I said, if I hadn't been the Iblis, I'd still be in that jail cell, unable to do anything that even a Low could do."

He frowned. "Then it wasn't one of our products. Like I said, the hardcore stuff isn't shipping yet, and no city police force could afford it even if we were delivering."

"So someone else is making these weapons?" I asked.

Dar snarled. "Not that I'm aware of. I know we've got some competition, but my information led me to believe they were still in the development phase."

If I hadn't known my brother since I'd been formed I

would have shivered. Dar could be a ruthless bastard if he thought he was being bested by the competition.

I shrugged. "Guess you were wrong. And if Phoenix PD has these things, then other cities probably do as well."

Dar began to pace. "Fuckers. Some fucking employee stole our secrets and sold them to someone else. That's the only way I can see this happening. I'm going to find out who, and they're going to regret it."

"Or maybe some other mage had the same idea as Kirby and Gareth. Before you go killing employees, let me look into it." I absolutely did not need Dar muddying the waters right now. "I've got a meeting with Gareth. I'll see what's going on at his end, and I'll get Terrelle to find out what other companies are selling similar products."

Dar stopped pacing. "You'll let me know? I'm part of your household right now. My interests are your interests. If there's a mage undercutting our prices…if someone beat us to market… I need to know these things, Mal."

And just like that, I'd achieved one of my goals without even having to lift a finger. "Of course, Dar. You're my brother. It would reflect badly on my household if your investments were being threatened by some outside company. I vowed to protect you when you joined my household."

He nodded enthusiastically. "Good. And I'll tithe the appropriate amount of profits to you, as is appropriate."

"Money is always of value, especially in the human world, but information is priceless. Especially information that reaches my ears before anyone else's." I'd learned to be a chameleon, to speak the language of angels in Ruling Council meetings, to work my way through the loopholes of the human legal and social system. Dealing with Dar just meant speaking his language, and that was something I'd learned to do when we were young and in the care of our dwarven foster parents.

"What sort of information are you looking for, Mal?" That wary look was back in his dark eyes once more.

"Well, in addition to the occasional heads-up about your political ambitions, I'd like you to keep your ear to the ground when it comes to high-level human politics. You're buddies with the president. He talks with other world leaders and gets information on things that are happening, or about to happen in their countries. I want to know those things. I especially want to know anything to do with angels, demons, shifters, or elves."

Dar nodded. "I can do that."

"I also want to be continuously up to date on Blue Fire. I want to know all the products you're going to be making as well as what you're selling where," I told Dar.

His eyes narrowed. "You not going to do some hostile takeover shit, are you Mal? Drum me out and rake in all the profits instead of your five percent."

I rolled my eyes. "No. I've got enough to do without having to negotiate contracts for weapons sales. And it's ten percent, Dar. Ten."

"I said ten. That's what I said. So…" He shifted his weight from one foot to the other. "You gonna tell that asshole angel of yours about your financial stake in Blue Fire?"

I snorted. "No. Well, maybe not. I'll definitely hold that in my back pocket until I need it. He knows about the company, though, and knows what they're making, so I can't keep that a secret."

Dar pulled a big glossy catalogue off the table and tossed it to me. "Here's our draft product listing including prices and descriptions. It's still undergoing a few modifications pending R&D results, so don't go sharing this with anyone. I'll email you our client and contract list. We do have a few custom products we're making but you'll need a security clearance to get information on those."

I folded my arms across my chest. "I'm the fucking Iblis, Dar. I don't need a damned security clearance."

He held up his hands. "Federal government says you do."

"Fuck the federal government. And since when did you give a rat's ass about following the rules."

He chuckled. "Never. Okay, I'll send that over as well. Just don't let anyone else see it. I don't want to lose our biggest contracts."

"You're not going to lose your big contracts."

"Not today, but if some asshole is out there selling similar products to the Phoenix Police Department, then he's going to want in on our contracts as well. We've got to make hay while the sun shines, Mal. I want to maximize profits, then sell my share just before price competition kicks in and margins decline."

Dar. I loved my foster brother. I glanced down at the slick catalogue. "Enough business. Asta's not back yet. The kids don't require any supervision right now. Let's go hunt down some food, some booze, and see what trouble we can get into."

At that moment I saw Lux fall past the window, screaming his lungs out. Half a second later Karrae did the same, waving her arms and legs frantically as she fell.

Dar laughed. "Your kid is a bad influence."

"Just how terrified are the humans walking below right now?" I was absolutely positive this had been Lux's idea.

"Probably shitting their pants. Toddlers falling off a high rise? I wouldn't be surprised if a few died of a heart attack."

I went over and looked out the window. Lux and Karrae must have revealed their wings and flown before splatting onto the pavement because they were now darting in and out of side streets, playing a game of tag.

"You mentioned food, booze, and trouble?" Dar asked.

I stepped away from the window, smiling and shaking my head. Food and booze, but I wasn't sure any trouble we could get into would top my son's. The kid was a freaking genius. And he was totally mine.

* * *

DAR and I stumbled back a few hours later drunk off our asses, but I quickly sobered up when I saw Asta waiting for me with papers spread across the dining room table. She wasn't alone. On her right sat an elf, and to her left was Rutter, one of my Lows. Lux and Karrae were sitting quietly on the floor a few yards away, putting together a giant puzzle.

"Guess I better get this over with," I muttered to Dar.

He laughed, slapped me on the back, then headed into the kitchen. I sat down at the table and picked up the pile of papers in front of me. It was bad enough that I had to attend Ruling Council meetings a few times a month, now I was stuck with this shit. Who the fuck decided to put me on a committee?

"Mistress, I'm on a committee," Rutter squeaked in excitement. "With an elf. And an *angel*. We're discussing minimum wage."

"Oh joy." I looked over the first sheet of paper. We spent what felt like the next twenty years discussing minimum wage and more. We could have just made a copy of the human regulations and called it a day, but no, we needed to go over each and every fucking section and subsection in excruciating detail. Clearly the universe was punishing me for something.

Rutter dozed off in his chair halfway through the meeting. I kept trying to do the same, but every time I closed my eyes, Asta would kick me under the table. Just when we were about to finish up, Karrae started having a meltdown about missing puzzle pieces, and Asta needed to attend to her before she blew up the building with her tantrum.

The elf and I stared at each other in awkward silence. I think her name was Leaf or something. She was dressed like she was ready to head into the office for a budget meeting, her blonde hair pulled back into a bun that revealed the long points of her ears. She fidgeted, fingering the amulet around her neck. I eyed the piece of jewelry, remembering what Kirby had said about the elves needing magic devices to protect them from death-by-iron.

"We're not all bad, you know," Leaf said to me, her voice soft and musical. "Most of us just want a place to call home."

"Which you had in Hel," I reminded her.

She sighed, glancing over at the snoring Rutter. "Hel was never really our home. I'm not sure this place will be either, but it's better than I'd expected. There was a time when we frequently came here, long before the war, before we left Aerie for our short-lived planet."

Karrae screamed, and I glanced over to see Asta trying to calm her while Lux watched the whole thing with wide-eyed concern. It was probably a good thing Dar and Asta had a dwarf. Lux was nowhere near as temperamental as their little angel.

I returned my attention to Leaf. "Why don't you guys just go back to Aerie?"

"And kneel before the Seelie queen?" The elf shuddered. "We defied her. We made a deal with the angels. We left. I doubt she would grant us mercy for any of those things."

Huh. It reminded me of the war between the angelic host two and a half million years ago. I guess no one could ever really go home—not the Ancients, not the Angels of Order, not even the elves who it seems had been bouncing around from place to place for a billion years or more.

"So this stuff really matters to you?" I motioned toward the stack of papers.

She shrugged. "It matters. It matters to the humans who don't want to be replaced in their jobs by lesser paid elves or demons. Every place we've ever lived, we have tried to recreate Aerie. I'm sure some elves will try to do that here as well, but I prefer to move forward and embrace what the Lady has set before us."

I thought of the elves in Iceland. "There are elves who would prefer to seize what they feel the Lady has given them."

Leaf smiled. "I used to be a princess in a castle where I was waited on by my changeling slaves. Every day was beauty and song and sunlight. But without contrast, beauty becomes a fragile, brittle thing. Here, in a world of gray, in a world where light and dark, where joy and sorrow always swing to a balance, here beauty becomes a powerful thing, forged out of the ashes of all that is ugly."

"Uh-huh." I had no idea what the fuck she'd just said. Elves. They never could just come out and say something without heaping a shit-ton of metaphors on top.

"Look, Karrae." Asta held up a puzzle piece. "I found it. See? The puzzle isn't ruined. All the pieces are here. It wasn't lost, it just had slid under the carpet."

Under the carpet. Just like Lux's rings.

CHAPTER 11

"I like this one." Lux pointed to a picture of a flash grenade that was supposed to render shifters, angels, and demons blind for a minimum of fifteen seconds. It didn't sound like a lot, but I'd been in enough battles that I knew what fifteen seconds could do.

Lux had teleported us back home after my meeting had ended and he and Karrae had finished their puzzle. We'd come home to an empty house and immediately snuggled up on the sofa to look through the Blue Fire catalogue.

I'd discovered that white-muzzled pistols and rifles were spelled to fire magical bullets. Some of those bullets negated magical barriers and could eventually break through all but the strongest wards. Some acted much like the elven nets had in taking away a demon's, and I assumed angel's, abilities. They wouldn't be physically restrained and the bullet's effects lasted between an hour to several days depending on the level of the demon.

This catalogue was absolutely out of date if the weapon I'd been shot with in Phoenix had been one of these. An hour to several days my ass. If Gregory hadn't forced his way through the effect, I'd still be wingless and drunk on my couch.

Turning the pages, I continued to read. Some amulets gave the wearer protection against physical projectiles, others against spells, others against the persuasive abilities of angels. The products went on and on, the language carefully worded to convince the reader that there was an imminent threat right outside their doorway—one that only Blue Fire could protect them against.

One thing I did notice was that none of the magical weapons and devices did lasting damage or killed. It made me feel a bit better about what Kirby and Gareth were doing. I was all for leveling the playing field, but with seven billion humans in this world, I didn't want to see the outnumbered demons, angels, and shifters slaughtered. As for the elves... well, I might want to see them slaughtered—aside for a few I'd kinda befriended.

Handing Lux the catalogue, I opened up my laptop and started going through the files Dar had sent me on all their customers and what they'd ordered. There was a lot to wade through, but one thing stood out—Blue Fire had not sold any products to the Phoenix Police Department.

Which meant there were at least two companies producing these sorts of weapons.

I closed the laptop and set it aside thinking that any further research into this would need to wait until my meeting with Gareth, and until Terrelle dug more info up.

"How did you and Uncle Samael do with the rings the other day?" I asked Lux, thinking about my ever-expanding to-do list.

Lux grinned. "Pile one all gone!"

Wow, that had been a huge undertaking. Of course with Samael helping, half those rings probably ended up with the wrong people, or stuck in someone's breakfast cereal box.

"Do you want to return a few more before bed?" I asked Lux.

He looked over at the lumps in my rug with a worried frown. "Scared."

I didn't blame him. I was scared too. The first pile had been the easy ones, and I'd still ended up shot and in jail. Who knew what the fuck would happen with this second pile.

"How about we do just one? I'll go with you, and if it gets too scary then you zap back home and let me take care of it."

He frowned. "Then how do you get back?"

Fuck. This not being able to teleport sucked giant donkey balls. "Okay, then how about this—if it gets too scary, you zap back, then find your father and he can come get me."

Lux took a deep breath and slowly let it out. "It won't be too scary. I can stay and help, Ma."

I walked over to the rug and pulled back the corner, revealing two piles. "Where does this one belong?" I picked up one of the rings, not wanting to go into this blind.

"Store," he told me.

That shouldn't be a big deal. We'd probably set off a few security alarms, but hopefully we would be in and out before the police got there.

My gaze drifted to the Blue Fire catalogue, and I remembered the splat of blue on my shirt in Phoenix, of being hauled off to jail. Suddenly I envisioned my little angel shot with one of those disabling bullets, unable to teleport home, terrified and without his powers while the human police decided what to do with him. Hopefully they'd be lenient toward someone who appeared to be a toddler, but from everything I'd learned in the last two days, I wasn't willing to bet Lux's life on that.

I put the ring back in the pile and scooted the whole thing over toward him.

"I'll be with you," I said, reassuring myself more than him. "Pick one out that you really want my help with, and we'll take care of it together."

He pawed through the jewelry. "This one," he announced, holding up a particularly large diamond solitaire.

I got up and stood next to him, reaching down to take his hand. "Okay, you get us there, and I'll make sure you're okay while you replace it. But if I say go, you need to go, okay? Get your little ass back here and go find your father. No arguments."

"No arguments."

Lux looked up at me, his eyes a clear aqua, then in a flash we were no longer in my living room, but in a huge area, dim aside from some emergency lighting along the floor. Display cases lined the wall to our right and were in rows down the middle. On the opposite wall was a large tapestry. To our left was a display of sofas and chairs with worn upholstery. The place smelled cool, but faintly musty in spite of the careful temperature and humidity controls. Lux gripped my hand tight and led me forward.

I took this opportunity to check out all the bracelets, necklaces, rings, and bejeweled combs in the display cases as we walked by. So far so good. I hadn't even heard an alarm go off, which was a bit odd given my estimated value of all the jewelry we were walking past.

I heard a low growl and the click of something large and hard on the glossy floors. Every hair on my body stood out. That sound…this place…suddenly I remembered I'd been here before. In fact, I'd been here quite a few times before.

"Hurry," I hissed to Lux. Did he have to put the ring back in the case? Could he just chuck it in the general direction of the display? Because we needed to get out of here right now.

He pointed ahead of us. "Two rooms. I think."

We ran to the end of the room then Lux stopped, glancing

left, then right, then straight ahead, a frown of confusion on his face. The growl was closer. I saw the floor lights glint off something red and gold.

"Just pitch it," I whispered.

"No," he told me solemnly. "Return to the rightful place."

Fuck that. I went to grab the ring, but he had a death grip on it. The growl behind us turned into a low rumble noise. An enormous clawed foot appeared in the doorway. Snatching Lux off his feet, I tossed the kid onto my shoulder and ran. My sneakers squeaked and slapped against the floor. I heard a roar, and ducked as flames licked the wall beside me. Thankfully the curators at the British Museum had done quite a bit of fireproofing over the last few years and nothing caught fire.

Tightening my hold on Lux, I raced through the museum, making a turn at every intersection, hoping to lose the pissed off dragon that was after us. I'd been on good terms with Sparky, but I got the feeling my kid stealing a ring from what he considered to be his hoard might be a deal breaker in our tentative friendship.

We were completely out of the jewelry area and weaving our way through historical clothing displayed through fireproof glass when I realized the dragon knew the layout of the museum far better than I did. I tossed Lux behind a display case of leather armor and ducked, taking the blast of dragon fire across my back.

"Throw me the ring and get out of here," I yelled. Lux stared at me wide-eyed as I shucked my burning clothes.

The dragon drew a breath in preparation, and Lux finally did as I said. I caught the ring he threw before teleporting away, and dove behind a case full of swords just as a wall of fire came my direction. I was trapped with the only way out being blocked by a huge angry dragon. The fireproof cases had proved to be indeed fireproof, but I wasn't sure how many blasts they'd stand before starting to melt. Then I'd not only have a dragon pissed off at me, but the museum curators as well. And I *really* didn't want the museum curators angry.

"Thief! Thief!" the dragon roared, stomping his feet.

"I'm not the thief. I'm the one trying to return the ring," I shouted back. "The thief is a baby. He didn't understand what he was doing. Haven't your baby dragons ever done something wrong before?"

He paused for a second, but I'd discovered that dragons weren't very logical when it came to their hoard, and Sparky was no exception. He let loose another blast of fire and I felt the case tremble.

This had to end. Now.

While Sparky sucked in another gulp of air, I stepped out from behind the display case and threw the ring at him as hard as I could, figuring I'd stand here and let him burn me into a blackened crisp a few times, just to get some of the anger out of his system. Maybe he'd be satisfied. He'd have his ring back. He'd have punished me for the theft. Then we could go back to being friends. Or at least frenemies.

Shutting my eyes tight, I waited for a wave of excruciating heat. Instead I heard a strange sound. Ack? Ook? Something like that?

Opening my eyes I saw Sparky stumble to the side, colliding with the wall and knocking several paintings off their mountings as he slid to ground. His mouth was wide open, giving me a lovely view of all his sharp white teeth. I could see the whites of his eyes as he stared at me in panic, his claws gouging the marble floor.

I frowned, wondering if dragons had heart attacks. Or strokes. Or epilepsy. Then I realized he couldn't breathe and the weird noise was him choking.

Fuck. I must have thrown the ring straight down his

throat where it got stuck. I wasted precious moments in amazement at how such a large creature could have a windpipe so narrow that a ring could jam it up. Then I wasted more precious moments pondering how I might perform the Heimlich maneuver on a dragon.

Sparky's eyes rolled backward and the claws were slowing down. Guessing I better do something or deal with the repercussions of killing a dragon and leaving its giant carcass in the British Museum, I summoned my sword and walked forward.

I'd intended to slice the ring out of Sparky's throat and hope for the best, but instead of a sword, my sentient weapon managed to appear as a giant hammer—like the kind the carnivals use in those ring-the-bell-and-win-a-prize games. Changing course from Sparky's neck to his belly, I cocked the hammer back and let it fly.

I'm not all that good at judging dragon anatomy, so it took five or six hits before the ring came flying out and Sparky took a deep breath. I braced for a blast of fire, but he stayed down, his body relaxing as the ring bounced off the back wall and rolled across the floor, coming to rest next to his nose.

It was a good time to make myself scarce, but Lux was gone and I wasn't sure how long it would take Gregory to come get me. I pulled out my cell phone and began to type him a message, letting him know that it wasn't an emergency, but that I needed a lift home and I'd be at the closest pub to the British Museum.

"Ma?" I turned at Lux's whisper to see him hiding behind a suit of armor. "Came back to get you."

He was holding one of the steak knives from my kitchen in his hand. It was absolutely adorable that my kid was ready to defend me against a dragon with a piece of cutlery.

"Thanks," I whispered back. I took his hand and we were

back in my living room. Lux was getting much better at this teleportation thing, but before I could praise him he wrapped his arms around my legs and held on tight. I removed the steak knife from his hand so he wouldn't accidently skewer me.

"Scary!" Lux announced with a shudder.

"Nah, it was just Sparky." I ran a hand through his golden curls, leaving a streak of soot. It made him look like a reverse skunk. "He's a real bastard sometimes, but he's not scary. I'll take you back in a few months when he's calmed down and you can give him a present to make up for stealing his ring."

Lux buried his face in my legs. I continued to stroke his hair, looking over at the two remaining piles of rings, wondering what the fuck the ones in the third pile belonged to.

"I'll help you with the rest of them," I assured the angel. "Don't be worried. If Sparky was the worst of that second pile, then we'll be fine. Let's do a couple more tonight, just to get some out of the way. If we can do a few each day, we'll have these done by the end of the week. There aren't that many left. Most of them were in the first pile and Uncle Samael helped with almost all of those."

He nodded, then sniffed, letting go of my legs to wander over to the rings. Looking down, he selected four and held them out to me. "These ones next."

These ones ended up being at the bottom of the ocean. Oceans. Plural. Lux had found rings from various shipwrecks, and as much as I tried to convince him that we didn't need to return these particular finds, he insisted. I ended up in scuba gear, fending off sharks and eels and other pissed off sea creatures while he took his own sweet time replacing the rings in the exact same spot he'd found them. We continued until there were only two rings left in the second pile, then decided to call it a day.

CHAPTER 12

The next morning there were more almost-dead things in front of my house. Six rats, four groundhogs, two opossums, and a partridge in a pear tree.

I was joking about the last one, but dead serious about the others. How these things managed mobility was completely beyond my comprehension. Most looked as if they'd played chicken with an oncoming tractor trailer and lost. I threw the poison theory right out the window and tried to think about who might have the skill and the motivation to curse me. Were they trying to send a bunch of live animals to harass me, and they suffered horrible injuries along the way, dragging themselves to my doorstep to carry out whatever my adversary's magic sent them to do?

As I was whacking one of the rats with my shovel, the rest of the menagerie attacked me. It was no fucking fun being bitten by a bunch of smelly half-dead animals. Groundhogs have always been my nemesis, and these were no exception. While I kicked, swatted, stomped, and tried to keep the rats from climbing up my legs, the groundhogs went on the attack. I'd just sent one of them flying into a tree trunk when the possum got into the game and sunk his sharp little teeth into my foot. Fucker bit clean through my sneaker. Grabbing him by the neck, I tried to pull him off me only to have a hank of hair and skin come off in my hand.

For a second I ignored the rats and groundhog still trying to get a piece of me, and instead stared down at the possum. I swear I saw its spine as well as the shiny strands of tendon holding what was left of rotted muscles together.

Ew.

Shaking off a rat that was climbing up my other leg, I took aim with the edge of the shovel and brought it down on the possum, cutting halfway through the animal. Smashing them wasn't killing them, maybe slicing would.

Nope. The back end of the possum still twitched. The front end still continued to gnaw on my foot. I hit it again, slicing it completely in half, and even that didn't kill it.

"Sam? What in the world are you doing?"

I looked up to see Wyatt standing beside my SUV, watching me do battle.

"Stay back. There's an undead rodent army trying to kill me. I don't know if they're infected with something like rabies, so don't let them bite you."

Wyatt took a few steps back. "Aim for the head," he told me helpfully.

"I cut one in half and it didn't do shit." This wasn't one of his video games, but just to test the theory, I squashed one of the rats with my shovel, then lopped it's head off.

"You've got to destroy the brain," Wyatt instructed. "Just cutting the head off won't kill them."

Right. I whaled away at the rat with the sharp end of the shovel until its head looked like hamburger on the pavement. It did seem to be working, so I continued that method with the rest of the animals. The possum head gnawing on my shoe was a total pain in my ass. I saved it for last since I had to nearly chop my big toe to bits to destroy its brain. Finally I killed the damned thing. And killed my favorite pair of sneakers as well.

As soon as all the brains were crushed, Wyatt approached, nudging one of the twitching bodies with a stick he'd picked up off the driveway.

"How long before the bodies die?" I figured he was the expert, so maybe he'd know when these things would finally be dead-dead.

"No idea. In the video games I usually don't stick around long enough to see when the bodies stop moving." Wyatt took the stick and nudged the rat body over to the edge of the driveway. "Can I ask why you've got zombie rodents attacking you?"

That was one of the nice things about having an ex-boyfriend-still-kinda-friend as a neighbor. Wyatt was completely unfazed by all the supernatural shit that happened in and around my house. If things got too weird, he just packed up his computers and went on vacation until they were a little less weird.

"I think someone cursed me." I ran a hand through my hair. "Any idea who might be pissed enough at me to do this?"

He laughed. "Everyone you've ever met?"

Very funny. I began to scoop up the body parts with the shovel and toss them into the woods.

"Seriously. None of the sorcerers I know can animate the dead. It's totally not an elven magic thing. I was thinking that with all your zombie video games, you might actually know someone in the necromancy community who could help me figure out who's doing this." I looked up at him. "Please tell me there's a necromancy community, and that you person-ally know one or two."

Wyatt gave me some major side-eye. "I don't know any

necromancers and I can't really help you with your real-life zombie problem."

"Well the brains suggestion totally worked." I kicked the last rat body into the woods. "So what's up?"

Wyatt didn't come around that much anymore. It sucked because I missed him, but I understood. We were no longer dating. Outside of riding horses and our both caring about Amber and Nyalla, we didn't really have much in common.

"First, I seem to have a roofing contractor doing repairs on my house. You know you don't have to keep doing this stuff, Sam."

Crap. I'd hoped he wouldn't notice, but I guess it was hard *not* to notice people banging away on top of your house.

"If I have to stare at your house every time I go up and down the lane I prefer it not be such a hideous eyesore. That roof is about to fall down on you. I don't want to have to come dig you out of the rubble in the middle of the night."

He shook his head but was smiling, so I knew we weren't about to have an argument. Good. I had weirdly complicated emotions regarding this guy and wanted us to be on friendly terms.

"Secondly, Darcie called and asked me to check with you about the bachelorette party. She said you're not answering your texts."

Shit. I'd been kinda busy, but I really needed to get going on this party. "Um Wyatt, can you do me a solid?"

He rolled his eyes. "What this time, Sam?"

"I need a venue to host the party with food and drinks. Oh, and I need a few strippers, and a ton of sex toys for party favors."

Wyatt tried to look pissed off. Tried. I counted the seconds as he contorted his face, finally giving up and laughing at the twenty second mark. A new record.

"Tell you what. I'll give you the phone number for

Amber's favorite local bar. They'll organize everything for you. Just make one phone call and give them the date."

He was the best. "And you'll handle the strippers and the sex toys, too?"

"No. The rest is up to you."

Okay, maybe not the *best*. I sighed, thinking I might at least be able to order some shit before I headed to Florida.

Wyatt moved in as if he were about to hug me, then took a look at the bite marks and animal goo all over me and decided against it.

"Fist bump?" I extended my knuckles.

"Fist bump." Wyatt did the same, smacking mine. "Check yourself for rabies or zombie virus, and always go for the brains."

"Thanks, Wyatt. Love 'ya."

He grinned. "Love 'ya too, Sam. And thanks for the roof."

I watched him leave, making sure he got home without any zombie rats attacking him. Then I went inside, washed up, changed clothes, ordered a whole bunch of sex shit off the internet, and went to Florida.

Actually, Gregory teleported me to Florida because I still couldn't do it myself. I thought about having Lux do it, but I didn't want to bring him along on the meeting, and I wasn't sure the legalities of having a winged toddler wandering around a major city alone. I already had one court date. I didn't want child protective services all up in my ass.

Gregory dropped me off a few blocks away so I could hide the fact that I was running on less than eight cylinders. I told him I'd text him when my meeting was done, and that if I didn't contact him by nightfall, he should look for me at the city jail.

Walking up to Blue Fire, I knew right away that this was a big money operation. Dar, Gareth, and Kirby's headquarters was in Miami. It was a huge gleaming white building with the name emblazoned across the top story in bright blue. Everything was white. The floor. The receptionist's desk. The walls. The only color at all was the company logo which was splashed here and there in strategic places. I decided given their contracts, I shouldn't go in with my wings out and sword in hand, but clearly I must not have hidden my identity well enough because alarms went off when I was ten feet from the receptionist's desk.

Silly me. I'd thought the alarms were to warn of an approaching hurricane or earthquake or something until two men shot me with a pair of white-muzzled guns—these a more compact pistol model then the one shown in the catalogue.

That left me on the floor, feeling like I wanted to curl up for a nap.

"What the fuck? I've got an appointment." I glared at the men who stood over me with their guns. They looked exactly the same from their SWAT team outfits, to their sunglasses, to their short, nondescript-colored hair. "At least post a 'No Demons or Angels' sign outside before you go unloading on visitors."

"This is a secure building," one of the men barked at me. "What's your purpose here?"

"As I said, I've got an appointment. I'm here to see Gareth. I'm a friend of his...well, sort of a friend of his. And Kirby."

The guards exchanged glances. "Iblis?" Guard One asked me.

"Yep. I'd show you my wings and my sword, but you fucking shot me so I can't."

Guard Two lifted his chin at the receptionist who dialed a number. She and another woman spoke, then I remained on the floor with weapons pointed at my head until she got a call back.

"Send her on up," Gareth told the receptionist through the speaker phone.

I'd expected better treatment after that, but I was wrong. The identical twin guards escorted me up to the top floor in the elevator, guns at the ready. Then they perp marched me through an office full of gawking humans to a big corner executive suite. They even went inside, prepared to blast me as I crossed the room and greeted Gareth. It was as if they'd expected me to attack him or something. I'll admit Gareth and I had disagreed on occasion, but it's not like I'd ever tried to Own him, or eat his heart or anything.

"This better wear off within the next ten minutes or I'm going to be pissed," I told Gareth as I shook his hand.

He gestured for me to sit, then waved the guards away. "The effect lasts an hour. Sorry for the inconvenience. Next time make an appointment and we won't have to shoot you."

Asshole. "I *did* make an appointment. Go shoot your assistant or whoever handles your schedule, because I'm supposed to be on there."

"Sorry."

He didn't sound sorry. I got the impression he'd known about this meeting and had just taken advantage of the opportunity for a little passive-aggressive payback for all the trouble I'd caused him over the years. That, or he thought a demonstration of their new products was in order.

"Quite the business you've got going on here," I commented as I sat. "You. Kirby. Dar."

He shrugged at the mention of my brother and switched to Elvish. "We needed an investor who had funds this side of the gates as well as connections. Your brother has both. His cash meant we could expand fast enough to meet demand and get the jump on any competition. His government and other connections meant we had customers lining up to order the moment we were introduced. It's going to be a struggle to keep up with demand, but we're the only company with the knowledge and technology to produce this sort of security."

I picked up a paperweight and tossed it from hand to hand. "I get that the humans might be feeling helpless, what with New Hell, demons and angels coming and going as they please, werewolves and other shifters who they'd thought were just regular human neighbors and coworkers last year."

Gareth nodded. "There are a few humans who are freaked about the shifters. We're expanding our line of home defense weaponry to sell to them. Unlike those idiots in Alaska, our weapons and ammunition won't be lethal though. The citizens asking for these won't be thrilled about that, but lethal bullets are difficult to create and insanely expensive. And our weaponry is legal where theirs isn't. Although, these people aren't particularly worried about the legality of their weapons."

I was relieved to hear that the Blue Fire weaponry wasn't going to kill anyone. Not that humans couldn't do that on their own, but nuking the West Coast would also destroy land that they clearly needed and valued as well as kill a whole lot of demons.

"As for New Hell and the demons," Gareth continued, "the federal government didn't like the idea of having to protect against demons spilling over into neighboring states. We've got a contract to provide a magical barrier instead. The only thing delaying installation of that is a modification that will restrict humans from leaving New Hell as well as demons. Unless, of course, those humans have appropriate permits."

Of course. Not that any of this bothered me. I didn't really want some of those demons running around all over the place either. Plus I'd made a deal for the US to stuff their criminals into New Hell. I could see where they might not want them walking right out the moment they got in.

"So *that's* project Woo-woo," I mused thinking the wall must be the top-secret shit Dar had been talking about.

"Actually, it's not." Gareth looked down at his hands. "Unfortunately due to some clauses in our contracts, I'm not allowed to go into details about that project."

I read between the lines. Normally that was a skill that completely escaped me, but I seemed to be getting better at all of this political mumbo jumbo. I blame all the endless Ruling Council meetings for that.

Blue Fire had a branch that specialized in retail sales for individual defense and home protection—as well as to corporations and law enforcement, no doubt. They had a branch that was dealing with the border between New Hell and adjoining countries. What the fuck did that leave? The president didn't think shifters were that much of a problem, and he was cozied up to Dar, planning to issue citizenship to demons in return for votes. That left angels.

"What's happening with the angels?"

I'd thought they were still stumbling around, getting used to life in a corporeal form, and occasionally meeting an unfortunate death until I'd had that talk with Gregory the other night about what the rebels were planning. Had the humans gotten wind of it? Was Project Woo-woo their way of preparing to defend against an angelic attempt to wipe them out?

Gareth eyed the closed door to his office, and continued to speak in Elvish. "Some angels believe that their mission is to stamp out sin and bring humans to what they consider a righteous path. Understandably, the humans don't want their interference, but these angels are insistent and they are powerful and invulnerable to traditional human means of defense."

"And you're providing the human governments with an equalizer," I mused.

"Reversible methods of long-term incapacitation, mostly. The majority of the governments want to make angels human so they can be subject to human laws and imprisonment."

I felt a bit sick at the idea of an angel—or demon—being permanently deprived of their abilities. To never fly again. To not be able to instantly fix physical injury. To not be able to change form, to cloak ourselves in ether or liquid or fire to suit any environment.

I'd cut them off from Aaru, and now Gareth wanted to take their wings.

"I don't like that." I added, "How reversible is reversible? What if the human with the antidote dies? Or it doesn't work? Will the effect eventually wear off?"

"We guarantee it for five hundred years, but I'm not really sure how long the effects truly last." Gareth shrugged as if the whole thing were of no real consequence. "It might be permanent without the antidote."

"And just how effective *is* this antidote? Because it better be one hundred percent, or project Woo-woo is a no-go."

"It works every time."

I squinted at Gareth, but couldn't tell if he were lying or not. He believed it to be true, but whether it had been tested enough was my worry. And how could he test it? It wasn't like he had a bunch of angels he was shooting then injecting. Was he running a clinical trial of this?

Wait. I'd completely forgotten that he'd said "mostly" earlier.

"So that's the majority of the anti-angel products. What's the rest?"

Gareth shifted in his chair, messing with a few of the papers on his desk. "A few countries want a weapon that will completely destroy an angel's corporeal form and prevent them from reforming."

I stared at him. "Kill them, you mean."

"Well…yes. It's not like they haven't killed humans since they've been here," he quickly added.

"Twenty." I glared at him. "Twenty people out of seven billion."

"Those twenty people had families," he argued. "Their lives mattered."

"Yes, and there was a two-hundred-page impact analysis on each one. Any angel found at fault was punished." It wasn't the same punishment as they'd had when they still had access to Aaru, but it was a punishment nonetheless.

"And how many angels were found at fault in those deaths," he shot back.

It was my turn to squirm in my chair. "None."

They'd truly been accidents. Aside from a few thousand of them, most angels had never been out of Aaru, never been in a physical form and had to deal with things like hunger, pain, or humans who tried to pick their pockets. There was a learning curve, and I thought only twenty deaths was pretty damned admirable, especially considering the number of people demons killed each year.

Not that I was going to share that with Gareth and his terminator machine, or whatever it was.

He settled back in his chair, hands folded across his stomach. "Humans are scared. This is *their* home, and suddenly it's overrun with powerful beings that want to take charge and control their lives. They want to fight back. Surely you understand that."

I did understand, but I also wanted to give Gregory and his brothers a chance to right this whole thing, to get control of the rebels, to get *all* the angels to back off and leave the humans the fuck alone.

"And you're shipping these lethal weapons now?" I asked.

"No. We're still testing and tweaking designs. The wall

will be ready to install in the next few weeks, and the long-term effect weaponry should be in production by then as well."

I stared at him, trying to tell if he was lying or not. I wasn't nearly as good as Gregory at that sort of thing, but I got the impression Gareth was telling the truth. He'd always been careful and exact about his magical items. Dar was bitching and moaning about how long it was taking.

He was telling the truth. Of course, if other companies were making the magical paintball weapons, they could just as easily be making the lethal ones. And if some other company was making this shit, that other company might not be as careful as Gareth concerning whose hands they wound up in.

"Can you tell me when the lethal weapons will be ready?"

"Those are in the final design stages and should be ready for testing this week. We hope to be shipping within the month."

Damn. "Can you stall on those and give me a chance to prevent this?" I begged him. It might not do any good if the other company had their own angel-killers, but if I could convince Gareth to hold back on his, it would at least limit the number in the hands of the humans.

He shook his head. "The contracts are signed. We've already received deposits. We've invested significant sums of money and mage-time in creating these items. We're not going to delay."

I held up both hands. "I know you've got a lot of money riding on this, but maybe I can work it so the humans will accept the incapacitation ones in place of the lethal ones. And maybe I can get them to agree on a reduction in the time before the effects wear off. I've got meetings with a bunch of presidents and prime ministers this week as well as a Ruling Council meeting. I'll get the archangels to tell the other angels to fucking knock it off. I'll get the humans to agree to a cease fire. We can all talk about this. Negotiate."

Fuck, I sounded so much like an angel right now.

Gareth shook his head. "I can't be in violation of my contracts as far as delivery dates and the product."

"Please Gareth," I pleaded. "Just let me see what I can do.

He sighed. "Fine. But you need to make this happen within the next week—preferably within the next few days—or it's going to be too late."

There would be no putting the genie back in the bottle, as the humans said, if Blue Fire started shipping the lethal weapons. Once these products were out the door and in human hands, they'd be in use. And even if we managed to stop production, there would be prototypes in circulation that other mages could use to make their own black market products.

I had a week. Actually I had days. Otherwise losing Aaru would be the least of the angelic host's worries.

* * *

GREGORY PICKED me up a few blocks away and teleported me back home. I had a shit-ton of stuff to tell him, so I grabbed us a couple of beers and pulled him down on the sofa beside me.

"We've got a problem," I said as soon as I popped the cap off my beverage. "There is probably more than one company creating magical weapons to sell to human governments and individuals."

"So, this Blue Fire and whoever sold those guns to the police in Phoenix?" the angel asked. "I've seen what that weapon in Phoenix did. Tell me about the ones this sorcerer's company is creating."

"The majority of them can strip an angel, or demon, of

their powers for a set period of time. The purpose of this is so the humans can incarcerate them for violating their laws. Gareth claims there's an antidote to negate the effect. Depending on the weapon, it should eventually wear off. The one they nailed me with in the lobby of their building only lasted an hour, but some are designed to keep going for a few hundred years. I get the feeling none of the antidotes have been tested and that Gareth has no idea how long the effects might really last."

"That's not so bad," Gregory mused. "I know the humans are very concerned about having no ability to defend themselves against angels. This might put them at ease, and convince some of our more intractable angels to follow human law."

That was not what I'd expected him to say.

"Here's the worse part," I continued. "Blue Fire is finalizing a weapon that can *kill* angels. And demons, but there are already human weapons that can kill us if we can't reform our physical bodies fast enough. This…I'm worried this might be a weapon that could even kill an archangel."

He chuckled, leaned over and kissed the top of my head. "Nothing kills an archangel."

"Devouring," I countered.

"It's the galaxy I'm concerned about you devouring, Cockroach. Not me or one of my siblings."

"That's not true. I'm young. Give me a few hundred thousand years and I'll bet I could devour the whole bunch of you and not even pause to take a breath."

"Yes, but you won't." He brushed his spirit-self against mine. "I have complete faith that you won't do that."

"You said once that you thought I was the one who would begin the apocalypse," I reminded him.

He shrugged. "Look around you, Cockroach. This *is* the apocalypse by heavenly standards."

He had a point.

"Either way, there *is* something that can kill an archangel. And I'm willing to bet there are other things you haven't thought of that might be able to kill even a being as powerful as you."

He smiled and shook his head. "These are humans we're discussing. I'll admit they've done a dismaying amount of damage with the gifts we angels gave them, but they are nowhere near advanced enough to come up with a weapon that would destroy an archangel."

"Even with the help of elven magic?" I asked. "They've trained some powerful sorcerers. Couple that with human technology, and they might produce a weapon that would surprise even you."

He thought about that for a moment. "I'll take it under consideration because you're concerned. I don't think it's possible, but I'll bring it up in the next Ruling Council meeting and we'll discuss."

I rolled my eyes because I knew where this was going to end up. Gregory and his siblings had changed quite a bit since I rolled into town, but they were still Angels of Order. There would be a committee formed and by the time they'd studied, discussed, and prepared a thousand-page report, there would be thousands of dead angels.

Oh well. I did my best to warn him. I'd try to convince the humans they didn't need to go killing angels. I'd try to convince them to stick with a less lethal weapon. But at the end of the day, this really wasn't in my hands—it was in the hands of the angels who made up the Ruling Council.

CHAPTER 13

The next day I went through my morning ritual of killing the undead animals milling about my front door. I'd checked my various wounds for rabies or something that might have turned the bitten into a zombie, but found nothing except the usual soup of bacteria that lives in dead flesh.

I had two appointments for the day and while the effects of the bullet Gareth's guards had shot me with *had* worn off within an hour, I was still dealing with the one I'd been hit with in Phoenix, so Lux dropped me off in Iceland then went to Harper's for a playdate with his Nephilim buddy Austin.

Iceland totally rocked. Lava fields. Glaciers. Volcanos. Hot springs. Northern lights. I loved Iceland—except for the elves. During the elven exodus, a group had landed here, and unlike most other countries, the Icelandic folk welcomed their elven overlords with open arms. Within weeks, the elves ended up in high government positions. Humans fought over who would have the honor of hosting an elf in their home. The lucky ones fawned over their guests, preparing them special foods, redecorating to suit their tastes, even giving up most of their house and sleeping in the garage so the elves could have privacy in the rooms of their choice.

I hated it, but what could an imp do when the humans she wanted to save were absolutely happy under an elven thumb?

One thing I noticed straight away was that Reykjavik was clean. Iceland had always been pretty environmentally conscious with geothermal electricity and other green power sources, but this was like the pollution clock had been set back thousands of years. It was as if the country was immune to the whole climate change thing. Elves. They were really damned good when it came to manipulating the environment, and they never could tolerate the slightest bit of trash.

I walked into the conference room to see four elves huddled around the end of the table, looking at pictures on each other's cell phones.

"Do you let him in the house?" one asked.

"I've been letting him sleep at the end of my bed," the other replied with a sheepish smile. "I can't help it. See how cute he is with those little round ears and floppy hair? He looks at me with those big blue eyes and I just can't say no. I've even been feeding him scraps off my plate."

"It's not good to spoil them," a third said.

"I'd spoil him, too. He's soooo cute." The fourth bent closer to better see the picture on the phone.

"He *is* adorable," the first said. "When he's old enough, I'd love to breed him to my Sadie. I'll bet they'd have gorgeous offspring."

The rest made approving noises, agreeing that the babies would be breathtaking. I walked around and peeked over their shoulders to see a picture of a dark-haired, light-eyed little boy of about ten on the first elf's cell phone.

Fucking elves.

Another elf came in and the others scurried to their seats.

I plopped down in a chair at the end and in a blink the table was filled with fruits and an assortment of beverages—no doubt in reusable and biodegradable bottles.

"Thank you, Iblis, for joining us today. I am the Prime Minister, Svelathia Lly. You may call me Prime Minister."

She smiled benignly, waving a hand and sending a plate loaded with fruits my way. I bit into a strawberry and nearly swooned as the flavor hit my tongue. Elves *were* good at weather and growing things, even if they were total assholes.

"We invited you here because we want to let the Ruling Council know that from this day forward, Iceland will not accept any demon or angel on our shores that has not received prior approval."

"Okay." I wasn't sure what I was supposed to say to that. Demons and angels were going to go wherever they wanted, approval or not. If Iceland was buying Blue Fire products, then those angels and demons would wind up dead, or in jail and stripped of their abilities. I'd spread the word, but that was all I could do.

"Applications for tourist visas and residency permits can be found on our website," the Prime Minister went on. "Processing time at the moment is approximately two to three years."

"Okay." Again, other than spread the word, there wasn't anything for me to do.

"We're also forming an alliance with other like-minded, forward-thinking nations. We're calling this alliance the Elven Union, not to be confused with the European Union. Henceforth we will be the EU in capital letters, and those other people will be the eu in lower case letters."

Like *that* wasn't going to be confusing as all hell. "Why don't you call yourself the Fae Union instead? So the acronym is different."

That would make them the FU, which in my mind would be just hysterical.

The Prime Minister wrinkled her nose. "We don't include other fae in our alliance. They're not welcome unless they go on the website and complete the appropriate paperwork, and even then I can assure you they will not receive approval."

I wasn't sure what the fuck elves had against other fae, but this had been a hatred stoked long before my time. From what Leaf had said the other day, it had begun before the war between the angels, before the angels had taken the elves under their wings.

"What countries are in the Elven Union?" I asked.

She named off Ireland, Norway, Sweden, Finland, the Netherlands, and France, then told me that the Ukraine and Poland were applying and some of the United Kingdom had expressed interest.

Damn it all. I couldn't believe this. I'd busted my ass to keep the elves from enslaving the humans, and they were marching right into cages behind the pointy-eared pied pipers.

"What about England? Has the U.K. split over elves, or are they all in?"

The Prime Minister smiled. "England doesn't want to be part of the EU or the eu. We're working on some of the other countries in the UK, hoping to win them to our side."

I left the meeting, wondering what Canada and Australia were going to say about this whole thing. Someone else in the Ruling Council had the other UK countries for their meetings. At the next meeting, I'd need to find out if this was really true or if the elves were lying. No one really minded if they took over Iceland, but if this Svelathia Lly was telling the truth and they had enough countries to form a union, then we needed to think about what that meant for the world going forward.

I texted Gregory for a lift to my next meeting, hoping that there was a grace period in the no-angel-or-demon-Iceland policy. Then while I was waiting, I sat on a park bench without the slightest bit of graffiti or bird poop on it and called Terrelle.

"Don't have a whole lot for you yet," she announced. "I'm still working on things, and would prefer to give it to you all at once. Plus I wanted to confirm some shit. Humans lie worse than demons, you know."

I *did* know. "Actually I wanted to ask if you know anything about the Elvish Union and which countries are currently or considering being in it."

She laughed. "Fucking elves. That crap is coming out of Iceland. They took over the whole country. They treat the humans like they're a bunch of spoiled pets. It's worse than it was in Hel."

I remembered the pictures in the boardroom and agreed. The humans here might not know they were slaves, but they were.

"So far the Elvish Union is a union of one. Iceland is the only country committed to the scheme. They've been talking it up, but the other countries aren't all that keen on having fae run their government or their lives. Svelathia Lly can say whatever she wants, but no one's buying. Unless the elves can prove some serious advantage to having them at the helm, no one besides Iceland is going to be coming to their little party."

That was a relief.

"Can I add a few things to your list if you've got time?" I asked. "Keep your ear to the ground on this Elven Union thing. Let me know if anyone seems like they might be leaning toward joining."

"Will do, boss!"

I hung up and contemplated the extreme cleanliness of

the park as I waited for Gregory. What would happen if I littered? Stuck some chewed up gum under the bench? Drew a penis on the statue of the elven Prime Minister? Would I get fined? Arrested? Shot with one of those guns that no one was supposed to have yet?

I decided against pushing my luck and played solitaire until Gregory came to pick me up.

* * *

I DIDN'T REMEMBER MUCH about my meeting with the Canadian Prime Minister because he was fucking hot and charming, and I spent our whole meeting envisioning what he'd be like in the sack. I think he'd said everything was fine. Everyone in Canada all got along with the shifters. They all got along with the demons. They all got along with the angels. No, there weren't any elves in their government, but he'd assured me that if one ran for office and was democratically elected, they'd welcome them just as they would a human. Just before I left, I remembered to ask him if they had any contracts with Blue Fire for weaponry or defense shit.

He'd replied that they were not so rude as to go shooting at guests in their country, or their own citizens who might occasionally turn into animals.

Which basically meant Canada was turning a blind eye to everything going on at the moment. Nothing to see here. Everything is fine. Good. That was one less country I needed to worry about. Maybe if the US started deporting angels, Canada would take them in.

Gregory picked me up and dropped me at home with a bottle of maple syrup, and a stuffed moose wearing a Mounty hat that I'd bought for Lux, then took off to take care of business. I felt bad for him having to haul me around everywhere when he had his own shit to do. It was inconvenient for me. It was inconvenient for him. I fucking hoped Terrelle figured out how to reverse this thing completely or I was going to need to fess up and ask the other archangels to take turns taxiing me around.

Lux wasn't home, which didn't particularly alarm me even though Harper was supposed to have dropped him off hours ago. When I'd first brought him here from Hel, he'd killed himself a few times every day. Luckily he was very good at recreating his human form, but I hadn't wanted to take chances, especially when a run-in with the chipper/shredder in my barn nearly left him dead-dead, so for months Lux had babysitters.

Since I couldn't convince any dwarves to apply for the job, Nyalla stepped up to take on the majority of the angel watching. So had Asta, Harper, Ahia, and Uriel. It really did take a village to keep a baby angel from offing himself.

Lux had learned quickly and now didn't require quite the level of supervision he'd originally needed. Between Gregory, Nyalla, and I we ensured he wasn't alone more than a few hours at a time. Unconcerned about his absence, I put the moose and syrup on the dining room table, made a sandwich, and headed out to visit the horses.

The three were out in the pasture, gorging themselves on grass. Boomer trotted over from the guest house, a bone in his mouth that I hoped was not from a graveyard. I ate my sandwich, petted my smelly hound, and thought about going for a ride with Lux later this week. I'd been worried after my meeting with Gareth, concerned that angels were going to end up filling prisons and cemeteries all over the world, but that Canadian Prime Minister made me feel I'd overreacted. There was no panic in Canada. Maybe I'd blown the whole thing out of proportion. Maybe all I needed to do was have Dar talk to his new bestie in the White House, reassure him that all was okay, and get Gareth to put the kibosh on the lethal weaponry part of project Woo-woo.

Brushing the crumbs from my hands, I gave Boomer a quick scratch behind the ears and headed back to the house. There were a few more meetings with world leaders to knock out and a handful of rings that still needed to be returned, then I could get on with the fun stuff in my life—like hiring strippers for Amber's Bachelorette party, horseback riding with Lux, and convincing Little Red to take a massive dragon dump on top of my neighbors' car.

The UPS truck was just pulling up as I walked through my living room. For a second I wondered what he was delivering, then I remembered my drunken internet shopping spree. I'd been inspired and pretty much bought out an entire sex shop worth of toys and novelty items.

Thankfully there were no more than four or five dead rats shambling around my driveway. The delivery guy ignored them and began unloading a lot of boxes from the back of the truck. I stood in the doorway and watched him, wondering if he would be interested in moonlighting as a stripper at a party. That brown uniform wasn't exactly form fitting, but when he bent over to stack the boxes on my floor, I noticed he had a nice ass.

"Wanna get naked in front of a bunch of horny women for money?" I asked as I signed for the packages. "One's a half succubus. You might even get laid."

Before he had a chance to respond, my living room erupted into chaos. Lux appeared in a flash of light, screaming and running toward me. Unfortunately when he'd teleported, he'd somehow also brought a troll with him—a very pissed off troll.

The UPS man froze. I wasn't sure if it was the little angel, or the troll, or the combination of the two that had fried his brain, but he was about to be squashed, so I shoved him aside and ran forward to confront the troll before he could attack either the delivery guy or Lux.

Correction, "she." Of course it had to be a female troll. They were bigger than the males, stinkier, and far stronger. Before I could even think to summon my sword, I found myself lifted into the air and slammed back to the ground, WWE style.

I landed on top of the boxes, and one broke open, spilling fat, twelve inch long, bright green dildos across the floor. A huge fist came my way and I rolled, narrowly avoiding being crushed. Another box burst open and red vibrators rolled out. Some genius had thoughtfully put the batteries in them pre-shipment, and they began humming and bouncing around.

That startled the troll enough to buy me a few seconds of time. I got to my feet and summoned my sword, completely unsurprised when the thing appeared as one of the green dildos—two feet long, because clearly my sword had size issues.

I had no time to think about how ridiculous I looked standing in my dining room holding a giant floppy green dildo because the troll recovered from her shock over the vibrators and grabbed for me. I danced out of the way, smacking her with the dildo-sword. It didn't do one bit of good, and with the next grab, the troll had me. My insides squashed together as she tightened her fist around my waist and lifted me over her head.

"No! Ma! Bad troll!" Lux squealed. A vibrator bounced off the troll's head. Then a pair of fur-lined handcuffs. Then Bobby the Blow-up Doll.

"Hey," I yelled. "That doll was expensive. Throw the cheap stuff."

I felt my ribs crack. Ignoring the pain, I continued to whack the troll with my dildo-sword. Lux didn't have the best aim and I was getting hit by as many of the vibrators and BDSM toys as the troll. Just as I was about to be snapped in half, Lux whacked the troll across the thigh with a sparkly riding crop.

The troll screamed, and without thinking I plunged my dildo-sword into her open mouth as far as I could.

The troll had a very active gag reflex. She made a horrible noise and dropped me to the ground so she could clutch her throat, trying to cough the dildo-sword out. I fell, landing on top of Bobby, his realistic cock sliding between my thighs.

Wow, this thing *was* nice. Those ads weren't lying. Curious, I reached down and flipped a tiny switch on Bobby's side. His hips angled mechanically back and forth, rubbing the cock across my crotch. It felt amazing. I could only imagine how incredible this would be if I were naked.

I rode the blow-up doll for a moment while Lux continued to smack the troll with the crop. Picking up a vibrator, I switched it on high and wondered if I could get off with my jeans on. Probably.

A crash tore my attention from the sex toys to the troll, who was now on the ground and beginning to turn an interesting shade of blueish-brown. Damn. This was the second time this week I'd caused a near suffocation. What were the odds?

"Uh oh," Lux announced, backing off on the beating he'd been delivering.

I got off Bobby and went over to the troll, yanking the dildo-sword out of her mouth and dismissing it into the ether. She sucked in a huge breath and opened her eyes. I took advantage of this momentary respite, helping the troll to her feet and handing her one of the non-sword dildos.

"Here. My apologies for nearly choking you to death with a dick. And my kid is sorry he accidently teleported you." I guided the dazed troll toward the door. "There's a nice bridge a bit north of here. Just hang a left on Route 27. You'll feel right at home. Bye. Have a nice life."

I shut the door and watched as the troll staggered down my driveway, past Wyatt's house and out of sight, the entire time clutching a floppy, twelve-inch, bright green dildo.

Turning to Lux, I grinned. "*That* was fun. If you've got any more rings belonging to trolls, then definitely count me in."

"Is it safe to come out yet?" a voice called out.

The UPS guy was cowering under the table. I knelt down and handed him his broken tablet. "Sorry about that. The troll's gone, although you might want to avoid 27 north for the next hour or so."

He scooted out, looking at the dildos scattered around the floor, then glancing at Lux who hovered a few feet off the ground, his wings flapping to keep him aloft.

"Sorry," Lux told the man. "Trolls are scary."

I shrugged. "Nah. They just get freaked out over strangers. *And* being teleported into a house. She'll be fine once she gets to a bridge and can hide out."

I brushed the dust off the UPS guy's uniform, straightening his shirt and feeling up his ass while I was at it. "So how about stripping at that party?"

"Not for all the money in the world." He scooted away from my roving hands and was out the door faster than Usain Bolt running the forty-yard dash. The brown truck actually spun its tires, tossing both gravel and undead rats as he tore down my driveway.

"Can I play with toys?"

I turned to see Lux clutching the moose in one arm and Bobby in the other.

"The moose is yours, but I need Bobby for a party. You can have him when we're done— if he's still in one piece, that is." I looked around at the mess of sex toys. "Give me a hand cleaning all this up and we'll go deliver another ring."

Lux set the moose on the dining room table, then patted its head before starting to pick up vibrators. I collected the dildos, thankful that I'd thought to buy extra since I'd sent the troll away with one. Hmm. Maybe I should buy a few boxes of these and give them out for Christmas. Or just give them out randomly to pizza delivery guys, my manicurist, the garbage people…

My mind wandered from sex toys back to Blue Fire.

"What do you think about angels who break human laws?" I asked Lux as I shoved the dildos back into a box. He was an Angel of Order. It would be good to have an unbiased opinion on these things.

"Which laws?"

Lux's question preceded a flood of telepathic angel-speak. From what I could manage to catch, the little guy felt angels should take the time to learn and respect the laws and customs of the land, but he had conflicted views about what should happen when human laws were in direct opposition to angelic laws. I hid a smile, wondering which of his uncles had been teaching him about angelic laws. Actually, Gregory might be the one doing the instruction. I got the idea he saw Lux as eventually taking a spot on the Ruling Council. Although that might be a few million years in the future at the earliest.

"Let's say you see a human beating someone up and trying to steal their money. What would you do?"

Lux set his mouth in a grim line, outrage shining from his eyes. It was especially adorable because he was holding a vibrator in one hand and a sparkly riding crop in the other.

"Punish bad human. Heal victim and give money back."

"Punish how?"

The little angel frowned. "Give warts? Or tummy ache?

Hit with stick?" The last was punctuated by a few swats of the crop.

"But the humans don't allow that," I told him. "Their laws say you should call the police. The robber will be judged by other humans, and a punishment decided by a designated human. You could get into trouble with the humans for punishing the robber yourself."

Lux let out an exasperated huff. "Too many human laws. Too slow. I see crime, I punish."

And that was the slippery slope even well-intentioned angels would find themselves on with the humans. It would start with a few minor actions like my scenario, and end up either with angels becoming vigilantes, or deciding to do the humans a favor and just run things themselves.

Mr. Hottie Canada might not be worried about this, but other world leaders would be. Gareth wasn't making a bunch of weapons unless there were buyers. Project Woo-woo was a go. I'd seen the paperwork on the President's desk, and I couldn't believe the US was the only country thinking about this.

I scooped up a handful of nipple clamps, dumped them in a box and looked over at Lux. I shouldn't give a shit about angels getting themselves de-angelized and stuck in prison. I shouldn't give a shit about some asswipe angels getting themselves killed trying to be not-so-benevolent dictators.

But Lux... He was an Angel of Order. As much as I tried to influence him, to turn him to the dark side, he was going to find himself in a back alley giving a robber warts and expecting the police to hand him a medal and thank him. A demon would just pop the fucker's head off, steal the money, and take off, but not Lux. I didn't want to see him in jail without his wings.

And I couldn't even bear to think of someone taking his life because the little guy misunderstood a human law or the duties of being a wedding ring bearer. I needed to do something about this situation before it escalated, before Gareth started shipping his weapons of angelic destruction. I needed to do something, I just wasn't sure what.

Reaching out a hand, I ruffled Lux's golden curls. "Your father isn't going to be back until dinnertime. Why don't we go return a few more of these rings, then you can help me find some strippers to hire for Amber's bachelorette party."

Lux looked up at me and smiled. "Rings then strippers. Fun."

Yep. Well, the strippers would be fun, the rings probably not.

The little angel's smile faded as he pulled the corner of the carpet back. "Uh, oh. Only very scary rings left."

I looked and saw he was right. Gregory must have helped him take care of the rest of pile two, because now all that remained were the six rings in the third pile.

"Then it's good I'm here to help you. We'll do them in order of scariness—easiest one first, okay?"

Lux took a deep breath then nodded. "These two." He picked them up. "And maybe this one."

Three out of six. I couldn't believe we were getting these done so fast. And outside of being shot in Phoenix, none of them had really been all that bad.

Rings. Bachelorette party planning. Cross that shit off my list, and all I'd have to worry about was a few more meetings and a potential war that could wipe out either all of humanity or all of the angels.

The first two ring returns really *weren't* so bad. I'd had some experience with vampires before and they'd always been polite and friendly to both angels and demons. This one was no exception. Eduardo looked to be only a few hundred years old, but he'd clearly been an important dude back in his human days. He accepted the ring and Lux's apologies with grace, then gave us a tour of his manor home while a vampire minion put together a light repast of cheese and wine for us to enjoy.

The next ring belonged to an elven princess who'd clearly fallen on hard times since the exodus from Hel. We found her working at a florist shop in Nebraska, assembling an elaborate funeral wreath of lilies and carnations. She was overjoyed to have her ring back. I didn't ask what magic she'd enchanted the object with, and she didn't tell me. Instead of being angry with Lux for the theft, she called him an adorable little angel and offered him a rose that she said would never die.

I was no fool, so I intercepted the rose, being careful not

to touch any of the thorns. Once we'd left, I set the thing on fire, watching the magic crackling in acrid sparks as the rose burned.

"Bad flower," Lux intoned.

"Bad elf," I corrected. I had no idea what would have happened if he'd pricked his finger on one of those thorns. That bitch was totally on my bad list. If she thought the florist job was beneath her, wait until I had her transferred to sewer cleaning duty or something like that.

"One more?" Lux asked, holding up a wide platinum band with sapphire chips embedded in it.

"Sure. We can take it back before we go home."

What the heck. Might as well knock one more off the list, then we could relax and enjoy some family time. I wondered what movie Gregory would want to watch tonight. For some reason, I was in the mood for horror, although those films always got Lux worked up. I really didn't want the little guy waking up in the middle of the night and using every last bit of salt in my kitchen to secure the doors and windows, or sitting just inside an open front door with a wooden chair leg and a crucifix he'd made out of braided straw.

Lux reached out for my hand and I took it. Instantly we were transported to a forest, only this wasn't like any forest I'd ever seen. Tree trunks were black as tar, clothed in delicate gray-green vines. The leafy canopy far above our heads only let in thin columns of gold-tinted light. Bird song filled the air, but the feathered beings were nowhere to be seen. As I looked around, the trees shifted and moved, revealing a path.

I frowned, thinking this was eerily similar to Doriel's forest back home in Hel. But we weren't in Hel, and Doriel didn't seem the type of Ancient to have a pretty little bejeweled ring.

Lux pointed down the path. I put a hand on his shoulder, angling him so he was slightly behind me. It wasn't easy walking down the path while keeping physical contact with the angel who was practically on my heels, but I had a feeling if I let go, he'd vanish.

It was a good thing I'd gone first, otherwise the spear would have hit Lux right between the eyes. As it was, I got it in the knee. There it lodged in bone and sinew, making me stumble so I took the second spear about four inches below my belly button.

The wounds burned, the magic in the spears going straight through my physical form to the spirit-self that I could neither heal nor recreate. Still holding Lux with one hand, I grabbed the spear and yanked it out of my guts, stabbing it point first into the ground.

"Hey! We're here to bring back your ring. And apologize," I yelled, trying in vain to pull the other spear from my knee.

"Sorry!" Lux hollered from behind me.

"Shoot us again and I'm leaving. I'll take the ring to the pawnshop, or one of those gold-for-cash places that'll melt it down."

The spear came free from my knee just as its magic was starting to gnaw past the edge of my spirit-self. The path widened, and in front of me appeared a mountain. Tossing the spear aside, I limped forward, stepping from a mossy forest path onto a stony one that climbed the orange-toned rock in narrow switchbacks.

The first thing that went through my head was that this was a fuckload of trouble to go to in order to return a ring. Didn't these people want their property back? You'd think they'd show up with their hand outstretched, or at least have a deposit spot with a "leave ring here" note. No, instead we were hiking all over the fucking place.

The second thought was that this mountain path wasn't any better than the forest one. I didn't get shot by any spears, but the sun was hotter than noon in Dis, and the path was barely wide enough for me to scoot along sideways. I'd thought about revealing my wings and just flying to the top, but I didn't want to risk getting hit with another spear, this time to my very sensitive wings.

Lux and I were both drenched in sweat and breathless by the time we got to the summit. Perched atop a peach colored plateau was a tiny stone house with a thatched roof. A twig wreath hung on the door, and those silvery gray vines crept up to the lintel. The door swung open and a bony hand ushered for us to come in. Lux huddled behind me and I swapped his shoulder for his hand, giving his fingers a reassuring squeeze.

I was prepared for the worst, for some ghoul to rush us the moment we crossed the threshold, for the house to fall down on our heads, for a hundred spears to shoot out from the walls and impale us. What I wasn't prepared for was a lovely cottage with a cheery fire, a vase of daisies on the table, and a set of comfy chairs on a richly colored Persian rug. The bony hand belonged to an equally bony woman with a beak of a nose and jet-black hair severely pulled back into a tight braid.

"You have rings?" she said in a thickly accented voice.

Lux peeked out from behind me, extending the sapphire-encrusted band. The woman took it from him, sighing in pleasure as she slipped it onto the pinky of her right hand.

"Other?" she asked.

Lux swallowed hard, then extend another ring—one that was identical to the ugly thing Gregory had given me as an engagement token. My left hand was behind my back, gripping Lux's. Holding my breath, I spun the band around, digging the stones into the palm of my hand and hoping she couldn't tell the difference between Gregory's reproduction and the real thing.

The old woman took the ring and frowned, turning it in her hand.

"We're very sorry about this," I said hurriedly, pushing Lux as I backed toward the door. "He's just a little angel, and he misunderstood. Didn't know. So very sorry. Won't happen again."

"Sorry!" Lux repeated from behind me.

"This isn't my ring," the old woman announced.

Shit.

"Get us out of here," I whispered, tightening my grip on Lux's hand.

Nothing happened.

"Now. Get us out of here," I repeated.

"Can't. Won't work," Lux whispered back.

Had she spelled the house to null Lux's abilities? Had she spelled the mountain? The forest? How far would we need to run before Lux could get us the fuck out of here?

"It's totally your ring," I lied. "And a very beautiful ring it is, too. I'm sure once you get it in the light over there by the fire, you'll recognize it."

"This. Isn't. My. Ring." The old woman grew six inches, her fingers lengthening into yellow claws. Then her eyes shot to my midsection, as if she could see right through me to the hand clutching Lux's. "You have my ring."

"Nope. I don't have your ring. I've got a completely different ring that just happens to look like yours."

A smart demon would have fessed up and traded for the reproduction. They looked the same, and an ugly ring wasn't worth battling some witchy old hag for. But this wasn't just any old ugly ring. It was the ring my beloved angel had given me, and I wasn't about to part with it. Greed was one of my top sins, and I tended to become very obstinate when others tried to take what I'd claimed as mine. The ring might have been stolen, but it was mine now, and I wasn't going to give it up.

The hag threw the reproduction ring at me. I caught it, threw it back at her, and ran, scooping Lux up and tucking him under my arm as I booked it across the plateau.

"Mine!" the hag screamed.

"Mine!" I screamed back, trying to move as fast as I could down the treacherous mountain path. I heard a huffing sound and risked a glance behind me. For an old woman, the hag was pretty damned nimble on her feet.

A rock slid under my feet and I nearly went over the side of the mountain, catching my balance at the last moment. My momentum transferred, and suddenly I was running down the switchback with a reckless speed I couldn't halt.

"Wings," I shouted at Lux, worried that I might drop him.

"No wings," he said in a matter-of-fact voice from under my arm.

Another rock came loose under my foot and I pitched forward, smashing my arm and Lux against the cliff face as I flailed with the other to keep my balance. I tried to reveal my wings, knowing their width would push me off the cliff and expose me to flying spears. They would also allow me to descend faster and with more safety than my crazy headlong stumble down the mountain side.

No wings. Just as Lux had said. The magic that had kept him from teleporting was also keeping us from flying. Would it also keep us from healing or recreating a damaged body? I ran faster, trying to decide whether a potentially fatal fall from the cliff was worse than a potentially fatal eviscerating if the witch caught up with us.

Halfway down the mountain I slipped again and this time couldn't keep my balance. "Grab me," I shouted at Lux heaving him onto my back as I pitched off the side of the cliff.

He wrapped his chubby arms around my neck, throttling me. I grabbed wildly as I fell, my hands slipping off rocks and ledges until my fingers finally closed around a branch. It bent, smacking me against the cliff face where I dangled, the thin limb all that stood between us and a hundred-foot fall onto a field of boulders.

"Uh oh."

The whispered words in my ear had me cringing. A spear whistled by, frighteningly close to mine and Lux's back. I tried to turn slightly to sandwich the angel between me and the cliff face and nearly lost my grip on the branch.

As I swung on the branch, I saw the spears and the fall weren't our only worries. The witch was levitating down toward us. And I could see right up her skirt.

"Some panties would have been a good choice," I shouted up at her. "Your crotch looks like a moldy, uncooked loaf of bread."

"Give me my ring!"

Figures that the witch would be more concerned about an ugly ring than whatever venereal disease she had going on between her legs. I shifted Lux around to my side, tucking him against my shoulder. He looked up at the hag floating slowly down toward us and said "Ew."

"I know. You'd think a witch could brew up some salve to take care of that." Another spear came my way and I let go of the branch with one hand to catch it. The good news was I now had a weapon to use against the approaching witch. The bad news was I didn't know how long I could hang on to the branch with one hand."

"Here." I handed the spear to Lux and gripped the branch with both hands again. "When she gets within range, stab her."

Lux swung the spear like it was a rattle. I let out an exasperated breath, wondering if it would just be easier to let go and deal with a few hundred broken bones. I glanced over my shoulder, noting that Lux's wild flailing of the spear did seem to be keeping the witch at bay. Although time was on her side. I couldn't hang here forever, and she certainly seemed to have no limit to her ability to float around mid-air.

"Give me my ring."

I'd never given up anything that was mine. Never. But here I was hanging off the side of a cliff, contemplating doing just that. I wouldn't have budged if the only consequence would have been my broken or dead body at the bottom of this cliff, but I couldn't do that to Lux—not even over something given to me by my beloved.

"Maybe we can come to some sort of compromise," I offered instead. "A shared custody sort of thing. Like you get to have the ring on alternate weekends, and for two weeks during summer break."

The woman stared at me, outraged. "It is *my* ring."

"Yes, but my fiancé gave it to me, and now I'm really attached to it."

She shook her head. "Your fiancé gave you a stolen engagement ring? You knew it was stolen, and you still said yes?"

My hands slipped a little on the branch. "Yeah. I'm a demon, an imp. The first ring he ever gave me was still attached to the hand—severed from the body, of course. Otherwise it would have been kind of hard to FedEx. I'm not sure shippers do cadavers. Actually I'm not sure they're supposed to ship severed hands either."

Her mouth dropped open. "He cut off someone's hand to give you a ring?"

"The hand was really the gift, not the ring. But severed

limbs rot, and I wasn't sure I could get it past security at the airport, so I kept the ring." I gripped the branch tighter, hoping maybe she'd think she got off easy since she didn't lose a hand and agree to my shared custody offer.

"It's love," Lux told her. "Rings are for love."

"You are crazy," the hag informed me. "And your fiancé is even more crazy."

"I know." I grinned. "That's why I love him."

She looked a bit taken aback at that. "But…it is mine. It was stolen, and I want it back."

My hands slipped a bit more. "Isn't that reproduction just as good?"

"No."

My arms were killing me. "How about every other weekend and *three* weeks in the summer? I'll even throw in Wednesday night so you can wear it out on dates if you ever get that crotch-rot taken care of, that is."

The hag glanced down between her legs, then glared back up at me.

"I can heal," Lux offered.

"No, he can't," I lied. I wasn't letting Lux anywhere near that hag's moldy beaver."

"I can," he insisted. "Heal hag. Swap rings every year."

The woman hesitated. My hands slipped again, leaving me clinging to the very end of the branch.

"Okay, but only because you have a psycho romance story involving severed hands and stolen rings."

The branch snapped. Lux resumed his strangle-hold on my neck as we fell. I tried to turn midair so I'd hit the boulders first, hopefully protecting the angel from dire injuries. The ground rushed toward me, then something changed. I felt a spark charging the air, like what happens the moment before lightning shoots across a storm-dark sky. My wings burst out and I swooped along the ground, a mere two feet away from the rocks below. I flew until I found a flat, grassy spot between the mountain and the forest, then landed, setting Lux on the ground beside me and rubbing my neck. The little angel had his wings out as well, and was dancing around in delight. The hag slowly descended like an oracle in a cheap production of a Greek play, smoothing her skirt once she was on solid ground.

Before I could protest, Lux danced over and punched her in the crotch. "Heal!"

The hag staggered backward, falling to the ground with her feet in the air. That left Lux and I with an unfettered view of her taco—which was a healthy pink and no longer looking as if bits might start falling off at any second. Huh. *I* was not interested, but I was pretty sure she might actually be able to get a date with a troll or a goblin now. Or a male hag, if they existed.

Or a female hag, if that's the way she rolled.

The hag held out her hand with the reproduction ring in her palm. I grumbled a plethora of curse words as I yanked the engagement ring off my finger. We both handed the rings to Lux who mixed them up behind his back, then held two closed fists out in front of him.

"Pick."

He'd instructed me to pick, no doubt because the hag would possibly know which was which even through his chubby little hands. I picked the left hand, because I always pick the left hand. Lux opened his fingers and the hag let out a frustrated huff, taking the other ring and jamming it on her finger.

"See you in a year, imp," she told me.

"A year," I lied.

Then she was gone, the forest was gone, the mountain was gone. Lux and I stood on a grassy meadow that seemed to go on forever. I dismissed my wings, jammed the ring back on my finger, then took Lux's hand.

"I think that's enough ring returns for the day. Let's go home."

"Pizza and movie?" the angel asked hopefully.

I squeezed his hand and smiled. "Pizza and movie."

CHAPTER 15

This time there were more than rats, possums, and groundhogs shambling around the front of my house. Let me tell you now that zombie deer are pretty fucking creepy.

They didn't hesitate to attack me. I grabbed Lux and he quickly teleported us inside the house. It was one thing for me to be mauled by decomposing undead. I didn't want Lux to be scarred by that sort of thing.

The zombie animals didn't go back to aimlessly walking around as I'd expected once we were inside. Instead they mounded up near the entrance to my house, clawing and biting at the wood. I grimaced, thinking I'd need to pressure wash to get all the gross rotting flesh off the door.

"Sam?" I turned to see Nyalla behind me, staring at the door wide-eyed. "I came home to those…things. There weren't as many of them then. I drove over a few and managed to get inside the house before the rest of them came after me."

"That's why I wanted you and Lux to use the back door," I told her.

"Well, I can't exactly drive my car around back."

I had a ton of shit to do with these stupid meetings, the rings, and the bachelorette party. But this was becoming a priority. Who the fuck had cursed me with dead animals, and how could I make it stop?

"I'll go out and kill them. Wyatt said to smash their brains, and that seems to be working so far."

"Wyatt? My brother knows about this? Are there half-dead animals outside his house, too?

I waved the question away. "No, I'm the only one cursed with zombie deer. And zombie rats, possums, and ground-hogs. Until I figure out how to make this stop, you might want to carry a gun when you leave the house. Aim for the head."

Nyalla came up beside me to look out the window. "What if they bite me?"

I snorted. "Then Gabe shows up and kills every last one of them." The archangel was even more protective of Nyalla than I was. After taking care of my zombie problem, he'd probably roam the countryside, squashing the brains of every roadkill, just in case.

"No, I mean what happens to *me*? Do I turn into a zombie? Do I need to have a month of rabies shots?"

I had no idea. I remember Wyatt telling me to check my wounds and see if there was any rabies or something. At the time there had only been bacteria, but I wasn't willing to stake mine, or Nyalla's, life on that.

"I think it's just a bite, although you'll need some serious antibiotics afterward. I'm not absolutely positive though, so perhaps you should only leave the house when someone can teleport you out."

Nyalla scowled. "I've got a bunch of friends coming over to help fill the penis squirt guns for the bachelorette party.

What am I supposed to tell them about the zombie deer in front of our house?"

I shrugged. "That there are zombie deer in front of our house and they should aim for their heads? I don't know, Nyalla. I'm doing the best I can here."

She threw up her hands, muttering something about having everyone go to the Eastside Tavern instead, then stomped upstairs.

The bachelorette party. Shit, I was really running out of time and I still had a lot to do.

I checked my texts and was relieved to see one from Wyatt giving me the name, number, and address of Amber's favorite pub. I made a quick call, keeping an eye on the undead out front. Just as Wyatt had said, it was easy-peasy. The owners of the pub were thrilled to be hosting Amber's bachelorette party, and would come up with all sorts of special foods and shooters without me even having to lift a finger.

"Ma?" Lux pointed at the zombies on the other side of the window. They were trying to chew their way through the glass and leaving spit and gore behind. "Ma, I help?"

"You're too young to be killing zombies, sweetie. Why don't you go get a beer and you can watch through the window while I take care of these things."

He grinned. "Ma funny?"

Oh yes, Ma would definitely be funny. Lux thought I was living a *Three Stooges* episode, and would be breathless from laughter watching me get my ass kicked by undead. I'd be annoyed if he weren't so damned cute.

I went out the front door and was mobbed and bitten a dozen times before I could grab my shovel. There were just too many of them, and after they'd ripped one of my favorite shirts from my back, I switched to my sword. The sentient weapon was not much more effective than the shovel, but the blade was built for penetrating rotting bone, where the shovel's edge wasn't.

By the time I staggered inside, I was unrecognizable from one of the zombie deer. Sure enough, Lux was red-faced and nearly passed out from laughing. He took one look at me and collapsed onto the floor in mirth.

"Ma funny!"

"Yeah, Ma is really fucking funny," I muttered as I headed up the stairs. I needed a shower. I needed to burn these clothes. And I needed to order pizza because in the midst of the shit-show that was my life, a few bright moments sometimes appeared and tonight was going be one of them. I was going to have pizza and movies with Lux, then Gregory would be coming over. He'd taken to spending nights here, and even though he didn't sleep, I liked having him in my bed with me. Then tomorrow we were supposed to do a family outing before the Ruling Council meeting. I couldn't wait. Too often it seemed like we were ships that passed in the night, doing the tag-team parenting thing. As much as I wanted some one-on-one time with my angel, I also longed for some family time with the three of us.

I never imagined these would be the things I cherished. As a young imp, I'd envisioned myself breeding with a mid-level demon, depositing my offspring in the best dwarven foster home I could afford, then forgetting all about it. After I devoured my practice partner, I'd vowed never to breed. Then after Ahriman…

But here I was, in love with an archangel, co-parenting an adopted angel in a hands-on way I'd never thought desirable, let alone possible. I couldn't imagine handing Lux over to another and never seeing him again. Yes, I longed for a dwarven nanny, but guiding a young angel as he matured was surprisingly rewarding.

I didn't want to breed. I didn't want to raise another

angel. But Lux was perfect. He was mine and he was perfect. And I was thrilled that Gregory felt the same way about our little winged guy.

After I got cleaned up, I settled Lux in with a movie and eyed the remaining rings as I waited for pizza delivery. Three. I couldn't believe we'd managed to return so many of them in such a short time, although I guess it hadn't taken Lux all that long to steal them. He'd done most of the first pile with the help of Samael. Gregory and I had helped with the second pile, and Lux and I had knocked out a good bit of the third pile. Now we were down to these three.

I wasn't ashamed to say these rings made the hair raise on the back of my neck. One was that nasty, rusty-looking gold thing. One was a pretty band with swirly script on both the inside and the outside. The other was some iridescent metal that shifted through a rainbow of colors. Every one of them burned with something powerful, something otherworldly. Every one of them was formed of unknown materials. I wasn't sure who these rings belonged to or what they did, but I'd be glad to get them off my dining room table and out of my house.

I eyed them, remembering the troll. Lux was afraid of delivering these on his own, but he still was trying to be responsible, make Gregory proud, and do this on his own. That troll wouldn't have killed him, but it would have been a horrible experience had she caught Lux. And if he hadn't been able to teleport home? It might have been hours before I realized he wasn't home, or with Nyalla or Hunter and gone to look for him. I couldn't take the chance that he'd do that again. I needed to keep these rings with me to make sure he didn't try to go off on his own and find himself with more than a troll after him.

The pizza delivery guy broke through my reverie, so I shoved the three rings in my pocket, then I went to answer the door. The pizza guy looked rather unsettled. It took me a few seconds to realize why.

My driveway was full of headless animals. The dude had carefully driven around the corpses, but I'm sure this wasn't something he usually encountered delivering pizzas.

"Um, we went hunting and…uh…didn't have time to field dress anything. We're going to eat first, then get right on it."

He glanced at the deer carcass a few feet to the left of the porch. "You might not want to eat these. They don't look like they're all that healthy."

I dug some money out of my pocket and quickly changed my story. "I know. We're culling rabid animals. They'll be composted or something. Just as soon as we're done eating our pizza."

Damn it. I was sick and tired of killing zombie animals, and I was doubly sick and tired of cleaning up the bodies afterward. I'd planned to just leave these in my driveway and hope that a few hundred vultures would swoop in overnight and hauled them off. If not, I was going to get my Lows to drag them all into the woods and hose off the front of my house and my driveway afterward. I hadn't thought about the impact this might have on random delivery people.

I handed the guy his money, sneaking a quick peek at his butt as he made change. "Hey, I'm looking for guys to strip at a bachelorette party. Do you think—"

"Sorry, I'm busy that day."

He shoved some money into my hand, snatched the five I held out to him, and practically ran for his car. I couldn't believe it was this hard to find a stripper. I'd assumed from the number of dick pics women seemed to get that guys would be lining up to get naked in front of a bunch of women—especially when there was a chance of getting laid. Was it me? Was it that the first guy I'd asked was hiding under my table from a troll and this second guy was swerving around a bunch of mangled headless deer in my driveway?

Wimps. There had to be some decent looking human guys out there who wouldn't be put off by dead zombie deer and trolls.

I shifted the pizza boxes in my arms and went back inside. "Pepperoni, onions, peppers, and olives for me," I announced. "Bacon and hots for Lux, and chicken with hot sauce—"

"For me."

An arm came around me, taking the boxes. Gregory planted a kiss on the side of my head, then carried the pizza over to the coffee table. He plopped down beside Lux, and I sat on his other side.

"How are my favorite angels today?" He wrapped an arm around each of us.

"Rings." Lux's face was solemn. "Scary."

I sighed. "Lux tried to deliver one himself and accidently teleported a troll back here. We beat her off with sex toys—I mean we subdued her with sex toys, although the other would have been really funny."

"Did you send her back?" Gregory asked as he took his arm from around me and leaned forward to open the pizza boxes.

"No. She left with a dildo. I think she's either under the bridge up 27, or the one where 97 crosses 26." I shrugged. "She'll be fine. Trolls are the least of our worries right now."

"I know." Gregory handed me a pizza slice. "I'm guessing we both have bad news. You tell me about yours first."

I had so much fucking bad news that I wasn't sure what to lead with. "Let's wait until later to exchange bad news. Right now I just want to eat pizza, watch movies, and chill on the couch with *my* favorite angels.

Which was exactly what I did. All too soon we'd put Lux

to bed and were back on the sofa. I snuggled against Gregory, wondering if the bad news could keep until morning.

"Okay, Cockroach. You go first. Tell me what happened today."

So much for waiting until morning.

I took a deep breath and began to count on my fingers. "First, the ring you gave me belongs to a witchy hag. She spotted the fake a mile away and damned near killed Lux and me, so I had to negotiate shared custody of the ring."

He looked outraged. "How could she tell? I made an exact replica of it."

I held up my hands. "I can't tell the difference either, but clearly she could. No biggie. I'll forget to return it next year and deal with it if, or when, she hunts me down. Second, the elves are trying to form an Elven Union. They've taken over Iceland and have plans to do the same to a bunch of other countries."

Gregory scowled. "Do we need to remove them from Iceland?"

"The human citizens will kick our asses if we do. Evidently the elves are duly elected officials, so we've got a choice here: we can respect the democratic process, or we can send in hitmen to take them out and put our own chosen leader in their place." I shrugged. "It's no big deal. Countries do that shit all the time. Then we can look shocked at the news of the elven assassination and claim we had no knowledge of this dastardly terrorist deed, all while we're making advantageous trade agreements with our puppet leader."

Gregory rolled his eyes. "Why don't we wait and see what the elves intend to do with their newfound power before we consider assassination. If they pose a problem, then we'll discuss what we should do. Did you have any further bad news to convey?"

Shit. I'd almost forgot. "Yeah, someone is sending dead animals to attack me."

"Is that what the headless deer carcasses are out front? I thought perhaps it was that gory human holiday you were observing."

"That's Halloween, and sadly humans don't decorate with deer corpses and body parts. No, someone has cursed me, or is trying to annoy me, or this is someone's idea of a sick joke."

"Dar?" Gregory suggested.

My brother would find this sort of thing absolutely hilarious, but I could only see him sticking with it for a day. Two max. "No, I don't think it's Dar."

"It can't be someone who *really* hates you, or they'd come up with a better scheme then pelting your house with headless deer," Gregory commented.

"They weren't headless when they got here. I made them headless. Because they're zombie animals, and Wyatt said I needed to destroy the brains."

Gregory nodded. "Yes, that's exactly what you're supposed to do. Wyatt *is* the expert when it comes to killing zombies. I still don't believe this is a serious threat, though. Zombie rats and deer wouldn't do much to harm an Angel of Chaos."

He had a point. "Okay, so it's someone trying to annoy me then."

"Someone who knows necromancy," Gregory added.

I turned to face him. "Holy fuck! If I find out who it is, maybe they can resurrect Elvis for our wedding! It would be the event of the millennia. Satan and the Archangel Michael married by the King."

"Judging from those deer out front, the King would be a skeleton at best, a semi-preserved rotting corpse at worst."

"I'm thinking the rotting corpse would be the best." I

pursed my lips in thought. "How the hell do I find this necromancer, though? And how much do I need to pay him to resurrect Elvis?"

Gregory chuckled, pulling me against him. "I doubt this necromancer can raise dead humans, or *they'd* be the ones banging on your front door instead of deer and rats. Also, I doubt a necromancer who is motivated enough to send the undead to annoy you would be convinced to do you a favor and bring Elvis back to life, no matter what you offered him."

I sniffed. "Says you. Anyone can be bought. You just have to figure out the price."

"Well, you would know that better than I." He chuckled. "Please tell me that's the end of your bad news, or do you have something horrible you need to share about Amber's wedding or this bachelorette party."

"I've got to find at least one stripper. Neither of the delivery guys today were interested." I looked up at Gregory.

"No, Cockroach. I will not be manifesting reproductive organs just to shake them at a bunch of human women."

"Spoilsport." I settled back against him once more. "Oh, and did I tell you about the troll yet? The one Lux accidently teleported into my living room?"

"Yes, you told me about the troll."

I frowned. "Wait, how come I get the troll, the nasty elf bitch, the hag, Sparky, and all the psychotic nutjobs and you're returning rings to sweet nice people who probably say 'thank you' and invite you in for dinner?"

"Just lucky, I guess."

I sent him a narrow-eyed glance. Lucky, my ass. "You were cherry picking the rings, weren't you?"

"I do not believe any of the rings have stones in the shape of cherries on them."

"You were taking the easy ones and leaving me the shit. That's totally what you were doing. Same with the meetings with the humans. I've got to deal with psycho elves and wheel-and-deal dude with his hamburgers, and you guys are being wined and dined with prime rib."

"You like hamburgers," Gregory pointed out. "The elves won't meet with us. You're best suited to speak with the US President since he has issues concerning New Hell. And I've heard the Canadian Prime Minister is very pleasant."

"He's hot as fuck, but that's not the point." I jabbed a finger against his chest. "I know the rest of you have more meetings than I do, but I got the crap at the bottom of the barrel, just like I did with the rings."

"I promise you that you are not getting the worst of the meetings. And as for the rings...I guess I've just been lucky."

Maybe he *was* just lucky. I mean, it wasn't like he knew where the rings needed to go. The only one who did was Lux.

Lux. That little sneak. He'd been purposely taking me along for the more dangerous confrontations. At first the realization angered me, then I remembered Lux loved me. He wouldn't do this because he wanted to toss my ass into the fire. No, he was bringing me along on all the most difficult ring returns because he trusted me to handle the situation. He trusted me to protect him.

His father was the most powerful and the oldest of all the archangels, but when it came to facing dragons and hags and other nasty shit, Lux came to me.

I smiled against Gregory's shirt. "Okay. I believe you. And I'll help Lux return the last three rings. You do whatever you need to do with the angels. Oh, and our wedding."

"I booked a floor of suites at the Wynn."

Holy shit. I loved this guy. *He* wouldn't have any problem getting strippers or hookers or anything at our wedding. I was totally putting the whole thing in his hands. Except, I would ask Rafi to check up on him, because Gregory sometimes screwed things up.

"Now it's my time to deliver bad news." He held me away from him so he could meet my eyes. "The humans have begun to wall off New Hell."

I nodded. "Gareth told me they were going to put up some magical wall that restricted demons and humans from leaving without approval. The president had also said something about restricting who could come and go from the area. I totally understand. I mean, if the dude is going to send convicted felons to live there, he'd want to make sure they didn't backpack their way out."

"You don't have a problem with this?" Gregory asked.

"Not really. I'll just teleport wherever I want to go. Or fly over the magical wall when I need to get in and out of New Hell."

"Even insects and plant life cannot cross the barrier. It goes deep enough underground that root networks cannot spread past it," Gregory commented.

I frowned. "How high does it go?"

"I believe airplanes can still cross, but they most likely need some clearance to cross the border or risk being attacked."

Well shit. So much for flying in. I'd just need to teleport back and forth if I needed to go there—not that I expected I'd be there all that often. As for airplanes, well this could be turned into an opportunity. Planes were going to get permission to fly across New Hell airspace plus pay a fee, or we'd shoot them the fuck down. Travel to Hawaii and Asia would become a very long flight if planes had to divert around New Hell.

"The wall isn't going to stop teleporting," I reminded Gregory.

"No, it won't, but this will pose a problem for many

demons as well as humans." Gregory grabbed the remote and turned off the movie neither of us were watching. "I have a second bit of bad news."

I sighed. "Lay it on me."

"A large number of angels that were on our side have changed allegiance and joined the rebels."

"How large?"

Gregory grimaced. "You don't want to know."

Shit. "Why would they abandon you and the other archangels to join the rebels?" I suspected the answer to that question, but I hoped I was wrong. I wasn't.

"Rumors have spread that they can never return to Aaru again, that their leaders—that's us—made a horrible error during the war and we are all forever banished."

"Do you think you can allay their fears? Give a rousing speech about a divine purpose here among the humans and lie like a demon?"

"I can, but I fear they will not believe it. Adding to the problem is the fact that the humans have not welcomed them the way these angels feel they should be greeted."

I couldn't blame the humans for being disillusioned. They'd expected demons to wreck things, not angels. Instead of curing cancer, feeding the hungry, and turning water into wine, they were either stumbling around like idiots or trying to shove kale and beets down everyone's throats.

No, it was the elves who were curing cancer, feeding the hungry, and turning water into wine. Go figure.

"What are we going to do?" I asked.

Gregory turned the television back on. "We're going to enjoy an evening together, then tomorrow we'll take Lux to visit the asteroid belt. This can all be addressed at the Ruling Council meeting. There's no immediate threat. We'll work together and find a solution.

I stared at him a moment. Gregory had never been one to

rush things—most angels weren't. Their timeline ran along millennia, not minutes. He was probably right. The rebels would be taking their time as well, planning and plotting, forming committees and focus groups and all that shit that angels did.

In the meantime, we had a movie to watch.

CHAPTER 16

As much as I wanted to explore the asteroid belt with my two angels, I decided it was good for Lux to have some private one-on-one time with Gregory. So after a breakfast of avocado toast, I waved them off, changed into my swimsuit, and headed out to the pool.

But not before grabbing a six pack of beer and a bag of Doritos. I mean, avocado toast? That wasn't a decent breakfast for demon *or* angel. I seriously needed to buy Gregory a new cookbook—one with real food cooked with real butter and bacon grease.

It was still chilly, but the sun felt warm on my skin as I lay back, shut my eyes, and snacked. This was the life. I had a glorious afternoon off—a few hours to do nothing but be absolutely lazy.

Except I *did* need to get off my ass and find a stripper for Amber's bachelorette party, but I could work on that later. I'm sure if I Googled, I could find a dozen places I could hire appropriate entertainment. But I wasn't going to bother with that now. Nothing was going to interrupt my lazy moment. Nothing.

Something bit down hard on my foot and I screamed, Doritos and beer spilling everywhere as I jumped up from the lounger.

It was an undead rat, and he'd brought friends.

Up until now, the curse seemed contained to the front of my house. What had changed that there were now zombie deer, dogs, and something that looked like it once was a cow shambling across my back patio and coming toward me? I summoned my sword and shouted for Boomer to help me, then began killing—starting with the motherfucker that was trying to gnaw off my toes.

Boomer's idea of help was to bay menacingly at the undead while safely remaining on the other side of the fence. I hopped around, feeling particularly vulnerable in bare feet and a bikini as I chopped the animated roadkill. A few of the rats stupidly fell into the pool and sank to the bottom, giving me an idea. I sliced my way through two dead dogs and ran straight for the cow.

I'd been cow tipping about a dozen times, but I'd never done it to a moving, rotting bovine corpse before. My arms sank into soft maggoty flesh until they hit bone. I pushed, shoving the cow over the edge of the pool and into the water. Unfortunately I couldn't get my arms free fast enough, and I went in as well.

The cow sank and I surfaced along with pieces of flesh and sinew. A splashing noise caught my attention, and I turned to see all the zombies leaping into the pool like lemmings off a cliff. I kept treading water, and they kept coming—and sinking. Waiting until I was sure there were no more, I swam to the ladder and climbed out. My pool was a disgusting mess of dead animals. I wasn't sure how much I'd have to pay my maintenance guys to clean all this out, but I'd need to do it fast before the whole thing started to stink.

I hosed myself off, made a quick phone call to the pool

company, then went inside. Terrelle was standing by my dining room table, eating my leftover chicken wings and drinking a beer.

"Got info," she said before I could yell at her.

"Go on." Depending on the info, it might be worth her eating what I'd been saving for my lunch.

"First, as you suspected, Blue Fire isn't the only operation in town. It seems word of their enterprise was leaked, and another sorcerer put together some weapons on the quick and dirty, and started selling them to individuals and local governments. They've undercut Blue Fire's price. Quality is shit, and there are some other problems, but availability and tight budgets are often the deciding factor."

I frowned. "Does Blue Fire know about this other business yet?"

"Nope." She licked hot sauce from her fingers. "The Woo-woo contract had already been in the works, so the other company wasn't in a position to bid on it. I don't think they would have won anyway. Your brother Dar is all up and cozy with the Prez. Do you know he's golfing with him at that swanky place down in Florida?" Terrella laughed. "I'd pay good money to see that game. I'll bet neither of them can golf worth shit. I can. I'm totally good at golf. Excellent, in fact. I've got a four handicap, I'll have you know."

"The cop that shot me in Phoenix was using the other company's weapon," I mused, ignoring the golf bullshit.

"Yep. You were really unlucky that day. Those crappy guns jam sixty-percent of the time. And they put the spell *inside* a paint ball. Sometimes it doesn't splat so the spell doesn't go off." Terrelle shook her head. "Yet another case of government using the lowest bidder and getting hosed."

This Noodle was worth her weight in gold. Or chicken wings and beer.

"And Gareth's weapons?"

"The guns are just like the ones in the catalogue. They've got a white barrel, and right now they can only shoot the magical bullets, although they're working on guns that can shoot either. It's going to be totally cool if they can pull that one off. Imagine just dropping the magazine, slapping another one in, and you can take out humans as well as demons or angels."

"Yeah, totally cool." I rolled my eyes. Totally fucking horrible, that's what that was. The only positive side of such a weapon is that the time it took a human to change magazines and pull the slide might be enough time for a demon or angel to either get away, or knock the fool's head off.

"Reliability is way better on the Blue Fire guns. They use a bullet, but it's not the round paint balls that are enchanted like the other company. These are *actual* bullets, so they cause physical damage in addition to blocking all demon or angel abilities."

"And reversing the effects?" I asked.

"On the long-lasting ones, you'd need an antidote. Blue Fire uses a potion to reverse the spell. Knowledge of the formula is tightly controlled in an attempt to avoid black market sales."

"And the other company?"

She shrugged. "They sell a counter spell paintball bullet."

"So I'd need to get shot again?" It hadn't been particularly painful the first time, but the idea that a demon or an angel proven innocent in a human court of law needed to be shot a second time pissed me off.

"Unless something else works." She waved a chicken wing at me. "And I'm still working on that. What I need is to get into the testing records, assuming these companies *did* any testing. I'm trying to get my hands on the actual spell itself, but both companies are pretty freaked about keeping that top secret. They didn't even apply for patents because they don't want to list even the bare minimum shit needed for the applications. I'm trying to go in the back door—and not the sex back door either, although I'm totally cool with that. I'm always up for anal. Or I can strap one on and pitch. I like—"

"Back to finding the antidote, Terrelle." Not that I minded hearing about her sexual proclivities, but I knew if both of us went down that rabbit hole, we'd quickly forget what the heck we were originally talking about.

"Yep! Gotcha! My best bet for finding out exactly how these weapons work would be to look at the notes for testing the spells and reversals. Fingers crossed, because if they didn't test, or I can't get those, then I'm looking at trying to break into some high security shit, and I'll need help."

"What kind of help? This isn't the sort of thing I can get caught doing. Or any member of the Ruling Council."

She nodded. "Oh, I get it. Politics and all that crap. Gotta be impartial and support human independence and sovereignty and all that. No, what I'd need for this kind of job would be a dwarf."

"A *dwarf*?" They were amazing when it came to enchanting weapons, and they made awesome nannies for demon children, but I couldn't imagine how one would help Terrelle break into some high security shit.

She tilted her head, wing halfway to her mouth. "Duh. They're nulls. They're the most null motherfuckers that ever nulled."

"Nulls."

"Nulls." Terrelle stuffed the wing in her mouth, bone and all.

I knew dwarves were good at nipping young demon naughtiness in the bud, but nulls? I thought back on my childhood, remembering that I'd created lightning, altered my form, set a building on fire with a dwarf nearby. Yeah, they'd put the fire out and fizzled the lightning before it destroyed that big oak, but that wasn't because any of them were nulls. They just had a way of quickly reacting to and neutralizing juvenile demon, and angel, mischief.

"So they turn it off and turn it on?" I asked. "How did I not know this?"

She crunched up the wing and swallowed. "Oh, the things you don't know. Many, many things, Iblis. Many, many things. Dwarves have a natural null ability, some more than others. They can expand the field of influence. They can increase the intensity too."

"You're fucking joking." All these centuries I'd underestimated the dwarves. Nulls. How useful was that?

"Nope. Most dwarves have a low-level null ability. About ten percent are powerful enough to go head-to-head with a mid-level demon. One percent can slap down an elven lord, a sorcerer, even an angel. Then there's the rare dwarf that might even be able to bring your archangel to his knees."

I laughed at that. I'd seen Gregory in action. He was the Archangel Michael. Nothing brought him to his knees. "So this null thing works on demons, angels, and elven as well as human magic."

"Depends. Like I said, some dwarves are stronger than others. Just like elves. Just like mages. Just like demons. Just like angels."

"Just like shifters," I added.

She shrugged. "I consider them angels light. Angels super light."

"Okay. So what sort of dwarf would you need to do this job? Because, let me tell you, they are not the most cooperative. I had to practically sell my fucking soul to get those weapons enchanted for my household. I can't even get one of them to come across the gates and nanny Lux. Dwarves have a long history of giving us and elves the middle finger when we need them for something, even if we're paying out the nose. They've got their mountains. They've got their society. They don't give two fucks about anyone else."

And that's the reason I'd always had mad respect for the dwarves. Growing up, the elderly dwarven lady who'd lived nearby had seemed like a goddess. Even nine hundred years later, I still thought she might be a goddess. Oma knew everything. Even the most powerful Ancient treated her with deference.

"Ideally the most powerful dwarf you can find. I'm not sure exactly what type of spells are on the other company's security systems, but Gareth has probably got some bad ass shit guarding Blue Fire's intellectual property. That's kind of his jam, you know."

My thoughts returned to Oma. How the fuck was I going to get the elderly dwarf to leave her home and cross the gates even temporarily? She didn't give a crap about money. Honestly, I didn't know of any other dwarves that I'd trust to do something like this. Maybe Dar's nanny, Andor. He seemed to be handling Karrae with no problem, but there was a big difference between keeping a little angel from killing half of Chicago and overwhelming a series of powerful magical wards.

I'd try Oma first. And if I couldn't beg or bribe her to do it, then I'd try Andor and just hope he and Terrelle didn't end up in some human jail awaiting trial. Or worse, dead.

"Then there's the other stuff you asked me to check into." Terrelle took a drink of beer, then wiped her mouth on her sleeve. "The Elven Nation stuff? I think a few countries might be interested after all. Humans are starting to get paranoid about demons and angels taking over, and the elves are putting it out there that they're humanity's only hope."

Right. Little did the humans know they'd be better off with the demons. Or even the angels.

"What countries are sniffing at the bait?" I asked.

"France, Ireland, Scotland, Wales." She frowned for a second. "And maybe Australia, although I think they're bluffing. I get the impression they don't trust elves one bit."

I had a meeting with the French Prime Minister tomorrow as well as the Ruling Council meeting. I'd tell whoever was handling those other countries to keep their eyes open. In the meantime, I needed to go to Hel and visit a dwarf.

I left a note for Gregory to come get me if I wasn't back from Hel by midnight. One of the uncomfortable realities of my life as an Angel of Chaos was that I could enter Hel through the gates, but only exit by teleporting—which I couldn't do right now. I was hoping to track down Doriel or one of the other Ancients and convince them to give me a lift home, but that might take a while. I had things to do, and being stuck in Hel for a few days wouldn't be convenient right now. As much as Gregory hated going there, he'd done it once before and I hoped he'd do it again if I couldn't find a ride.

I left Terrelle with the contents of my fridge and drove to Columbia. The contractors had made progress on replacing the destroyed mall. The entire steel structure had been erected and the concrete poured. The huge building was only a hollow shell, and I wasn't sure how long it would take for the workers to finish and new shops to move in.

Today the gate was over by where the parking garage was supposed to be. Beatrice was perched on top of a bulldozer, wearing a hard hat and drinking a giant iced coffee. The gate guardian waved me over and hopped down.

"Hey! I haven't seen you in ages. What's up?"

"I need to use the gate." I'd dropped the ball on our weekly lunches since I'd started teleporting everywhere. We'd need to start doing that again. There hadn't been any place nearby for lunch since the mall had been destroyed, but that was no excuse. I could easily pick something up and we could hang out here and eat carryout until the mall was back in operation once more.

She pointed toward the shimmering spot ten feet away that only demons, angels, and elves could see. "The guys are making a run to Chipotle for lunch. Want them to pick you up anything? Ricky's buying today."

"Nah, I might be a while. Thanks though." It was good to know she'd made friends with the construction workers. I knew she and Snip were an item, too. What had been a horribly isolating job guarding the gate to Hel wasn't quite so lonely anymore.

"Lunch next Wednesday?" I asked, then I suddenly had a better idea. "What if I get someone to give you the night off and you can come to Amber's bachelorette party."

"Amber's what party?"

I wasn't sure Beatrice even knew Amber, but surely one more person wouldn't matter, and the gate guardian really needed a night off.

"It's a human tradition. Amber's getting married, so she and a bunch of girls get together and get drunk and watch strippers."

She stared at me as if I were speaking a foreign language.

"Seriously. It'll be a blast," I said. "I bought a whole bunch of dildos and vibrators, and squirt guns shaped like penises that we can fill with booze. I haven't been able to hire the strippers yet, but I'm working on it. Maybe these construction workers would be interested? Amber's a half-succubus, so there's a good chance they might get laid."

I pulled out my phone and sent a quick text to Gregory, letting him know someone else needed to guard the gate that night, then texted the date, time, and location to Beatrix.

Her phone dinged. She pulled it out of her pocket and looked down at my message. "Um, okay. I'll give it a shot.

And I'll ask if any of the guys want to be entertainment for the evening. I don't think they'll go for it, though. They talk like they're a bunch of wild horny teenagers, but I get the feeling they'd be too scared to actually get up on stage and get naked in front of a bunch of women."

Damn. "Ask anyway." Maybe I'd get lucky and one or two would be interested. I hoped so because time was running out.

* * *

OMA TOSSED HER LONG, gray-silver braid over her shoulder. "You want me to leave my home and my husband, go to the human world, and help a demon steal a sorcerer's grimoire."

Yeah, that was pretty much the gist of it. "We need to figure out a way to reverse the spells so angels and demons are not completely at the mercy of seven billion humans."

Her bushy white eyebrows shot up. "It's about time demons and angels got their comeuppance. Can't be top of the food chain forever, you know. Personally, I think humans ought to have the final say over their own world."

"But what if we're innocent and they withhold the counter spell? What if some dickwad shoots one of us because he just doesn't like demons, and we have no way to reverse it?"

Oma shrugged. "Maybe don't get shot? Maybe start being polite and not starting things you can't finish? Say, where is this Gareth anyway? I might want to buy one of these pistol things. Might keep the lot of you from eating all my food and pestering me all the time."

That last bit was said as she pushed a huge bowl of hot spicy stew in front of me. Oma always bitched and moaned about demons, but I got the idea she secretly liked us. She'd often provided me with a safe haven when I was bullied as a young imp. She was skilled in divination, even if her prophecies were couched in confusing symbols and double-talk. And every time I visited her, she fed me.

"We don't want to take away the ability for humans to defend themselves, we just want to have a reversal of our own. For rare and extreme cases. It would only be available through appeal to the Ruling Council."

She snorted. "Oh, like they're in a position to judge. They've screwed up a lot in their billions of years. They might be angels, but they're no angels."

How old *was* Oma? And how did she know any angels if she'd never left Hel? I eyed the woman, realizing that the little I knew about her was pretty damn miniscule.

"Oma, please. We need this information. There are seven billion humans. The angels are locked out of Aaru. There's nowhere else for them to go."

"That is complete and total nonsense and you know it. They can go to Hel. They can go to any number of planets in any number of solar systems, in any number of universes. They're *angels*. It's not like you cut their wings off when you banished them. Don't fall for their 'woe is me' sob stories, Az. Tell them to stop whining, take their lumps, and learn from this opportunity they've been given."

"I don't know what I did when I banished them. It just happened. Things were bad. I didn't want Gregory to get killed. I jumped the gun and tried to do what he was going to do and banish the rebels, and we *all* fell."

Oma reached out and smoothed my hair. "I know. When you are a chaotic instrument of fate, then you need to shoulder the blame and resentment of others. Now finish your stew and I'll read your future."

I did as she said, savoring every bite. It brought me back to my childhood when I'd sat at this very table, eating stew and carving drawings into the table with my claw. It all seemed so long ago, even though I wasn't even a thousand years old yet. It all seemed so long ago.

When I was done she took the bowl and hocked up a big loogie. Then she swirled the spit around in the bowl, eyeing it intently. I was not even remotely tempted to peek over her shoulder.

"Ten." She stuck the bowl in the sink. "One of the ten."

That was it? I'd expected some cryptic shit about triangles and cats, but "ten"?

"Will you cross the gates and help us break into Blue Fire?" I asked one more time, knowing her answer wouldn't have changed.

"No. Angels and demons will need to start treating the humans more as equals. Otherwise many of you will be experiencing the human prison system."

Or dead, I thought sourly. I stood and pushed my chair back under the table. Before I could leave, Oma came up to me, reached up for my face, and pulled it down toward hers. I panicked for a second, thinking that maybe she was going to kiss me or something equally horrible. Instead she rested her forehead against mine and breathed out through her mouth.

Everything felt heavy. My limbs, my eyelids, my hair piled up on top of my head. I could no longer reach my store of energy or even gather it up from the air around me. I knew without trying that I wouldn't be able to transmute, that I wouldn't even be able to summon the tiniest of spark. But unlike when I'd been shot, or collared, or netted, I still felt my spirit-self right there. It wasn't like when Gregory had coated my energy with that slippery stuff either. My wings revealed themselves, making it incredibly crowded in the small cottage. My sword came straight to my hand, although I sensed it could do nothing a plain old sword couldn't do.

It was exactly like when I'd been a young imp and I'd been

about to do something like set one of my siblings on fire, or send a lightning bolt into a nearby house. I was still an Angel of Chaos, an imp, I just couldn't do anything either an angel or demon could do at the moment.

This was Oma's power. This was the feeling of being in a null zone. It was similar to what my foster parents had been able to do, but this was *more*.

Oma let go of my face and stepped back to the sink. "There. Can't have you going around like that. It isn't fitting. Now go on back to your angel and your humans, to your Lows and all of those you've taken under your wings. Scoot. Get going."

I left because that's when Oma usually got her stick. I might be a grown imp, but I still didn't want to get whacked with Oma's stick. It wasn't until I was halfway to the swamp that I realized what she'd done. All the little jagged remnants of the spell that I'd carried around since that cop in Phoenix had shot me were gone. I was completely free, and I hadn't had to go through the pain of Gregory trying to smash through the magical barrier. I hadn't had to drink some potion or be shot again with another bullet. All it had taken was a dwarf—a dwarf who had the power of a null.

CHAPTER 17

I could teleport again. This made my life so much easier. I'd gotten back from Hel with enough time to kill and dispose of the zombie animals around my house and meet with the pool maintenance people.

They were *not* happy. It seems when I'd told them I had some dead animals that I needed removed from my pool, they'd thought frogs or a turtle or two. They had not expected a bunch of rats, two badly decomposed dogs, and a cow.

The nets they'd brought were totally inadequate for the job, so they called in for some sort of heavy equipment, informed me that my pool would be out of service for a few days, then got to work scooping up drowned zombie rats and various body parts that had come loose from the cow and were floating on the surface of the water.

I went inside and left them to it. Gregory and Lux weren't back yet, and Nyalla was off doing wedding stuff with Amber and Darcie, so I sat down with my laptop and sent emails to every place I could find within a hundred-mile radius that had anything remotely to do with strippers. Gentlemen's clubs. Exotic dancers. Escort services. Singing telegram and balloon delivery. Anything. Then I sat back, watched the pool guys try to winch the cow carcass out of my pool, and thought about dwarves.

It seemed that being a null had a whole lot of advantages I hadn't even thought of. Oma hadn't just negated the effects of the paintball bullet while I was in her presence, she'd completely cancelled it out. Could other dwarves do that? If so, then we really didn't need to steal intellectual property and reverse engineer an antidote. All we needed to do was convince a few dwarves to cross the gates when we needed them, and to nullify a spell or two.

Although knowing dwarves like I did, reverse engineering an antidote would be easier than getting them to cross the gates. So far, Andor had been the only dwarf I knew that was willing to do so. And even if he was willing to give us a hand every now and then, I wasn't sure Dar would agree to loan him to us. My brother had become especially greedy and selfish when it came to his childcare.

But the dwarf didn't work twenty-four seven. He got regular days and evenings off. Maybe I could get him to consider a side job? I'd have to tell Terrelle that the dwarf thing was a no-go unless I could talk Andor into it. Maybe she could steal the spell book without a dwarf. She *was* pretty sneaky.

The cow carcass was half out of the pool when it's spine broke and the rear half slid back under the water. I heard the guys cursing clear through my triple paned French doors. It made me laugh. I was whole again. I could teleport. I could feel my spirit-being in all its entirety. Suddenly nothing else mattered. The rebel angels, the angel-killing weapons, the Elven Union, the three rings in my pocket that I still needed to help Lux return—none of it mattered. I was whole. My angel and my kid were off having fun on a bunch of asteroids. For the moment there were no zombie animals scratching at my front door, and the guys out back were cleaning out my pool.

Right now my life was perfect—or it would be if Terrelle hadn't drunk all the beer in my fridge.

* * *

THE FRENCH PRIME MINISTER, much like the Canadian one, didn't seem to have any issue with angels or demons living in his country. They needed to be gainfully employed, paying taxes, and have appropriate identification, but he made it clear that the French welcomed those of other cultures, although they would not make exceptions for angels or demons who broke the law.

And the elves? Oh, the French loved the elves. They had incredible taste in art, were highly knowledgeable about wine. They prepared the most exquisite meals, grew fruits of the highest quality. They were environmentally conscious, selfless in caring for the sick and the hungry.

Basically the elves were a combination of Jesus and Doctors Without Borders. The French Prime Minister assured me that there were no elves in governmental office, but of course any public servant with a brain had an elf as an advisor. It would be foolish not to, when they had so much to give the world and were so dedicated to helping the human race.

Fuck me.

From there I went to Ireland where I had no official meeting and had to gather all my information by hanging out in pubs—which was going to be the highlight of my day. I encountered only suspicion and denial of any knowledge of elves, angels, or demons in the first two pubs, but by the third I finally found a group of drinkers who'd had enough pints that they were ready to talk.

Especially once I started buying rounds.

"I bloody well like those demons," one woman told me. "They can hold their liquor. They can fight. They're fun. Angels aren't fun, but we don't get many of them around here."

"How about elves?" I asked them.

They exchanged knowing glances. "Gotta be careful with the fae, you know. They act like they're giving you the sun and the moon, but it all comes with a bloody big price. Don't accept a gift from a fairy, my gran always said. 'Cause it's no gift."

"And don't be takin' any food or drink from them," one man said with a wag of his finger.

"The elves seem to think that Ireland is with them, that you're going to join their Elven Union," I said.

The burly guy chuckled. "You learn ta respect the fae. Leave them offerings and flatter them, but never ever follow them anywhere. You gotta be clever, stay one step ahead. You gotta let them think you're worshiping the ground they walk on, when the whole time you're making sure there's a way you can escape when they try to tighten the noose."

I left with a much greater appreciation for the Irish than I'd ever had before. And I left fairly drunk, which made my next few visits somewhat hazy. I remember some dude in England telling me they weren't going to belong to no EU whether it was with big letters or little letters. I couldn't understand a damned thing the Scottish people said, and by the time I got there, I was too drunk to even remember what the Welsh people said.

Giving my phone a bleary-eyed glance, I wondered if I had time to swing by Australia before the Ruling Council meeting. I was supposed to meet with their Prime Minister some other day, but I'd discovered there was just as much value in chatting up the drunken locals as there was these official meetings.

I'd be cutting it close, but I figured I had time for a pint or two, so I headed down under, roaming the streets of Melbourne before I found a bar that looked promising. Warm light spilled out the big windows in a welcoming glow. Inside the bar was all polished wood and brass with a row of taps that seemed to go on for miles.

It was just after midnight there and everyone in the place was far more plastered than I was. In spite of the level of inebriation, there were very little spills on the floor, and although most of the patrons were a bit disheveled, they still had all their clothing on. I ordered a beer at random, grabbed it off the bar, then sauntered on up to a group of loud, rowdy guys.

I immediately won them over by buying them a round. It took about twenty minutes to get their orders because each of them was drinking a different beer, each with an incredibly long and complex name. I'd been to a place like this in Baltimore, down by the convention center, where all the beer geeks hung out, so I immediately tried to impress them by throwing around words like Saison and Gose.

I had no idea what I was talking about, and thankfully they were too drunk to notice. I'd been all snobby to Samael about his drinking Natural Light, but beyond a few IPA's I didn't know jack shit about this stuff.

"You're American," one of them said to me after taking a few careful sips from his glass and commenting on the faint banana ester in his Belgian-style Dubbel.

"Sort of." I'd lived there for the last forty some years, and although Samantha Martin had been a citizen, the Iblis technically wasn't. Although according to the president, that would soon be remedied.

"Can't believe those demon wankers took your entire West Coast." A guy with a blond man-bun toasted me with his beer. "Surprised you didn't nuke them."

"Glad they didn't," a college-aged guy muttered. "Stupid Yanks would have destroyed half the planet."

"Still, s'not fair a bunch of supernatural wonks swoop in from nowhere and start snatching up the real estate," Man-bun argued.

"S'not fair," a bald guy muttered into his beer.

"So I take it you're not a fan of the demons?" I tried for a casual tone, reassuring myself that they couldn't know who, or what, I was, and even if they did, Gareth hadn't started shipping his serious weaponry yet.

Or had he? He wasn't supposed to be building the wall yet either, and the damned thing was more than halfway done according to Gregory.

Man-bun waved his hand, sloshing beer over the edge of his glass. "Demons. Angels. They're all the same. Take stuff. Order us around."

"I hate kale," the bald guy added.

There was a general consensus of murmurs as all the men agreed that kale was not good food.

"Beetroot though…" bald guy continued.

The others nodded in unison, agreeing that the enjoyment of beetroot was one of the few redeeming qualities of angels. I shuddered, not understanding how anyone could like that shit.

"What do you guys think about the elves?" I asked.

That question was greeted by a shout so loud I nearly dropped my beer.

"Elves are the *worst*," Man-bun insisted. "They try to fix your hair."

"Fix your houses," bald guy added.

"Take away your beer." Beard guy glared. "They only like

wine. I mean, wine is okay, but I'm not giving up my beer."

"Yeah. They don't like beer," college guy agreed. "Or playing football, or skateboarding, or surfing. Did you hear that they showed up at Byron and kicked everyone out? Said they were making it better for coral and phytoplankton."

The group grumbled about how none of them gave a shit about those idiots that called themselves surfers down at Byron, and how they probably deserved to be kicked off the beach anyway. That was followed by a lot of bragging over what they'd do if either elves came to kick them off their surf spot, or those shitty-surfers from Byron showed up to hone in on their beach territory. I didn't understand half of what they were saying, but the idea that these guys would kick anyone's ass was laughable. In the end, the consensus was that none of them liked interfering elves one bit.

"One tried to fix my broken arm." Bald guy held up an arm that didn't appear to be broken. "Maybe I *want* a broken arm. Maybe it gives me something to talk about with the guys. Maybe it gets me respect because I tried to do that pop shove-it 360 with a Blunt Fakie, and no one else has got the guts to try that with their deck."

"Yeah. Don't fix our broken arms," Man-bun yelled. "We don't want your help, you pointy-eared, non-surfing, cool-hair-hating elves."

I blinked. "So what are you doing about the elves? And the demons? And the angels?"

College guy leaned in with a conspiratorial grin. "Drop bears."

I shivered. "Fuck. No."

"Yes. Drop bears. We've been training them. Elves are terrified of them."

I was terrified of them. Cute koala things with sharp teeth and a vicious attitude. They usually hunted by waiting for prey to walk under the tree where they were hiding, then they dropped down on them and tore them to shreds. Merciless carnivores, they'd been coming through wild gates faster than we could shove them back. Most humans hunted them. Figures that Australians would embrace them and decide to put them to good use.

"You're sending drop bears after angels and demons as well?" I could see how most demons would run screaming from the things—most angels as well—but I didn't see how it would drive them from the country.

"We're sending drop bears after everyone," Baldy announced. "And if the drop bears don't work, then the magic stuff the ADF bought will."

I frowned, assuming this ADF was the military.

"They bought some no-wings guns," college guy said. "They don't hurt humans one bit—it's supposedly the same as getting hit with a paint ball bullet. But hit a demon or an angel, and *bam*."

"Bam?" I asked weakly. I knew about bam. I'd personally experienced bam.

"Bam! No more supernatural powers,"

"Then we beat the crap out of them," Man-bun said, trying to look tough and failing.

Shit. Was Gareth already shipping his stuff internationally? Was this other company? As freaked as I was about these weapons, I was honestly more afraid of the drop bears.

I bought another round, excused myself to go to the bathroom, and got the fuck out of Australia. Returning home, I found both Dar and Terrelle standing by the French doors overlooking my pool patio. They were drinking the beer I'd just restocked and watching zombie animals shambling around the pool.

"Five bucks says the rat goes in first," Terrelle said.

"Rats are smarter than that. My money's on the skunk," Dar replied.

I went to get my own beer, dismayed at the dent that they'd made in my supply. Then I joined them at the door. The zombie animals were dangerously close to the pool that had just been emptied and cleaned out. Thankfully the company hadn't returned yet to fill it up since there appeared to be several undead squirrels twitching at the bottom. Fuckers. I'd have to call the pool people to clean it out once more. Maybe I should go ahead and put the cover over it and fill it once I'd taken care of the zombie situation—*if* I could take care of the zombie situation, that was.

The thought depressed me. A huge part of my summer was usually spent by or in this pool. And now some undead shit was about to ruin that for me.

The rat plunged over the edge to the bottom of the empty pool and Terrelle held out her hand. "Live rats are smarter. Dead ones? Not so much."

Dar grumbled something and handed her a five. "Lost at golf, and now this. Hope this losing streak ends before the next election."

"I thought the plan was for you to lose golf," I said. "That way you'd win in the long run politically."

"True." Dar moved away from the door. "I still don't like losing, though. And that guy is horrible at golf. I had to actually *work* to lose. And you know how much I hate to work."

We went over to sit on the couch as Terrelle continued watching various animal corpses fall into my pool.

"So, what did you learn?" I asked Dar.

"A lot, most of it having to do with his food preferences and vast conspiracies by the media, certain racial groups, and various nations. Luckily paranoia works to my advantage."

"Yes, but does it work to *my* advantage?"

"That depends on how much you like the angels. I mean, we've both got certain angels we like, and I've been promised those particular angels will be exempted from any laws."

That's pretty much what I'd been told in my meeting. "So he's going forward with the immigration policies thing? No angels except those with special permits?"

Dar nodded. "And it's coming sooner than you think. Law enforcement is going to be tasked with disabling and turning any angels they apprehend over to immigration for deportation. It's a version of stop-and-frisk, and since angels aren't human, no one is concerned about the constitutionality of the policy."

"But where are they going to deport to? Throw them through the gates to Hel? Toss them into New Hell with the convicts and demons? Load them into a rocket and shoot them to the moon?"

"Not the moon thing. That's too expensive. And I've been told they're not going to New Hell without your permission, since the Prez thinks you're pretty damned cool, and he doesn't want to get on your bad side. Besides, he thinks you'll charge him for any angels he deports to New Hell, so he's planning to toss them through the gates."

Which would be instant death for angels neutralized by the magical weapons. A death sentence might be justifiable for an angel who was a real danger to humanity, but just for existing and trying to make a life here? They wanted to go home, they just couldn't.

But, of course, there was one problem with the president's plan.

"Humans can't activate the gates. They were designed that way on purpose so people didn't go accidently falling into Hel." Much like the zombie animals were falling into my empty pool.

"They can now." Dar smirked. "It's one of Blue Fire's offerings."

"The archangels made the gates to Hel. They can just as easily disable them," I pointed out. That would be a pain in the ass for demons, though. Seattle was in New Hel. Maybe I could convince Gregory to keep that gate open so demons could come and go as we pleased without having to find an Ancient to teleport them.

"Then Blue Fire will have to make a one-way set of teleportation stones. Why do you care, Mal? *Our* angels won't be deported. And the less angels that are living here, the easier it will be for us to do what we want. And think of the money we're going to make!"

Back before I'd been an Angel of Chaos, I would have agreed with him, but things were different now. "I'm the reason they can't go back to Aaru. It's my fault. None of them want to be here. And now they're going to die because of something that's not their fault."

They wouldn't all die, though. After word got out about what the humans were doing and what sort of weapons they had, the angels would band together and what Gregory feared would come to pass. It would be war, and it wouldn't just be the rebel angels against the humans, but all of them. They wouldn't just sit back and wait until a cop caught them, took their wings, then shoved them to their deaths, they'd launch a preemptive strike. And even with Blue Fire weapons in hand, millions of humans would die before they managed to exterminate all the angels. Possibly billions.

And there was a slim chance that the angels might win. If they started to get the upper hand, the elves would jump in and promise humanity help as long as they let the elves run things. And faced with no good decision, the humans might take that deal.

I ran through all the possibilities in my head, and didn't see this ending well at all.

"Anything else come out of your trip? Either with the president or with Gareth?"

"I managed to push Gareth along on deliveries. We've got

some asshole out there undercutting us with shitty merchandise. Besides price, they're shipping faster than we are. I told Gareth we've got to get product out the door within a week of order, and to get going on the Woo-woo deliveries before the government tries to back out and use this other company instead."

Fucking hell. I was running out of time.

CHAPTER 18

I was early to the Ruling Council meeting. Gabe had barely called the meeting to order when I snatched the agenda from him and tossed it across the room.

"I'm going first. We've got a problem. We've got a serious problem and I don't want to waste time talking about stupid shit."

For once no one argued. In fact, I was a bit flustered by the six pairs of eyes turned attentively toward me.

"Uh…there's guns and other shit. Some places have the weapons now, and the rest will in the next week or so. It's no fun, let me tell you, and it's not fucking easy to break either. And the Elven Union, and rebel angels, and human governments aren't going to take any shit from angels."

Thankfully Gregory explained it all in a more coherent manner. That's when the whole room erupted into bedlam.

So much for Angels of Order.

Gregory slammed his fist onto the table. "One at a time. Uriel, you first."

"What restrictions are there on who gets these weapons? Because, trust me, there are humans in this country who wouldn't hesitate to shoot anything with wings and claim self-defense."

"The shifters faced something similar up in Alaska," Ahia chimed in. "It helped to get the majority of humans on our side, to portray us as victims."

"It helped that most of the humans in Alaska were already familiar with shifters and had been working beside them in peace for almost two centuries," Raphael added. "There are packs in other states and parts of the world that are facing discrimination and even violence. Many shifters feel safer continuing to pose as humans."

"I still think a concerted PR campaign might help," Ahia insisted. "For angels as well as shifters."

I snorted. Obviously there would be no PR campaign for demons. Kinda hard to paint theft and violence in a positive light.

"There's a bigger problem here than angels being jailed or possibly killed." Nyalla's voice shook with emotion. "This world belongs to the humans and the other species native to the area, not elves, not demons, and certainly not angels. I spent eighteen years of my life enslaved to the elves in Hel. I'm not about to sit here discussing PR campaigns when seven billion of my people are facing the same slavery I did either by angels or elves. Or death by angels who want to wipe us out, like we're pesky ants ruining their picnic."

"Darling, the problems are interrelated." Gabe put his hand over Nyalla's. "If angels fear they're going to be sent to human jails, or that they might even be killed by a random human on the street, they'll be less likely to protect humans in the coming war between us and the rebels."

Nyalla yanked her hand away. "Maybe if angels actually abided by human laws, they wouldn't worry so much about jail or being killed. We shouldn't have to pander to their egos to save ourselves from genocide."

"Nyalla's right." I'd never been so proud of my girl. "I'm as worried as you all are about these weapons, but if there are angels out there wanting to rid the world of humans, then humans need to have a means of defending themselves."

I couldn't believe I was saying that. Maybe it was because I'd spent almost a thousand years worried I'd be killed by an angel that I had some sympathy toward the humans in this. I hadn't been anywhere near the top of the food chain in Hel, and living among the humans I'd always been careful not to draw the attention of any angels. I understood not wanting to get killed.

It sucked that the angels couldn't go back to Aaru, but that didn't give them the right to take over here.

Everyone turned to Gregory, who had been unusually silent throughout the discussion.

"As concerned as I am about the weapons and the potential for misuse, I agree with Nyalla that our priority is to ensure this war of ours does not adversely impact the humans and their world."

"An odd statement given that you've led the Grigori for the last ten thousand years," Gabe commented drily.

Gregory scowled at his brother. "The original Grigori, the tenth choir, were to ensure the positive evolution of the humans. *My* Grigori were to try to mitigate the wrongs of the first group and allow the humans to evolve naturally with minimal intervention on our part. Those who wish to exterminate humans and take over their world make the sins of the tenth choir seem minor in comparison."

"Exactly how do you propose we protect the humans?" Uriel leaned back in her chair and shook her head. "There are seven billion of them and seven of us on the Ruling Council. Even if we divide up the world, none of us can protect a billion people."

"We can't protect humans acting like we're a bunch of

security guards," Ahia said. "We need to support the humans as they protect themselves, all while we're taking out the rebels. Angels need to know that this sort of thing won't be tolerated, either by us or the humans."

"Cockroach, what do you think we should do?" Gregory asked.

I shrugged, feeling exhausted by the whole thing. All this thinking, planning, and multitasking…. I wasn't an Angel of Order, and I was damned tired of trying to act like one. "Fuck if I know."

Gabriel waved my words away. "Ahia, you and Raphael will be in charge of the PR campaign. Make sure humans know there are powerful angels who are on their side, and that we're willing to partner with them in defending their lands and people. Nyalla, you can help. A human liaison will be particularly important here."

"Uriel and her human household can assist us," Raphael added. "She received a lot of positive press after her actions in taking down that human trafficking ring."

Gregory nodded. "Gabriel and I will continue to work on locating and eradicating the rebels and those who support them. The Iblis will gather as much information as possible on these weapons, including possible antidotes, and present at the next Ruling Council meeting."

"And the elves?" I asked.

Gregory shrugged. "At this moment, the elves are the very least of our worries."

Normally I'd agree, but after meeting with them in Iceland, I was worried the sneaky motherfuckers were going to be more of a problem than anyone thought.

I hoped I was wrong, because we already had enough to do without adding another war into the mix.

* * *

INSTEAD OF GOING STRAIGHT HOME after the Ruling Council meeting, I went to Florida. I'd tried being an angel, negotiating and smoothing shit over between everyone. It wasn't working—at least it wasn't working fast enough. I wasn't like the other angels. I wasn't even like Dar, who could play a long strategic game to get what he wanted. I needed change, and I needed it right now. So I was going to fall back on those old demon standards of threat and intimidation.

The white edifice of Blue Fire sparkled in the sunlight. I walked right on in the door and up to the receptionist's desk. Knowing what was coming, I did a quick pivot and duck, summoning my sword as the guards shot me.

The bullets flew over my head. Thankfully my sword appeared as a tall shield because the guards adjusted aim and fired once more. I had little faith that my sword would be of any use at all against these weapons. I was wrong. The bullets bounced off the shield as if I were a demon Captain America. I felt their magic coat my shield and experienced a second of panic before the weapon absorbed everything without any damage whatsoever.

Ha. Score one for the imp.

Another round of bullets hit the shield. Unsure how many more my weapon could take, I got to my feet and rushed the guards, smacking them with the flat of the giant shield as the receptionist screamed in the background.

I'd never fought with a shield before. Figuring one quick blow wouldn't do much, I pushed the two guards backward, pinning them against the building wall. Peeking over the edge of the shield, I reached around and punched them in turn. Then I added a little demon energy into the mix. The pair went down, and stayed down.

The receptionist had fled the building at this point, so I pocketed the two guns as well as the guards' key cards, and took the elevator upstairs. When the doors opened I saw people racing toward the stairs clutching laptops and files in their arms.

"Hurry," a man shouted as he ran by. "There's a demon in the building. We've got thirty seconds until lockdown."

The demon was me. And lockdown? What the fuck good was that going to do? Were they locking me out or me in? Plus thirty seconds meant these people were probably all going to be stuck in the stairwells between the eighth and first floor.

I fought against the tide of panicked employees to Gareth's office. It might be ten more seconds until the overall lockdown, but I knew the moment I saw the door that the sorcerer's security had kicked in the moment I'd walked into the building. As curious as I was to see what would happen if I hacked at the magically secured door with my Iblis sword, manners prevailed so I knocked.

Gareth got up from his desk to look out the side window. I smiled and waved, then waited for him to unlock the door and let me in, figuring I'd resort to bashing at it with the sword as a back-up plan.

The sorcerer unlocked his door, then clutched an amulet around his neck. The alarms stopped, and so did the people racing toward the exit. Ushering me in, Gareth said a few choice words to me in Elvish.

"Hey, your people shot at me first. If they'd kept their fucking guns in their holsters, none of this would have happened." I shook a finger in the sorcerer's face. "You can't just shoot at any demon or angel that walks through the front door, especially me. It isn't polite. Actually it's damned insulting. You make a habit of that, and you're going to find your building and all its occupants reduced to subatomic particles."

"You aren't able to do that sort of thing," he fumed.

"No, but I could devour the whole fucking thing. Same

end result. And I know an archangel that can incinerate a moderately sized solar system. I'm pretty sure wiping out an eight-story building won't take much effort."

"That would start a war," he snapped.

I shrugged. "I don't give a rat's ass about starting a war. Luckily for you my beloved doesn't want war. He wants to allow humans autonomy. He wants angels to live in peace beside them. But if humans are going to start taking pot shots at anything with wings, and some things without, then he might just change his mind."

Gareth sat back down at his desk. "Are you threatening me?"

"Nope. Just telling it like it is." I sat down across from him. "And here's what's going to happen. You'll deliver only the non-lethal weapons. The ones that kill angels are no longer available through Blue Fire or anyone else. If I hear of them being sold and trace either the sale or the spell back to you or this company, you're going to be spending the rest of your life in Dis."

He sputtered, and I held up my hand.

"Oh, there's more. Weapons are only to be sold to law enforcement communities. No private sales whatsoever. You can build the fucking wall. You can continue with the elf amulets that protect against iron. You can create and sell security devices that allow people to keep angels and demons out of their homes. Any other product you want to make needs to be cleared through me first. Is this clear?"

Honestly, I had no illusion that any of these rules would stick. The weapons would get stolen or sold or smuggled, and there were going to be private owners who managed to get their hands on them. And restricting Blue Fire wouldn't do shit if that other company was distributing to every dude with a PayPal account. I could fly around every fucking day trying to shut down small operations and private mage-labs.

I was an Angel of Chaos. I was going to let the chips fall where they may. All I wanted to do was slow this shit down and buy us all a little time to get control of a potentially explosive situation between humans and angels. Getting Gareth to limit his distribution, knocking the crap out of the other company—it might give us a week, it might give us a year. But even a week was better than what we had now.

"We have contracts," Gareth argued. "And I don't care how powerful these angels are, they're not going to win in a war against humans. My weapons mean there might be a world left for us to live on after the dust settles. Stop my sales, the fulfillment of my contracts, and humans will start bringing out things that will not only destroy angels, but decimate this planet."

I leaned forward and put my elbows on his desk. "Picture this. Some dickhead of a leader decides he doesn't want angels in his country, so he starts killing them. Four, five die before the rest of the angels find out what's going on. Then they start wiping out the humans one city at a time. Humans try to nuke them, but angels teleport so all they're doing is blasting away at their planet. Two months later all the humans are dead, and the angels are chilling out on an empty world with the cockroaches and whatever else is okay with radiation."

I paused and watched as Gareth steadied his breathing.

"Or we angels have time to align with human governments and sign treaties about what countries we're welcome in and which ones we're not. That way when the police start shooting angels and stuffing them in jails, there will be powerful archangels standing there supporting them. That way when lethal weapons eventually find their way out in the open, both human governments and these powerful angels will denounce their use and work together to bring those who take the law into their own hands to justice."

Gareth shook his head. "It'll never work. The humans aren't going to work with angels. They're afraid of them. They want to defend themselves, and they feel powerless against celestial beings."

"Humans have always partnered with those more powerful than them. They've served rulers, generals, CEOs. They've aligned themselves with demons, even sold their souls to us. You think nations aren't going to line up for an alignment with the Archangel Michael? The Iblis? Please. The President is already serving me hamburgers in the Oval Office. He's golfing with the demon mayor of Chicago."

I stood and started toward the door. "I'm done asking, Gareth. I'm telling. Do as I say."

"Or what?" he snapped.

I turned and smiled. "I've been in Ahriman's dungeon before. It's not pleasant for a demon, and I'm sure it will be worse for a human. None of your magic will work there. It's cold and damp, and there's shit prowling around that's been there long before I took over."

CHAPTER 19

J came home to find Lux barricaded in the house with an entire menagerie of dead animals prowling around the perimeter. As I went to pull out my sword I realized a few of them weren't animals, but human corpses. Great. I really *was* living through the zombie apocalypse. Once I got all this angel and human shit taken care of, I really needed to deal with the necromancer who was cursing me with animated dead. The elves were sliding down farther onto my list, because I couldn't continue to live like this.

It took me about an hour to dispatch them all. I'd given up dumping them in the woods and instead just piled them up beside the driveway so the mail and delivery guys could get through.

Lux watched me through the window, greeting me with a hug when I came through the door.

"We should move," he told me.

"I like this house. I'm not moving because some asshole is recreating a *Walking Dead* episode in my front yard. We'll figure it out." I ruffled his curls, thinking about what we could get into tonight. Maybe ice cream then a free fall off the cliffs at Maryland Heights? I could call Candy and see if she and some of the pack wanted to do a four-legged run along the towpath, just for old times sake. I wasn't sure Lux was capable of changing into a canine form at this point, but he could always fly above us as we ran.

"Rings."

I sighed, realizing that my Angel of Order child was not going to delay his duties further.

"We've only got three left." I dug them out of my pocket and set them on the table. "Sure you don't want to wait until later this week? I was thinking we could get ice cream instead."

He pursed his lips, tapping them in thought. "One ring, then ice cream."

It was a good compromise.

"This one's pretty," I commented, picking one of the rings up and turning it over in my hand. It was a solid band with some weird inscriptions on it. Even though I felt mildly compelled to put it on, I wasn't going to. I'd sat through that twelve-hour trilogy *and* the other movie, and I knew exactly how things went when people started shoving other people's rings on their fingers. "How about we take this one back?"

"Very scary," Lux intoned.

"The ring?" I wasn't getting any scary vibes from it, but what did I know?

"The place," Lux said. "It's scary."

"I'll be right by your side. Nothing is going to happen to you when I'm there."

His eyebrows shot up.

"Or I can go myself. Just write down the address and show me on Google Maps, and I'll do it."

Lux shook his head. "No satellite maps. No address."

Great. I thought about the weird place where that hag tried to steal my engagement ring and kill us. If that was the sort of place we were going, then I really didn't want to take Lux there. But I had no idea how I'd figure out where it was without an address or Google Maps. Lux was pretty good at communicating abstract ideas, but if I'd never been there before, I wouldn't have the foggiest idea how to teleport there on my own.

I knelt down in front of him. "Then you'll need to be brave and take me there. If it's too scary, you go straight home. I can get home myself. I'll carry the ring and come back just as soon as I replace it. Okay?"

His blue eyes met mine. "Exact place? Da says the rings should be in same spot."

We'd already fudged that quite a bit. If this place was as Lux feared, then I was going to pitch the thing and get the fuck out of there.

"Of course. I'll return it to the exact same spot," I lied.

"It's very scary," he warned me.

I'd been smacked around by a troll, burned to a crisp by a dragon, shot by the Phoenix police, and cursed by a hag. Better me than Lux. Hopefully this time whatever he was scared of would be something like a circus clown, or a Picasso painting, or a creepy looking house.

Well, maybe not a clown. I think I'd rather be burned by a dragon than face down a clown.

"I know, but I'm very scary too." I tried for a ferocious, toothy expression and he giggled. "We've only got three rings left to return. Let's do this one, then we'll get ice cream."

"Okay." He put his hand in mine and I'll admit my insides felt a little gooshy when he did it.

"Good, my brave little angel. Take me there, and show me where, or who, I'm supposed to take the ring to, and I'll do it. You can go right back home if it's too scary."

He smiled, rendering my insides even more liquid, then we were off, teleporting to wherever the heck he'd stolen this ring from. I got that weird nauseous feeling I did when I was tagging along on another angel's teleportation, then suddenly it was as if I'd hit a brick wall. I felt Lux's hand ripped from my grip, then I felt myself fall.

I hit the ground in the middle of a busy street. Cars slid and shrieked as they tried to avoid driving over top of me. The smart thing to do would have been to immediately teleport out of there, but instead I rolled to the curb and stood, dusting off my clothing.

"Are you okay?" A young man pulled over and eyed me with concern.

"I'm fine, thanks." Actually I was stunned. What the fuck had just happened? And where was Lux? I tried to reach out and locate him but came up blank. Did my Lux-locater have a distance limit? Was he on Neptune or something? Although I'd been to Neptune before and never had any problem getting there and back.

A sick feeling wormed its way through my guts. There was only one place I'd experienced such an abrupt refusal when I'd tried to enter.

Aaru.

Lux must have gotten in. And he'd gotten in before if he'd managed to steal a ring from there. I'd suspected he could, but hadn't wanted to test that theory while he was so young and defenseless compared to the Ancients who were currently occupying the home of the angels.

Shit. I pulled the ring from my pocket wondering who he'd stolen it from. What Ancient in Aaru was missing a ring? And no doubt really angry about it?

Worse, Lux was there without me, probably facing a pissed off Ancient without the ring he was supposed to return. My pulse went into overdrive. I had to get in. I had to get in and get him out. But I'd tried before and no amount of force, pleading, or stabbing the barrier with my sword was going to gain me entrance to Aaru.

I tried to teleport there a few more times. I stood outside the barrier and screamed for Lux. I even put the fucking ring on every single one of my fingers and my toes to see if that got me in.

Nothing worked. Terrified, I went home and paced the floor, thinking of which Ancient I could bribe to go in there and bring Lux back safely. I certainly couldn't trust Remiel. Fuck. Remiel. If he discovered that Lux was in Aaru, he might snatch him up and never give him back. Was Doriel in Hel or New Hell? Would she go for me? Could I somehow manage to find Samael? I reached out with my Iblis skills, but couldn't manage to pinpoint the location of either one of them.

I pulled my cell phone out and dialed Samael's number, but it went straight to voice mail. Doriel's as well. They were either in Hel with no cell service, or somewhere here with no cell service, or just not answering their fucking phones.

Eyeing my contact list, my finger hovered over the number for Gregory. I couldn't call him and send him into a panic as well. There was nothing he could do to get Lux back. I needed an Ancient, and I needed one right fucking now.

I teleported over to the guest house, nearly knocking Snip down the basement stairs. Shooting my hand out, I steadied him.

"I need you to get every Low you can to find an Ancient. Any Ancient. In fact, tell every Ancient that you can find that I need them to go to Aaru. Immediately. It's urgent. Huge reward. Fucking huge."

Snip frowned. "Mistress are you okay?"

"No, I'm not okay," I snapped. "Lux is up in Aaru and I can't get in. I don't know if he's okay or not. I need an

Ancient to go in there and find him and bring him back. I'll pay a reward for whoever returns him to my home safely."

Before Snip could reply I had him in Hel, at my house in Dis where it looked like two dozen Lows were setting farts on fire. I didn't wait, I just dropped Snip off and got back to my house even before he started to throw up from the vertigo.

I'd hoped to find Lux there when I returned. I yelled. I screamed. I searched the place from attic to cellar. I put Boomer and Diablo on the alert. Then I ran out the front door to go tell Wyatt. That's when I ran into a small army of undead.

Okay, maybe not an army. A platoon? A cohort. Whatever. It was more than twelve, and they stank like two-day-old roadkill on an August afternoon. I so did not have time for this shit, so I summoned my sword and started cutting through them, screaming in frustration as their headless bodies continued to grab at my legs.

Remembering that I'd needed to pulverize the brains last time, I dragged a bunch of headless zombies across the driveway and chopped the fuck out of their heads with my sword. The whole time, my eyes burned with tears.

Breathe. I needed to breathe. None of the Ancients up in Aaru would be stupid enough to hurt Lux. Remiel might try to keep him, but I knew even he wouldn't harm an angel I'd claimed as my own. Lux would be fine in Aaru. He was a being of spirit. Nothing would harm him there.

He'd been scared to go there alone, had thought it was a frightening place. I remembered my first time in Aaru, the first time I'd been forced to shed my corporeal form. It had been one of the most terrifying moments in my life. The thought of Lux alone and scared, wondering where I was, twisted my chest into a tight knot.

"Ma?"

It took me a second to realize the voice wasn't some sort of panic-fueled hallucination. Turning around, I saw my little angel standing in the doorway of our house. Adrenaline abruptly receded, leaving me weak and shaky. I tried to breathe, tried to force my legs to move.

"Ma!"

Lux did the moving for me, rushing into my arms. I crumpled to the ground, holding him tight and burying my face in his hair.

"Ma, where were you? Lost in scary place?"

Breathe. Breathe. "Yeah, I got a little lost, so I came home. I was getting worried. What took you so long?"

He laughed. "Lost too! You return ring?"

The band felt heavy in my pocket. "Yep. Took it back where it belonged. There's no need to go back."

I felt him nod. "Everything is the same there. Nothingness. Itchy skin. Lonely place. Big lonely place."

Yes, I'm sure it was. Aaru was huge, and four or six Ancients would never be enough to make it feel less empty.

I stood up and took his hand. "I'm going to do the next two rings by myself, okay? You take me there, then come straight home and wait here for me. I was very, very worried about you. That place is big and I was afraid I wouldn't be able to find you, or that maybe you couldn't find your way out and back home again."

He looked up at me, his blue eyes huge. "I was lost, but a man showed me the way."

Remiel? One of the other Ancients? Had Snip gotten one to go to Aaru and retrieve Lux? Although I'd expected they would have been here with him for the reward. "What man showed you the way? What did he look like?"

Lux shrugged. "Nothing. No body. No voice. Just angel talk."

I stared down at the little angel. "No body? Was he fire? Light? A rock? Anything?"

"Nothing," Lux insisted. "No body at all."

How the fuck could that be? None of the Ancients could shed their physical forms in Aaru and none of the angels who *could* shed their physical forms there were able to get back in.

Was someone the exception to that rule? Or had someone been left behind when I'd banished every angel in heaven? Was this "man" even an angel? I'd assumed only angels could exist in Aaru, but honestly that wasn't a question I'd ever thought to ask.

I needed to find that out. And I needed to corner Samael and see if there was some way he was able to get in and be without a physical form, because if there was one Ancient who could make that happen, I was betting it was him.

And it if wasn't him, then who the fuck had given Lux directions home?

But all that would need to wait. First I needed a good stiff drink or six. Then I needed to clean up the dead bodies off my driveway before Nyalla got home.

My phone beeped a reminder. I dug it out of my pocket and glanced down as Lux and I walked back into the house.

Shit.

Forget cleaning up the dead bodies. I needed to shower, change my clothes, and grab anyone I could find with a dick, because tonight was the bachelorette party.

"Yeah!" Amber punched the air with her empty shot glass.

All the ladies wearing felt penis or vagina hats cheered. The rest of the bar cheered, saluting us with beverages of their own. The patrons at Billy Wampus Watering Hole were very entertained by our raunchy drunken antics. The country dive bar was so far off the beaten track that I'd worried half the party would get lost and end up pulling up to the gates of Camp David wearing penis hats and demanding to know where the strippers were.

Luckily all the locals knew how to get to Billy Wampus, and they'd been more than happy to give directions to women who were ready to Party—with a capital "P."

"This is the best Bachelorette party ever," Amber slurred on Darcie's shoulder. Darcie teared up and told Amber that she loved her. They both had a drunken argument about who loved each other most while I scowled.

Where were *my* hugs and declarations of affection? I was the one who'd chosen this locale. Actually, Wyatt had chosen it. This had been Amber's favorite party spot when she'd been an underage teen. The locals all knew her and had been thrilled to host her party, happily providing food, shots, and free jukebox selections.

Sadly, there weren't many jukebox selections. In a modern age of twangy-pop country music, Billy Wampus's music hadn't budged an inch since the sixties. Waylon Jennings. Conway Twitty. Patsy Cline. Loretta Lynn. Merle Haggard. Buck Owens. Johnny Cash. Glen Campbell. Tammy Wynette. The closest thing they had to modern was The Oak Ridge Boys. Not that I was complaining. I swear if someone had queued up Achy Breaky Heart, I might have bludgeoned them with a giant green dildo.

The booze selection was equally limited, and *that* I wasn't happy about. Wyatt hadn't let me know about that little factoid when I'd been asking for a good place to host the party. No vodka. No gin—not that I drink that Pine-Sol flavored crap. The rum was a bottle of Bacardi Gold that the bartender had to wipe a thick layer of dust from. Billy Wampus was a whiskey bar. Whiskey and more whiskey—ninety percent of it from Kentucky. The one bottle of "import" was Crown Royal, which was doled out with a sneer.

Luckily I liked Bud Lite, because that was one of eight beer selections, all of them domestic and none of them craft. I asked them what they did for Saint Patrick's Day, and the manager told me they put green food coloring in a keg of Coors and charged fifty cents extra a glass for it.

"Strippers!" One of Amber's friends screamed.

"They'll be here soon," I promised. Then I pivoted so she couldn't see my smile turn to a grimace. I'd ordered the party favors. I'd gotten Amber a gift I knew she'd love—an all-expenses paid trip for her and Irix to one of the premier sex clubs in Europe. I'd booked this place, threw my credit card on the table and refused to accept donations from the others to help defray the cost.

But the strippers… None of the delivery guys I'd accosted had been interested. The professional organizations I'd contacted had been booked up through the summer. I'd begged vampires, werewolves, the homeless people camped out at my condemned properties at the end of the canal walk. Finally, out of desperation, I'd asked the one group I knew would enthusiastically be on board with this project, and who would be available.

The doors of Billy Wampus flung open. "We're here!"

I lifted a finger in the air and the jukebox began playing Rhinestone Cowboy as half a dozen Lows swaggered into the bar, wearing only chaps, cowboy hats, and a smile.

I clapped my hands. I was the only one. The Lows had clearly spent a lot of time and effort choreographing their routine in the thirty minutes between when I'd told them about this gig and their arrival. Their moves were completely synchronized, even though quite a few of them hadn't mastered the art of creating a convincing human form. Pick sauntered up to a redhead, hopping on his bow legs so that his long thorny member bounced in her face. The woman recoiled, her spine hitting the back of the chair with an audible whack.

"Uh, Sam?" Nyalla sidled up to me, patting Rutter on the head as he shook his hips at her.

I waved a hand at her. "Shhh. They're going to do splits for the finale. Do you know how difficult it is for Lows to achieve that level of flexibility? Quite the thing to watch."

"Sam, I adore your Lows, and am especially fond of Snip, but most of Amber's guests are human, and they don't find most demons sexy or attractive. Especially Lows."

"Are you kidding me?" I pointed at the dancers. "Lows are a fucking blast. They'll do anything you want them to do.

They're used to being ripped apart by high level demons, so human rough play is nothing to them. They're enthusiastic. Loyal. And available at the last minute because I couldn't find anyone else willing to do this." I turned to her. "Do you think a few of the party will fuck them? Because I kind of implied they would. Maybe if the girls had a few more shots of Jim Beam…"

"I really doubt it, Sam." Nyalla waved at the crowd. "I mean, do they look like women who want to have sex?"

They didn't. They looked like women who were about to flee the room. There was one human, not actually in our party, who was clapping and wiggling her hips over by the bar, but that was it.

Damn it. I waited for the routine to end in the splits, because I didn't want to hurt anyone's feelings. Then I shooed the Lows over to a corner of the bar, bought them a round of beers and shots, and turned to address the party-goers who were still in a state of silent shock.

"Okay. Sorry about that. My bad. I've been informed the entertainment was a total flop. Hopefully if you all drink a few more shots, you'll forget all about it."

Behind me I heard the door slam open, felt a gust of hot air that was tinged with the faintest odor of brimstone. The women's expressions went from shocked and disgusted to enthralled.

"I heard there are some *very* naughty women at Billy Wampus tonight."

The voice was deep, with a rasp like manicured nails on velvet—and I instantly recognized it. I turned and saw before me the Fallen who'd been Aaru's most beautiful archangel.

His white-blond hair was tousled under a black Stetson, as if he'd just rolled out of bed and plopped that hat on. He wore chaps and a G-string of black leather that was tight enough to reveal all that lay underneath. Every glistening, darkly tanned muscle was defined along his chest and arms. His pecs firmed as I watched, his biceps rippling as he lifted his arms and pointed at Amber.

"Especially you. I've been told you're the naughtiest of all."

Amber audibly sucked in a breath. "Punish me. Oh God, punish me.

Samael smiled, and my legs trembled. "I'm not your god, and I don't punish the naughty, I *reward* them."

He snapped his fingers and Conway Twitty's "I'd Love To Lay You Down" came on the juke box. Several of the women not in our party screamed. Others sighed. All of them, even the men who had been lurking along the walls waiting for a woman drunk enough to possibly take them home, focused their rapt attention on the Fallen angel.

Samael danced, giving each woman in the party a moment of his smoldering attention before turning to where Amber sat. His eyes were hooded, the blue gaze under the lids intense and focused as he made his way to her. She stared at him breathless, not making a sound as he dug his one hand into her blonde hair and straddled her. The muscles in his thighs bulged as he lowered himself down, grinding against her. Then he jerked her head to the side, roughly kissing her neck.

That drew a desperate whimper from the bride-to-be's throat. Thick pheromones filled the air as Amber lost control of her succubus nature. Before the entire bar turned into one giant orgy, Samael slid his hands down to Amber's hips and spun her sex magic away from the others and into himself.

He whispered something into her ear, and her head leaned back, eyes closed as she shuddered with orgasm. I'll admit I was pretty close to the same.

Then the youngest archangel smiled. Amber slipped

down in her chair, eyes dazed and Samael stood and flexed, queueing up another song on the jukebox.

"I'm here all night ladies," he said in a husky whisper. Then he reached out and pulled Darcie to him. She grabbed his ass with both hands as they began a slow dance.

Nyalla chuckled. "Lows. I should have never doubted you, Sam. I can't believe you actually convinced Samael to do this."

I hadn't. I wasn't even sure how he'd known about the bachelorette party. Maybe Lux had told him? Maybe he'd figured it out from all the sex toys being delivered to my house. Maybe the Lows had told him. Either way, I was glad he was here totally pulling my ass out of the fire.

Either way, I was taking credit for this. And I was absolutely getting him to come dance at my bachelorette party as well.

CHAPTER 21

The party went on until the bar closed. I think a few of Amber's friends may have gotten lucky. I drove all the Lows back home. A few of them threw up in the back of the Suburban. I left it there and went into my house, trying to decide whether I should make the Lows clean it up, or just burn the damned SUV.

Gregory would have been thrilled, because for once I didn't bother going to sleep. Instead I made a pot of coffee and watched the sun come up—and watched undead roadkill come out of the hedges and crawl around my driveway.

Terrelle wandered into the dining room, looking over my shoulder at the zombies. "You really need to do something about those things."

"I know." I drank the rest of my coffee.

"That party last night fucking rocked." Terrelle looked at my mug. "Is there more coffee? Did you make breakfast yet? Is your angel-lover here, because he makes damned good pancakes."

"Yes. No. No. No." I patted her on the shoulder as I turned

to go into the kitchen. "I'll get you a mug, but you're on your own for breakfast."

"Splash of milk in my coffee, please," she called after me.

I rolled my eyes, filled two mugs of coffee, and reached into the fridge for the milk. I was pretty sure it was expired, but Terrelle probably wouldn't notice.

"Oh wow. Cool." I heard her say.

I walked in, handed her the coffee, and saw that she was looking at the two rings I'd left on the dining room table.

"No, not so cool," I told her. "Lux misunderstood something and stole a few hundred rings and now he has to return them. Since he's a little guy and I got shot trying to return one, I've been helping him."

"These aren't human engagement rings." Terrelle nudged one aside.

"No. We returned the human ones already. These are what's left of the ones Lux is calling super scary."

She picked up the one she'd been nudging. "What's the writing on this one? It looks Elvish, but it's not."

I squinted down at the ring. "No idea."

Terrelle pulled out her phone and took a few pictures of the engraving, then texted them to someone. "I wish you'd let me see the others before you returned them. It's rare for me to get my hands on museum pieces without getting arrested. And I'll bet you had some sweet magical pieces beyond these two."

"Like the one some witchy hag tried to kill me over," I commented, twisting my engagement ring around my finger.

"I'm pretty sure this one is Andvari's ring." Terrelle picked up the other band and held it up.

"Who the fuck's Andvari?" Maybe he wouldn't be pissed about Lux taking the ring. I was assuming Terrelle knew him, so he was possibly a demon? Maybe one of the Ancients? If so, I hoped he was still slumbering. That would be ideal. I'd just sneak in, plop the ring in his lap, then get the hell out.

"Andvari is a dwarf. He's a fish shifter."

I had never heard of any of the dwarves being shifters, but I'd recently realized I knew a whole lot less about dwarves than I'd thought.

"Awesome. So he's in Hel? Do you know his family name? Which mountain and community he's a part of?"

Terrelle shrugged. "No idea. I read about him in a book. He lives in the land of the dark elves."

Who the fuck were the dark elves? I thought through all the elven kingdoms, wondering if she meant the elven Kingdom of Klee which was in the mountains. They tended to have much darker skin coloring than the other elves. It made sense. Dwarves lived in mountains. The Klee lived in the mountains. Most of the Klee had declined to make the exodus when the other elves left Hel, so it shouldn't be too hard to visit them and ask where I could find this Andvari dude.

"Hopefully if you return the ring it will end the curse."

"What curse?"

"From what I read, the ring was created to attract wealth, specifically gold. Loki stole it from Andvari, as well as all the dwarf's gold."

I recoiled. "He *stole* from a dwarf? This dude had the balls to actually steal shit from a dwarf? I'm guessing he's dead now?"

"Not really. Loki dies a lot, but he never really dies."

Huh. Kinda like me.

"He's a trickster god. An imp."

I wasn't liking where any of this was going. *I* was an imp. I didn't believe in gods as the humans seemed to, but I knew many beings that the humans called gods were real. Was the mythological Loki actually a demon, an imp, who'd had the balls to steal from a dwarf?

"Andvari couldn't do anything about the stolen gold, but he cursed the ring."

That sounded right. Dwarves were very good at enchanting things. Usually weapons were their favorite items, but I could totally see one enchanting a ring. *And* cursing it when it got stolen.

"So what does it do? I'm assuming it makes the person poor since it was originally meant to attract wealth?"

"Nope. It brings death and ruin to whoever possesses it."

Terrelle sounded far too cheerful for that sort of pronouncement. I looked at the ring that she was still holding. "Sucks to be you. It's yours now. Enjoy."

She dropped the ring on the table. "Oh no. It's in your house. It's in your possession. Just because I pick something up to examine it, does not mean I own it. Nope. Nope, nope, nope."

"Too late."

"You can say that all you want. Doesn't make it so."

Terrelle glared at me. I glared at her. Then I wondered who I could pawn this ring off to before death and ruin showed up on my doorstep.

Doorstep.

"Motherfucker!"

I snatched the ring up off the table and threw it across the room. Then I crawled around looking for it because the only way I'd probably be able to get rid of the zombie shit showing up at my front door would be if I returned it to this Andvari dude.

"The zombie animals. I'm cursed. I figured it was a necromancer cursing me, but it's this fucking ring." I found the rusty-gold band behind the umbrella stand and blew the dog hair and dust off before returning it to my pocket.

"So take it back." Terrelle shrugged. "Find Andvari and get him to end the curse in return for his magic ring. Or give it to someone else—not me—and let it be their problem."

Giving it to someone else was definitely the easiest of the options, but I'd learned that the easy path often led to a whole lot of shit down the road. I didn't know anything about what triggered the curse. It would suck if I gave the ring away, only to find out that it had to be sold, or stolen, or certain words needed to be said to complete the transfer of the curse as well as the gold band. No, my best bet would be to take it back to the original owner. If Loki stealing the ring had started the original curse, then I'm sure Lux "stealing" it a second time was the cause of my current woe.

"Uh, Iblis? Have you looked out your front door lately?"

"What now?" I grumbled. Swinging the door open, I immediately slammed it shut. In addition to the various undead rats and other animals, half a dozen corpses were shambling around my driveway. More human zombies. Just what I needed.

"Great. Fucking great." Normally I'd just send Boomer out front for a snack, but he was refusing to get anywhere near the undead. Sucks when the one time you really needed a corpse-eating dog, he was hiding behind the barn and refusing to come out.

"You find out all you can about this Andvari, and that other ring as well," I told Terrelle. "Oh, and get out some cereal and milk for Lux's breakfast. I'm going to go take care of my zombie problem."

"On it, boss!"

I left Terrelle pouring Frosted Flakes into a bowl, summoned my sword, and did battle in my driveway for the next half hour. The human undead were much more difficult to kill than rats and deer. Even smashing their brains didn't seem to stop them. Cutting them apart meant I had dismembered arms and legs coming after me as well as whole zombies. Even my Iblis sword seemed less than effective at keeping these fucking things dead.

This had to stop. It had to stop now before I ended up barricaded inside my house, hoarding toilet paper and living off ramen noodles and canned baked beans.

After reducing the zombies to a bunch of twitching, diced-up flesh and bone, I went inside, pulled the ring out of my pocket, and showed it to Lux.

"Sweetie, where did you get this one from?"

Lux swallowed his mouthful of Frosted Flakes, took the ring from my hand, looked at it, then handed it back. "Dirt."

"Is this Dirt a human? A demon?" Dirt definitely sounded like a Low's name to me.

"No, dirt. In the ground."

"What, like buried treasure?"

He shook his head. "No, just the ring. No other treasure."

Well it was gonna be really damned hard to return a ring to nobody, but I was going to give it a shot. "It was in the very scary pile. What's so scary about it if it was just lying on the ground somewhere."

"Cursed ring."

I'd never wanted to face-palm so bad in my life. "You purposely picked up a cursed ring and took it home?"

He nodded. "Sacred duty."

Oh for the love of everything unholy. Only my kid would decide his duty as ring bearer meant picking cursed rings up out of the dirt and bringing them home. Wait. Was *I* the one cursed, or was Lux?

Thinking back, I remembered putting a bunch of the rings on my fingers when I'd first found Lux with them. Had this ring been one I'd worn? Had putting it on been the trigger for the curse, or just taking possession of it? So far the zombies had only been congregating around my house, but neither Lux nor I had worn the ring consistently, and I think I'd only left with it in my pocket once or twice.

Did that mean the zombies followed the ring and not the owner? I really fucking hoped so, because that meant I could just bury this thing back in the dirt and let the undead hang out there instead of my house.

"Let's do a little experiment," I told Lux. "I want to see if we can take the ring back, okay?"

He nodded, and took my hand. In a gut-wrenching flash we were off. It took the usual amount of time for us to get there. I was prepared when we arrived and this time didn't fall over to crash into anything. Not that there was anything to crash into. We were in a plowed field. It could have been anywhere, but now that my own teleportation skill was working, I could tell we were somewhere in southern Italy.

"Show me where you found it," I told Lux.

"Right here." The little angel pointed to a spot on the ground.

Here goes nothing. I dug the ring out of my pocket, dropped it on the dirt, then scooted a few inches of soil on top of it.

"I'm going to stay here," I told Lux. "You go home and hang out for a few minutes. I want to see if there's still a bunch of twitching body parts outside our front door, or any new ones have shown up."

He vanished and I stood there in the middle of a field, hoping no farmers appeared to yell at me or chase me off. I didn't want to lose this thing, leaving me stuck with these zombies and a cursed ring I couldn't find to try to break the curse. Lux might have been able to find a small band of gold in the middle of a field, but I doubted I'd be able to, and I worried he'd not be able to find it a second time. It would be just my luck to misplace the fucking thing, or have someone else come along and scoop it up.

Although if someone else found it, then maybe they'd be cursed instead. I looked around, realizing the chance of someone stumbling across a ring in the middle of a field was pretty damned slim. I was surprised Lux had found it. He must have some special ring radar going on because this was as close to a needle in a haystack situation as I'd ever found.

It seemed to be taking Lux a while so I sat down in the dirt, nearly planting my ass on the crawling remains of a rotting fox.

"Fuck!" I jumped to my feet, summoned my sword but before I started chopping, I realized the error in my plan. Was this zombie fox coming for me, or the ring? How could I be sure? Using my sword to mark the spot where I'd put the ring, I jogged back a few yards and waited to see what the fox would do.

It took a while, but he turned and shuffled toward me. And as I waited, a few others joined him—the skeleton of a bird, and something that might have once been a cat. I frowned, still not sure if the undead were just heading for anyone near the ring, or me in particular.

Lux appeared by my side. "Lots of dead at home," he informed me. "Rats. Cats. Deer. People."

More people? Fuck me, I did not want to have to keep dealing with people zombies shambling around outside my house.

"Okay, let's try something else." I walked back to the ring with Lux. "You stay here, and I'm going to go away for a while. If any zombie animals try to attack you, blast them. If they keep coming and you're scared, then come back to the house. Okay?"

He nodded. Leaving my sword to mark the spot where I'd buried the ring, I teleported, but instead of going home, I went to the nearest city, bought a can of soda, and found a cemetery.

I wasn't sure exactly what the fuck I was doing. So far none of the undead had been anywhere except my house. Admittedly they didn't move all that fast. Perhaps by the time the dead had risen and slowly made their way toward me, I'd been gone. Living out in the country, there was a whole lot more roadkill within spitting distance of my house. And I *was* there for long stretches of time, plus the ring had remained there.

I picked up the phone and called Terrelle.

"Hey, are you at the house?"

"Yeah, I'd be by your pool if it wasn't for all the dead shit crawling around your house. I'm thinking I might want to move into a hotel until this curse shit gets lifted."

I hung up on her. Okay, there were still zombies around my house, even though neither I nor the ring were there. Meandering around the cemetery, I didn't see any corpses clawing their way out of the ground. Of course, these dudes were six feet under and sealed in both a coffin and a grave liner. That shit wasn't easy to get through—and I knew this personally. If this experiment was going to work, I'd need to either stay here much longer, or find a dead body that didn't have to fight its way through concrete and dirt to the surface.

There was a graveside funeral occurring at the newer end of the cemetery, so I made my way there, drinking my soda and trying to figure out how the fuck I was going to break this curse. Lux appeared beside me with a flash of light, nearly making me drop my drink.

"Dead fox is still moving," he told me sadly. "And dead bird and cat. Lots of others came too."

Ugh. Did that mean they were heading toward the ring? If so, why were there still zombies in my driveway? Should I just leave the ring in the dirt and hope the effect eventually wore off?

"I think I'm going to have to try to find this Andvari dwarf," I told Lux, not wanting to take my chances on this.

Lux nodded. "Where is Andvari?"

I sighed. "Fuck if I know. I need to go to Hel anyway to see Doriel. I'll start with the Klee, since according to the legend he seems to have lived in their mountains. I'll track the dwarf down and give him the ring in exchange for breaking the curse."

"I help?" Lux looked up at me with his big blue eyes.

I ruffled his hair. "I got this one. You hang out with Nyalla and get ready for the wedding."

There was a piercing scream, quickly followed by shouts and more screaming. I looked over at the source of the noise and saw the attendees at the graveside funeral running across the grass as they raced for their cars. The casket rocked on its stand, toppling over onto the ground. The lid popped open and an impeccably dressed corpse struggled to his feet.

I started to laugh. Maybe this cursed ring wasn't all that bad. All sorts of impish ideas flooded my mind, and for a second I thought maybe I'd just keep the thing.

But then I remembered the dead cow in my pool, and changed my mind. Constantly having to fight off zombies was too high a price to pay even for some truly funny pranks.

Nope. I needed to get rid of this ring and the curse. I just needed to figure out where Andvari was then give the damned thing back to him.

CHAPTER 22

*D*oriel was the Ancient I'd given responsibility to for the demon area now known as New Hell. She'd promptly done what every Angel of Chaos since the beginning of time had done and delegated. Thus, instead of spending her days in meetings and administrative crap, she was back in Hel, sunning herself on a rock while members of her household entertained her.

I'd tried delegating, but unlike Doriel, I had an angel who insisted I actually get off my ass and take care of things myself. It sucked, but it was the price I paid for falling in love with an archangel.

"Iblis!" Doriel opened one eye and adjusted the reflective thingy she was using to make her brown skin more of a fire-engine red.

"We've gotta talk business." I sat down on the rock beside her.

Doriel's face scrunched up with distaste. I'm sure my face had the same expression on it.

"What's there to talk about? Things are wonderful in New Hell. It's just like here except with more humans."

"I'm sure New Hell is lovely," I assured her. "But the humans are complaining, which means the angels are complaining, which means I won't get any sex—angel or otherwise—until everyone's less bitchy about stuff."

Doriel folded up the reflective thingy and sat up. "Which humans are complaining? Because the humans in New Hell seem to be quite happy."

Right. Given how many of them had fled the area, I thought not. Perhaps Doriel's idea of happy and the humans' idea of happy were miles apart? I'd gotten sick of hearing Nyalla talk about how the human government was financially stressed trying to take care of all the refugees from California and the other states. Some humans who'd owned property in Seattle and San Francisco, and other high-priced areas were asking for reparations from the demons.

We all knew how *that* was going to work out.

"There are tech companies still operating in New Hell," I told her. "And there are a shit-ton of orchards, farms, and wineries. The president and his minions want a treaty where they can get a percentage of harvests and stuff at a reduced rate because we stole their land."

Doriel's eyebrows shot up. "And what did you tell them?"

"That of course we'd be happy to agree to that sort of trade agreement."

The Ancient laughed. "And, of course, we have no intention of actually doing so."

"Right. They can bite my ass. It's not like they're giving sixty percent of the gross domestic product to the natives they shoved out when they pulled up on their boats from Europe. It's not like they gave land and start-up funds to the descendants of the Africans they snatched up and enslaved. There's legal precedent and whatever for this kinda thing. They're not getting jack shit except a "sorry, too bad.""

Doriel chuckled. "So what's there to discuss?"

"Did I mention I like having sex with my angel?"

She sighed. "Fine. Just tell me what we're doing."

"We're assigning someone from your household to a committee with some dudes at the White House. Make sure you pick someone you particularly need to punish so that they can prove their loyalty and earn back their position."

Doriel's eyes narrowed. "Is this a human committee or angel committee?"

"Human," I assured her. "But whoever you pick can't kill the humans."

"Can they flip tables? Eat all the snacks? Spit in the water pitchers?"

"Sure. Can't expect a demon to forgo all fun."

Doriel nodded. "So what's the line in the sand for us?"

"I haven't decided. They want first rights to buy food, wine, and tech up at way below the going rate. Have them agree to everything. If we get caught, we'll figure it out."

She nodded and began unfolding the reflective thingy.

"I'm not done," I told her. "There's an issue about the border between New Hell and the rest of the world."

"Yeah, yeah. Let me guess—humans can come and go freely, but demons only can with a hall pass."

I was impressed by how quickly Doriel had been picking up human slang and modern culture given that she'd been pretty much asleep in hell most of the last millennium.

"Actually no. The president decided he doesn't want other humans to leave freely from New Hell, because they're paying us to stick their violent felons there."

Doriel shook her head. "They're paying us for that? Humans are stupid."

"That may be true, but now humans need approval to leave New Hell. Same as the demons."

Doriel shrugged. "No skin off my nose. I don't care if the

humans stay or go. Most of them are more like demons than humans anyway."

"I told the president that if he wants to restrict demons and other humans from leaving New Hell, then they're the ones who need to do it. They're already working on putting a magical barrier up around the border. I'm assuming humans will be patrolling on their side as well, checking papers or fingerprints or some shit. I just wanted to let you know so you could warn any demons they'll get killed if they try to hop the magic fence."

Doriel unfolded her reflective thingy and sat back. "I'll let them know. Not that any of them will heed my warnings."

Not. My. Problem.

That done, I headed east to the mountains. It would have been easier to just teleport there, but I'd been in a nostalgic mood lately, so I took to the air and flew.

The elven lands were crumbling. Hel's natural climate was chipping away at the weakening environmental spells the elves had put over their kingdoms. What had been lush forests were now dried, dead trees, sand beginning to cover the meadows. Here and there were patches of green where some elves remained, struggling to keep the desert at bay. Only the highest elves had the ability to command wide-spread control over the weather and environment, so I had no idea how these groups were managing. It was sad seeing the forests vanish, but they'd never really been natural to Hel anyway.

The mountains were definitely natural to Hel, and unlike their brethren, the Klee elves didn't fight the landscape of Hel. They saw the beauty of their stark lands, and only modi-fied what they needed to produce food. As I approached the capital city, I hovered, giving them plenty of time to notice my arrival and see that I was not intending to attack.

After circling a few times, I slowly made my way down,

landing at the edge of the marketplace. For the most part the elves ignored me. Not many demons made their way here, and those who did were no threat to the scrappy mountain residents. I made my way through the crowds not to the palace, but to the place I figured I'd find what I needed—the library.

The building was tucked into the side of the mountain. Inside, stone shelves rose up four stories with gold ladders that rolled magically along the racks. Cases lined the center of the room, filled with scrolls and maps. I ignored everything, heading straight to the elf at the reference desk. He had dusky brown skin, dark golden eyes, and white braids in a complex top knot. He warily watched as I approached.

"I'm looking for a dwarf," I told him.

His thin eyebrows shot up. "In the library?"

"As convenient as that would be, I doubt he's in the library. His name is Andvari and he's a fish shifter. He's said to live among the dark elves."

"A *fish* shifter? I have never known a dwarf to be a shifter. And there are no dwarves living among us. They all live in the mountains to the west."

"Maybe they moved? I've got no idea how long this Andvari might have been living here."

The librarian frowned, then put a book on the counter, paging through it. "There might have been dwarves living in these mountains before we got here. Perhaps in the early days we shared this territory. That would have been quite a long time ago, though."

The elves came to this region just after the Ancients. We'd been banished during the war, and the elves were given a choice—life with the angels, or with us. They chose us, figuring we'd be less likely to interfere with their lives. They were wrong.

Demons weren't big on traditional education, but history

was something every young demon learned. We needed to know of Aaru, of the war, of the unjust way we were treated. Nothing I'd studied had said anything about dwarves and elves sharing territory, but then again, that wasn't the sort of thing a demon teacher would have bothered with.

The elf whispered a few things under his breath, then held up his hand. A book appeared from nowhere, and he began to leaf through that one.

"Ah yes. There were dwarves here in the early days. Some of them relocated. The rest died out."

I leaned over the counter. "Is there any mention of an Andvari?"

He shook his head. "No, but the elven histories don't go into any detail about these particular dwarves—or any dwarves actually. You'll need to check with them to see if this Andvari is still alive or not."

My mouth dropped open as I processed what he'd just said. "Two and a half million years ago? You think there might be a dwarf still alive from then?"

I'd always assumed dwarves had life expectancies numbering in the five digits. Either Andvari was long dead, or Terrelle was wrong and he'd perhaps been descended from the dwarves who'd lived here, or he was the Methuselah of the dwarven race.

"I doubt it, but then again I don't know much about dwarves." The librarian shut the book and returned it to its place on the shelves with a flick of his wrist.

I got the feeling I was being dismissed. Not that it mattered, because the information I needed wouldn't be found here. Hopefully it would be found among the dwarves. And I knew the dwarf I was going to visit first.

Oma wasn't surprised to see me, although she complained for five whole minutes about demons coming and going and eating all her food. Then she set a huge plate of bread, cheese, fruit, and pickled fish in front of me, along with the biggest mug of ale I'd ever seen.

"I'm still not going with you to rob a sorcerer," she told me. "So if you're here to pester me about that, then you can leave right now."

"I'm not here for that," I said before stuffing one of the pickled fish into my mouth.

"Good. And I'm glad to see that you haven't been shot again. It seems you've been taking my advice to heart."

I'll admit I was being more cautious. Me. An imp. But the thought of being stuck in a human prison, or even dying had me concerned. At the end of the day I was pretty sure my impulsive chaotic nature would get me in hot water as it always had, but there was no sense in being even more foolish than I already was.

"I'm actually here looking for a dwarf that most likely lived in the mountains among the Klee—the dark elves, as legend says."

She shook her head. "Those dwarves left for the western ranges over two million years ago. It's doubtful any of them are still alive, but if you know their family name, I might be able to tell you who the descendants are."

Here was the sticky part. "I don't know his family name. I've been told he was a fish shifter."

"That's not dwarven magic." She sat down across from me. "Perhaps he had an amulet that allowed him to change form?"

"Maybe. Or perhaps he was just a good swimmer?"

She laughed. "Now *that* would be rare. Most of us can tread water and paddle short distances, but we're not known for have strong swimming abilities."

"If I knew the dwarven families who'd descended from those who lived in the eastern mountains, maybe I can track down the ones I'm looking for. The original dwarf was named Andvari."

She frowned, as if trying to remember something, so I went on.

"Legend has it that Andvari was a dwarf who was a fish shifter. He lived among the dark elves and was very rich. He was robbed by Loki who took all his gold and a ring that was spelled to attract wealth."

"He owned a ring spelled to attract wealth? That he traded an elf for?" she asked.

I shrugged. "I got the feeling he'd spelled it himself, because after it was stolen, he switched the enchantment to a curse."

She got up and walked to a shelf full of books and knick-knacks. "That's a *very* specific skill. Any dwarf can enchant metals, but the ability to cast a wealth spell is rare. And the ability to reverse the spell into a curse without even having possession of the ring? I don't even know how that might have been possible."

"Could he have put the curse on the ring with a trigger in case it was stolen?" Dwarves were especially paranoid about people stealing stuff from them. I could see someone preemptively cursing an object, with the spell taking effect as soon as someone other than the owner touched it, or put it on or something.

"That was my thought as well." She pulled a book off the shelf and brought it back to the table. "Let me see if there are any notes in this regarding a wealth ring. If it was stolen, Andvari might have put out a reward for its recovery, as well as the details of the curse so the finder would turn it in for the bounty rather than keep it themselves."

I ate my cheese, bread, and pickled fish as I watched her page through the book. Finally she pointed at a page, squinting closely at it.

"The Troutswiftsons. It looks like they continued offering a reward for twenty generations."

"Troutswiftson?" That had to be the weirdest dwarven family name I'd ever heard.

Oma wrinkled her nose. "Those eastern dwarves were odd. It seems this family earned their fortune not only catching, processing and selling fish in Hel, but in the human world as well. Trout and pike were their most popular products." Oma looked up, a dreamy expression on her face. "Oh, I love trout. I haven't had it in so long."

I made a mental note to get Oma some trout. If we could arrange for grocery deliveries and Amazon Prime in Hel, there was no reason I couldn't get her some fresh fish.

"This curse is very unpleasant," she went on. "It seems whoever possesses the ring gets ruin and death instead of wealth. The reward offer warns the finder not to wear the ring, and to handle it with gloves on, just to be safe."

Had I put it on? Again I tried to remember when Lux first brought the rings home, and I stuck one on each finger. Had this ring been one of them? I still couldn't remember.

"Does the reward notice define ruin and death?" I asked, wondering if the undead rats were just the tip of the curse iceberg.

"No, but let me go back a bit farther now that I know their family name, and see if I can find anything else."

I drank my beer, then admired the childish artwork I'd carved into her table as she continued to search the book.

With a sigh, she closed it and returned it to the shelf. "Andvari died twelve thousand years after the theft. I could find no details on the specifics of the curse, but I would assume it would follow whoever wore the ring last."

Which was probably me. Fuck my life.

"Does the curse end when the ring is returned?" I asked.

"Yes, but there's a bit of a problem in that there are no descendants of Andvari Troutswiftson left alive."

"No one? Not even a fifth cousin twice removed? Anyone?"

She shook her head. "No. Dwarven genealogy is very thorough. The entire line has died out."

I stood and started to pace. "Then how do I break this curse?"

Oma chuckled. "I suspected as much. You have the ring. And, of course, you put it on."

"With my luck? Of course I did—I must have since I've got an entire undead army camped out around my house." I stopped pacing and turned to her. "Please tell me you know of a way to break this curse. Is there a dwarf I can give the ring to, or someone who can reverse the spell?"

She shrugged. "Convince someone more foolish than you to put it on?"

It wouldn't be hard to do that, but Lux would have a fit. Damn it, why couldn't my adopted kid have been an Angel of Chaos? This would have been so much easier if his moral code was just a little bit more on the flexible side.

"Lux found it in the dirt. Do you think if I bury it, or throw it into the sun, or..."

Her eyebrows rose. "Whoever had it probably died long ago, and the curse went dormant with their death. I'm going to assume it was buried with them, and the curse was reactivated when your son found it and you put it on."

"How about a sorcerer? Maybe one of them could break the curse?" I thought of Gareth and winced. After throwing my weight around in his office and threatening him, I doubted he'd be at all sympathetic to my plight. And I was sure no amount of money would persuade him to even attempt reversing this curse.

Oma shook her head. "Dwarven magic is unlike elven

magic—which is what human magic is based on. A sorcerer might be able to give you something to protect you against the undead, but they wouldn't be able to reverse the curse."

"How about a necromancer?" I was grasping at straws here. I didn't know any necromancers. Wyatt didn't know any necromancers. For all I knew, it was a completely lost magical art.

The dwarf pursed her lips in thought. "Perhaps. Although their magic is not the same as ours, they have fundamental control over the dead. If the curse is simply raising and sending the dead to attack you, having a necromancer work a counter-spell might do the trick. If there is another component to the curse, such as financial losses or bad luck, those would still remain, though."

I shoved another pickled fish into my mouth and rose. "Thank you, Oma."

Dealing with financial loss or bad luck wouldn't be nearly as horrible as zombies everywhere I went. Fuck, with my weird chaos, bad luck always walked by my side. And although losing money would suck, I'd find a way around that.

I needed to get back home. And then I needed to scour the human world in search of a necromancer.

CHAPTER 23

I got home to find my house under siege by zombies. This time the rats and other roadkill were substantially outnumbered by human corpses. My horses and the goat were holed up in the stable. Boomer was inside cowering under the dining room table. Lux was peering worriedly out the front window. Nyalla, on the other hand, was entertaining. Standing next to her by the French doors looking out at my pool patio was a woman with short, bright green and blue hair, and an old guy who looked like he'd just come inside from gardening. I assumed they had something to do with Amber's wedding, although I couldn't understand why Nyalla would have invited them to meet here and have to run the gauntlet through a zombie apocalypse when she could have asked them to join her at the nearest Panera instead.

"Most unfortunate," the man said as if he were looking at sub-par rose blooms instead of zombies dragging themselves around my patio.

"Sam!" Nyalla turned around with a smile. "I'm glad

you're back. This is Tamika Pickens. She's a paranormal investigator."

The woman with the cap of mermaid curls came up and shook my hand. "Sorry there wasn't anything I could do. Ghosts are more my thing. Have you tried bashing in their brains?"

"I've been doing that, but more just keep coming," I told her. Nyalla had been busy, and I was thrilled she'd made the effort to assist with my undead problem, even if the Scooby crew couldn't help.

"And this is George." Nyalla did the Vanna White thing toward the gardener. "He's a necromancer."

My brain did that screechy noise. "A *necromancer?*"

Nyalla was friends with a necromancer? How the fuck did I not know that? I eyed the man, thinking he didn't exactly look like the sort of guy who'd be in Nyalla's social group. Maybe she'd found him on the internet? I should have Googled necromancers after that first dead rat showed up at my door. I sprang forward to shake the man's dirt-smudged hand, then asked the most important question of the decade.

"Can you resurrect Elvis? I'm marrying the Archangel Michael in Vegas and we'd really like the real thing to officiate instead of an impersonator. Except we'd like him to look like Elvis and not like a corpse that's been in the ground for decades, so maybe resurrect him back to 1977. Actually, can you resurrect him back to 1960 when he was really hot?"

He shook my hand. "Satan…you're not quite what I expected."

I waved away the compliment. "Now, about Elvis —"

"As Nyalla can attest, resurrection is a very difficult process, fraught with disastrous consequences if the slightest part of the ritual is off."

I shrugged. "I'll take my chances. Elvis—"

"Elvis has been dead for too long." His expression was

stern. "You're better off with an impersonator than a skeleton that lacks the vocal cords to speak, let alone sing."

"Fuck." I sighed in disappointment. "I was really hoping for the real Elvis at my wedding."

"Weren't we all," the man drawled. "Now, let's return to the immediate problem of undead surrounding your house and attacking the residents. Have you been able to locate the person who cast the curse?"

I shook my head. "He's been dead for millions of years. He didn't curse me specifically, but a ring. So far I haven't been able to find a way to break it."

"Ah. Unfortunate indeed." He walked back over to the French doors and looked out.

"Can you break the curse?" I asked hopefully, digging the ring out of my pocket and extending it to him.

He held up a hand and backed a few steps away from the ring. "Charms and curses are not part of my skill set. I can provide a barrier along your driveway and entrances so that you and others can come and go without being attacked, but that's all I can do. From what I can see, this problem is only going to get worse. I suggest finding a descendant of the original mage, or possibly one of their students, because ending the curse is the only way to truly stop this."

Fuck. "I appreciate any help you can provide," I told him, thinking that at least the pizza delivery people wouldn't cut me off, and I wouldn't need to worry about Nyalla being bitten every time she tried to leave the house.

He turned to Nyalla. "I'll put something temporary in place, but I'll need to come back in a few days. Until then, make sure you have a weapon with you when you come and go. And tell that little boy I'm so sorry this is happening to him."

I frowned. "What little boy?"

"The cursed angel," Tamika chimed in. "He's a cute little fella, too."

I swear my heart stopped in my chest. "Lux? He's not the one who's cursed. I'm the one who's cursed. He stole the rings, but I think I put the cursed one on…"

Damn it. He'd giggled and tried some on as well. Suddenly it all made sense as to why the zombies were mostly around the house, and why they'd only started showing up elsewhere when Lux had been with me, even momentarily. Me being cursed I could deal with, but my little angel? That moved this whole thing from a pain-in-the-ass inconvenience to an emergency.

"He's the one that's cursed." George gave me a sad smile and headed toward the front door with Tamika at his heels. "I'm sure you'll find a way to break it. I hope so, anyway. Angels are practically immortal and it would be horrible for that little guy to have to deal with zombies attacking him for billions of years."

That was not going to happen. I glanced helplessly outside at the shambling rats, rotted people, and road kill, and felt a surge of anxiety. I couldn't let this go on. I couldn't let poor Lux spend his life like this. I had to do something. I had to find someone to break the curse.

CHAPTER 24

Gregory's arms came around me and he kissed my cheek. "How was your day?"

"Oh, just fucking lovely. One of the rings Lux picked up is cursed, and that's why I've got the entire cast of *Walking Dead* extras outside my house. Worse, zombie shit is now starting to appear wherever he…I mean, wherever *I* go. I can't return the ring to the fucker who cursed it because he died over two million years ago and doesn't have one descendant left to break the curse. Nyalla managed to find a necromancer but all he can do is pop by every week or so and basically do the pest exterminator version of a whole-house bug spray. I'm gonna have to fucking deal with this shit for the rest of my life."

"A necromancer? Can he resurrect Elvis?"

This angel clearly knew what was important. "No. He says Elvis has been dead too long, so we're out of luck there."

"Well, can he at least keep the zombies out of your pool?" Gregory honed right in on one of the few good things that had come out of today's events.

"That's something the necromancer can do as well as keep them away from the entrances and the driveway. Although he did say drowning them would be an effective control technique. I considered it for all of five seconds, but I like swimming in my pool too much to use it to drown zombies."

"Understandable."

I felt his chest shake with laughter and turned to swat him. "It's not funny. Well, the dead guy crawling out of the casket at the graveside funeral was funny, but the rest of it isn't. The necromancer isn't sure he can keep up the protection zones forever. If I can't find a way to end this curse, I'm going to wind up having to deal with zombies everywhere. No one is going to want to ever deliver food to our house again. I'll bet we won't even be able to get package delivery or mail service." I frowned. "Maybe I'll have all my mail forwarded to Wyatt's house. The zombies seem to stay away from his place, probably because he's gotten quite the reputation for killing the undead in his video games."

"You'll be fine." He kissed my forehead. "I love you, Cockroach."

"Yeah, I love you too," I said with far less enthusiasm than usual. "It gets worse."

"Worse than a cursed ring and zombies following you everywhere?"

"Much worse." I took a deep breath because I hadn't wanted to tell him this. But he needed to know. Lux was just as much Gregory's child as he was mine, and the archangel needed to know. "The necromancer said I'm not the one with the curse, Lux is." I watched the smile vanish from Gregory's face. "I don't want to worry the little guy so I didn't say anything to him. Nyalla knows. The wedding is tomorrow, but the very next day I'm devoting every moment of my time to getting this curse broken. I'm just letting you know that I won't be attending Ruling Council meetings, or meetings with world leaders, or meetings with Asta about Elven labor relations laws, or taking that last ring back. I don't care if I have to go through the genealogy of every fucking dwarf in Hel, I'm going to find someone who can break this damned curse."

"Understood." He touched my cheek. "I'm not worried. We'll protect Lux, and while you're interviewing dwarves, I'll see what I can do to help."

Actually, there was a lot he could do to help. Zombies weren't a problem in the asteroid belt or on most of the planets in the galaxy. He and Lux could explore the universe and not worry about zombie anything off-planet.

There wouldn't be undead in Aaru either, but I wasn't willing to send Lux up there with a bunch of Ancients. That would be an absolutely last resort—as in last, last resort.

"So how was your day? Bet it doesn't top mine in terms of suckage." I forced a smile, trying to think of something besides the fact that my little angel had managed to get himself cursed.

"I think it might come close." He looked around my house. "Can we take a brief trip? There's something I want to show you."

"Lux is upstairs with Nyalla getting ready for the rehearsal dinner," I told him. "I've got time as long as we're back in ten or fifteen minutes."

He gathered me close, and in a blink we were no longer in my living room.

"Is this Ireland again?" I looked around at the rocky ground, the farms, the cluster of houses a quarter mile down the road from us.

"Scotland."

He walked down the side of the road and I followed. A few cars passed, the drivers eyeing us curiously.

"And why are we in Scotland?" He'd said his day was

shitty—well, the Angel of Order equivalent of shitty. For all I knew that could mean this road wasn't exactly straight, but Gregory tended to be a bit more particular in what he found shitty and not shitty.

"Three dead angels." He stopped and with a flick of a finger, three bodies appeared.

I immediately looked around, searching for a wild gate and didn't see one. "How the fuck did the monster-things get here from Ireland?"

He shrugged. "Swam? Flew? Teleported? None of the humans have seen anything odd, but as far as I can tell these angels died the same way as the other ten."

I shook my head, baffled. "So, we've got toothy killers roaming the world and taking down groups of angels?"

Gregory walked over to one of the dead. "It appears that way."

I looked around once more. "I don't see a wild gate like I did last time." Following Gregory, I knelt down and examined the dead angel. "But yeah, I agree that the cause of death appears the same."

"Perhaps the wild gate at the last location had nothing to do with the deaths." Gregory began to pace. "Perhaps that was just a coincidence, and something else is preying on angels."

"But what killed them? It wasn't hellhounds. This doesn't seem like the sort of damage a demon would do." I looked up at him. "Humans? I've gone through the Blue Fire catalogue and haven't seen any weapons that would do this, but they're not the only game in town. Another company sold those weapons to the Phoenix PD. Maybe they've got a weapon that does this. Or maybe some other company does."

I'd assumed from how far apart the other dead angels were that they'd been killed by multiple attacking creatures, but what if the chewed-up physical bodies and spirit-selves weren't actually chewed, but torn apart by some sort of projectile weapon?

"It's a possibility," Gregory agreed. "If a human weapon did this, then they're distributing to at least two countries."

I stood and watched him pace. He'd been unconcerned when I'd told him about the Blue Fire weapons, but seeing something like this firsthand had clearly shaken him. Ten angels dead in Ireland, and now these three here in Scotland. What the fuck was happening? Humans might be uneasy about angels in their midst, but I didn't get the impression from anyone I'd spoken to that they would just start exterminating them.

"And why were they here?" I mused.

He stopped and frowned over at me. "What?"

I gestured toward the dead. "These three angels. Why were they here, together in the middle of fucking nowhere Scotland? Same with the ones in Ireland. Ten angels? Out on a country road next to a cow field?"

Was this a pastural appreciation club where they all met once a week or something? I had no idea what angels liked to do for fun. For all I knew they were out here admiring the dirt or the grass.

"I don't know." Gregory scowled. "None of the dead angels were part of the rebellion. They were from different choirs. I'll need to ask and see if they knew each other. Living here in the human world has been difficult for many angels. Perhaps they were coming together to commiserate, or share tips on life in a corporeal form?"

"In the middle of fucking nowhere?" I repeated. "That's the sort of thing you do in a coffee shop, or a pub, or over dinner at someone's house, not by the side of a barely-traveled road in the country. I know you angels aren't all that savvy about this sort of thing, so let me clue you in here: Either these guys were getting ready to set up and do some plein air painting, or they were purposely meeting out here in a place where no one would see them and tell. They didn't want other angels—as in the Ruling Council—to know they were meeting each other. And they definitely didn't want you all to know what they were talking about."

Gregory slowly shook his head. "It seems an unnecessary precaution, Cockroach. There are less than twenty thousand angels and our ability to sense each other is not the same here as it was in Aaru. I can't imagine why angels would feel they would need to journey to a remote location to meet in order to avoid detection."

I shrugged. "Well, you'd know better than me."

He sighed. "You are right, though. My concerns are not just with how the angels died and why, but what brought them together in these areas. Did their killer lure them here? But that is something I will need to investigate on my own, and not now. Now, we have a wedding rehearsal to attend, and a little angel to protect from an army of the undead."

He took my arm and we were back in my house.

"I wish I could have been more help," I told him.

"Me too. I'm not sure whether it would have been better for you to have found a wild gate in that spot or not. At least then we'd have some idea what happened to those angels."

"I'll put Terrelle on the human weapon research, while you're figuring out why these angels are meeting up. But right now, we need to get ready."

Gregory waved a hand across his chest and instead of his usual jeans and polo shirt, he was suddenly in a dark gray silk suit. I only wished I could get dressed that fast—and look so good in formal attire.

The rehearsal at the church was thankfully brief. I was distracted the entire time, eyeing entrances and hoping this wasn't one of those churches with dead priests in some crypt beneath the nave or a little graveyard beside the chapel.

We practiced walking up the aisle, then as the minister went over the ceremony, I broke ranks with the other bridesmaids and walked over to peek out the tall stained glass window.

Fuck. Just as I'd feared there was an acre of white headstones just outside where I stood.

We finished up and I practically snatched Lux from the alter steps and teleported him to the restaurant.

"Ma?" Lux reached out and touched my arm, a puzzled frown on his face.

"I'm just in a hurry to get a drink and some appetizers," I lied. "Aren't you hungry? I'm starving. Here, have a mushroom stuffed with crab meat. And a glass of wine."

I shoved a plate and glass into Lux's hands, then went to check the building.

"Are there any cemeteries nearby?" I asked the hostess. "A farm? Lots of roadkill? A wooded area? A dumpster with rats and mice?"

The woman took a step away from me. "No! Why would you ask that?"

Relieved, I looked out the front door, just to check, then wandered around past diners and waitstaff, to peer out windows and doors. Satisfied that any undead would need to shamble several miles to get here, I returned to Lux and grabbed a glass of wine for myself.

The dinner was lovely, but I barely remembered what we ate. I didn't want Amber's wedding ruined by zombies. If it had been me that was cursed, I might have found a way to back out of my bridesmaid duties, but I couldn't ask that of little Lux. And I didn't want him to know. I didn't want anything to change in his life because of this.

Just one day. I just needed to get through one more day,

then I could turn Hel upside down to find someone that could break this curse.

Just one more day.

CHAPTER 25

"Are you sure?" Nyalla frowned at me. "You love getting your nails done. And your hair. There's mimosas, and brunch."

I looked out the front window. There were no zombies in my driveway or by the door. There hadn't been any by the pool. Clearly George knew his shit. But I was well aware that a fucking hoard of undead were in the woods beside my house, and lining the edge of the pool patio.

I needed to protect Lux. I needed to keep him safe. That was more important than getting my hair done and drinking mimosas.

"Cockroach, go have your fun. Be a bridesmaid." Gregory handed me a cup of coffee. "I'll take care of Lux. I'll make sure he's at the church at the requisite time."

"But not before the requisite time." I was worried that the longer Lux was in any particular area, the more time dead shit would have to rise up and make their way toward him.

He kissed the top of my head. "Go. I am perfectly capable of taking care of our child."

I was such an idiot. Of course the Archangel Michael

could keep a bunch of zombies from Lux. Mimosas. Mani, pedi. Brunch. I took a deep breath.

"Okay."

But I worried the entire time we were getting buzzed and being fussed over by salon employees. When we were done, a fleet of limos drove us over to the church, and we went into a side room to get dressed.

I kept looking out the window at the cemetery. Did the dirt look disturbed? Was that a live animal moving about in the gardens, or a dead one?

"You look wonderful, Sam." Nyalla gave me a quick hug. "And the bachelorette party was amazing."

I did look amazing. The ugly puce dress wasn't as horrible as I'd expected. My hair was piled up in a cascade of dark curls. My makeup was Instagram ready. I picked up the bouquet of creamy white flowers I was supposed to carry down the aisle, and forced a smile.

"I'm going to head out for some fresh air. I'll be right back."

Nyalla frowned. "The guests are arriving. We need to line up in ten minutes."

"I'll be back," I assured her. Then without waiting for a reply, I snuck out the back door and into the graveyard.

The dirt was definitely disturbed. I went from headstone to headstone all the way to the back of the church graveyard. Looking over the dense green hedges, I let out a stream of curses. Not fifty yards away was another cemetery—this one huge with several mausoleums along the left side.

Something grabbed my leg and I yelped, spinning around. A skeleton grinned up at me. Bony fingers raked down the skin of my calf and he leaned forward to bite my shin. Kicking, I managed to get my leg free just as I felt hands clawing at my back.

I shrieked and jabbed an elbow back into something

squishy. A foul smell filled the air. Where the fuck had these things come from? I was surrounded by corpses, all of them coming for me. Lux might be the one cursed, but I was the one who these fuckers were attacking.

Shit. The curse. Death, ruin, and tragedy to the cursed. The curse wasn't just about losing wealth or having zombies pounding at your door, it was about losing the things you loved most. And what did Lux love most? Me. Gregory. Nyalla. His friends, his uncles and aunt. No wonder these fuckers were attacking me.

I summoned my sword, and started slashing. Zombies bit at me, grabbed my dress, clawed my skin. Unwilling to ditch the bouquet I was supposed to carry down the aisle, I wielded my sword one-handed, resorting to smacking the undead with the flowers as I tried to kill as many as possible.

Faint sounds of organ music issued from the church. Damn it. The wedding was starting, and here I was out in a graveyard. Lopping off a few more heads, I pushed past the zombies and took off. I dismissed my sword as I ran up the church steps, hesitating just a second before I walked over the threshold, still amazed that I could enter a church without bursting into flames. The organ music swelled, and I looked up to see other bridesmaids waiting at the narthex with their paired groomsman.

"It's about time you arrived," Gabriel snapped. His eyes widened at the sight of my dress and he didn't say another word. I'd rendered him mute. Hopefully it was a permanent condition.

"Go, go," Nyalla urged me. Then her eyes widened as well.

I put my hand on Gabriel's arm. Luckily the angel's sense of decorum and appropriate conduct overcame his shock at my appearance because he turned and walked by my side down the aisle.

Glancing over to the left, I saw my Lows occupying the

pews, sitting right beside human friends and family. Halfway down was Gimlet, picking his nose and wiping the snot on the bibles. I bit back a laugh, wondering why he hadn't come to the wedding as Samael. I guess he still wasn't quite ready to rejoin his family. I knew who Gimlet was. Lux knew who Gimlet was. But Samael had his personal energy so tightly locked down that to everyone else in this church, he was a Low.

Here, but not here. Well, he was going to have to come to terms with all this pretty damned soon, because the youngest archangel was *not* walking down the aisle as my Maid of Honor in the form of Gimlet.

Dar and Asta sat on the groom's side of the aisle, Karrae between her mother and Andor, the dwarven nanny. Leethu sat in the front row with Uriel on one side and Amber's mother on the other. It was nice of Amber to recognize the demon as a parent. I wondered how her human mother felt about sitting next to a succubus. I wondered how her human mother felt about having a daughter who was half-succubus.

I took my place beside Darci, ignoring her dismayed gasp at my appearance, and watched the other bridesmaids and groomsmen walk down the aisle. The music changed, everyone stood, and there was the bride.

Amber was absolutely beautiful in a creamy lace gown that was snug enough to show off her curves, but not so tight that she looked like she was ready to perform a Superbowl halftime show. Wyatt walked by her side, his arm linked with hers. He seemed pleased about the whole thing. That was a relief. I know he had been left with some rather mixed feelings about demons after our relationship, finding out that his sister was a changeling, and discovering that his biological sister had been a slave in Hel for eighteen years. I'd expected to see a for-sale sign out front of his house for the last year. He might not like all the comings and goings at my house, but I knew he'd worked out an odd sort of friendship with Gregory, and he clearly loved Amber as well as Nyalla. I guess that meant he was somewhat accepting of all the shit-show I'd brought into his life.

Although to be honest, the shit-show had been in his life long before I'd arrived.

Amber's eyes widened in shock as she saw me, but she quickly composed herself and smiled at Irix for the rest of her walk down the aisle. At the altar, Wyatt placed his sister's hand in her fiancé's then bent down to kiss Amber's cheek before taking his seat beside his mother.

The minister began. "Dearly beloved, we are gathered here today—"

"What happened to you?" Amber whispered furiously to me. "Your dress is in shreds. Your hair is a wreck. Your bouquet looks like you were using it to beat someone. And is that blood? That's blood, isn't it?"

"Yep." I tried to fluff up my bouquet a bit and two more roses toppled from their stems to the floor.

"Amber?"

She turned to Irix. "Huh? Oh, I do.

The minister turned to Irix. "And do you, Irix take Amber Shania Lowry to be your lawful wedded wife, to have and to hold—"

The church doors shuddered. Shadows darkened the sunlight coming in from the windows. I winced and fidgeted, wishing this minister would hurry the fuck up.

"I do." Irix stared adoringly at Amber. Loud thumps came from the door.

"Should someone let them in?" Darcie whispered at me.

"No!" I grimaced and lowered my voice. "No. They need to stay outside."

The minister spread his arms wide. "Irix and Amber will

now exchange rings as a symbol of their love and commitment to each other."

Lux stood and approached the altar. Everyone in the church said "Awww," even though my little angel was buck naked instead of wearing his little tuxedo. His wings were outstretched, his golden curls shiny, his blue eyes sparkled with joy. My chest felt like it would burst with love.

He shot me a quick grin, then extended the crimson pillow toward Amber and Irix.

"Thank you, Lux." Amber beamed as she and Irix untied the rings from the pillow.

Really? My naked kid got a "thank you," while I got whispered-scolded for having blood on my torn dress. It was so unfair.

The banging on the door grew louder. Several guests turned to frown at it.

"Irix, please place your ring on Amber's left hand and repeat after me—"

I eyed the shadows on the windows nervously. With the stained glass I couldn't quite see how many were out there, but I was willing to bet they were banging on the glass just as the others were banging on the door.

"Amber, please place your ring on Irix's finger and repeat after me—"

I heard the shattering of glass from the front of the church. The doors shuddered.

"Hurry the fuck up," I snapped at the minister.

He blinked at me in shock. The church door flung open.

"Now. Say it now," I shouted.

Someone screamed.

"I now pronounce you man and wife," the minister said just before he dived behind the organ.

Irix bent down to kiss Amber, and I ran down the aisle, ditching my ratty bouquet and summoning my sword just as the zombies poured into the church. Halfway down the aisle I found myself pushed backward and nearly trampled as the wedding guests fled the zombies and rushed toward the altar.

Jumping to the side and hopping from pew to pew, I forced my way through the crowd. The Lows seated toward the back were smacking the zombies with bibles and psalm books. I lopped off as many heads as I could, trying to reach the door before every dead person and animal in town shambled their way in.

I caught a glimpse of Gimlet, and suddenly he was no longer the Low. Samael reached across a pew and grabbed me by the waist, throwing me through the air toward the doors. I fell a little short and dropped to the ground on top of several ripe corpses.

As I struggled to get to my feet amid the slimy gore, I felt someone grab the back of my dress and haul me upward. Samael punched several of the zombies back outside. I heard the stained glass windows begin to break, and glancing around I saw angels and demons fighting to keep the undead away from the humans crowded together in the front of the church.

"What the fuck is going on?" Samael shouted as he pushed the door closed. "Did you try to resurrect Elvis and it backfired? Why is there an army of undead trying to storm the church?"

"It's the damned ring," I yelled back, putting my whole weight into keeping the door closed. "Lux found it. It's cursed. I tried to take it back but the owner has been dead forever. I've buried it. I've thrown it away. Nothing works. It curses whoever possesses it."

The door hinges groaned. A crack appeared in the wood and splintered.

"I hate cursed shit. Hate." Samael frowned and stepped away from the door. "So it curses whoever possesses it?"

"Hold the door, dickhead!"

I'd barely gotten the words out of my mouth when the door burst open. I fell backward, scrambling to avoid the dead, rotted corpses that were once more pouring into the church. I heard Karrae and Lux shriek, and saw Andor shove them behind him. The dwarf picked up a zombie and tossed it into the pews, protecting the little angels.

"Destroy the brains!" Gregory shouted, still convinced that Wyatt's technique would work here. I hated to tell him, but headless zombies were just as much of a pain in the ass as ones with their brains intact.

I turned my attention back to the undead coming through the main door when Samael appeared before me. He had one of the zombies in a head-lock and was dragging him down to the floor. "I've got him. I'll hold him. You get the ring."

Okaaay. I wasn't sure what the fuck he was trying to do, but I was too curious to just ignore him. Dismissing my sword, I knelt down and helped Samael straddle and restrain the zombie.

"Put the ring on his finger," Samael ordered.

Could an undead "possess" the ring? Hell, it was worth a try.

I pulled the band from my bra where I'd stuffed it since this ugly bridesmaid dress didn't have any fucking pockets. Grabbing the zombie's hand I shoved the ring over a swollen, putrefied finger. The flesh tore free, oozing a yellowish liquid and bunching up around the dude's knuckle. Pushing the ring down over the flesh, I was pleased to see it helped hold the ring on.

"Got it!"

We both jumped free and watched. Nothing happened. Well, nothing except the humans screaming and the zombies still trying to kill everyone in the church.

"Wait. Let me try something." Samael grabbed the zombie

and vanished, appearing a second later without the corpse. "Did that work? They should follow the ring or something."

I looked around. Rafi was trying to rip heads off and stomp on the undead. Gregory was slashing with his sword. Uriel had grabbed one of the kneeling benches and was bludgeoning the zombies with it. Gabe had formed a barricade with pews to protect the humans and was stabbing the undead with a broken chair leg.

"Didn't work!"

Samael vanished again, returning with the ring-wearing zombie. Twisting the guy around, he snapped the corpse's hand off at the wrist and shoved it at me. I managed to get the ring off and back into my bra before the zombie came toward me. Calling my sword, I kicked the guy to the ground, and started chopping.

"Any other ideas?" I shouted as bits of rotted flesh flew from my blade.

"Nope. Guess this is your life now. Iblis and magnet for the undead." He laughed and tossed an arm at my feet.

This was so not funny. "It's not me that's cursed, you asswipe, it's Lux."

He stopped laughing at that. "*Lux* is cursed?"

"Yes, he's cursed." I slashed a zombie in two. "Fuck these things. Fuck this ring. Fuck that Loki bastard. And fuck that dwarf Andvari who should have at least had the courtesy to put an expiration date on this fucking cursed ring."

Samael stared at me. "Andvari? Fish-shifter Andvari? This ring is *Andvari's* ring?"

Suddenly everything clicked into place. That motherfucker. How the hell was he Loki? I guess the same way he was Gimlet. Maybe the humans got the story mixed up and blamed a Norse god instead of Satan. Maybe Samael blamed it all on Loki rather than take responsibility for this fuckup. Maybe Samael had been calling himself Loki at the time.

Either way, this was his fault, and this ring was his to deal with.

"You! This is all your fault you motherfucking cock-sucking son of a bitch!"

Samael backed up, hands raised. "Hey, it was a long time ago."

We could discuss that later, right now I had a church full of zombies to deal with. "How did you get it to stop? Undead haven't been attacking you for the last two million years. How the fuck did you stop it?"

Samael shrugged. "I gave the ring to a human, and made it their problem."

And that's exactly what *I* would have done if I didn't have a judgmental archangel for a fiancé and an Angel of Order for a kid.

"I guess the ring got passed around among humans until the last one died without unloading it," Samael went on. "Probably got buried with him and that's where Lux found it."

I thought furiously as I continued to slice and dice zombies. I just needed to find a person near death and give them the ring. I looked over at Gregory, knowing that wasn't going to fly. Plus there was always a chance the funeral home people would remove it and keep it, or that some relative would take it. Or a hospital worker, or someone at the morgue. Or grave robbers would snatch it. No, this ring needed to be gone forever, but how could I ensure that when Andvari was the only one who could break the spell?

The hoard of undead was slowly but steadily pushing us back to where the humans were huddled together. No matter how fast I cut them down, they just kept coming. Glancing to either side, I saw the angels were having the same problem. Soon we'd be backed to the altar, forming a barrier around the humans and hoping the curse ran out of undead before one got through to the humans.

Damn it, this needed to stop, and it needed to stop for good.

"What about Aaru?" I shouted to Samael. "Take possession of the ring. Go to Aaru. Give it to one of the Ancients there. Give it to Remiel and tell him to put it on."

Except Remiel wouldn't put the ring on just because Samael, or anyone told him to. Even if he did, the moment he left Aaru, the undead would be all over him. Ah well it would serve him right for being such an ass.

"I'm not going to Aaru." Samael scowled. "I'm never returning to Aaru. Ever. Never, ever, ever. Get someone else to do it."

I swung my sword in a wide arc and beheaded three zombies in one blow. "None of us can get in. I can't. None of your siblings can. Leethu, Terrelle, Irix, and the Lows can't teleport."

"Then find someone who can. Zip back to Hel and find an Ancient to do this for you, because I am *not* going to Aaru."

"You are such a fucking dick. I don't have time to go to Hel and convince an Ancient to put the ring on and go stay in Aaru forever. By the time I manage that, there will be tons of humans dead." Plus, knowing demons, there was a good chance the Ancient I convinced to do this would either decide to leave Aaru and I'd end up dealing with the same fucking problem in Hel, or they'd realize it was cursed and gift it to a random human as Samael had done.

I swung the sword one-handed and dug the ring back out of my bra. "Take it. You got us into this mess, you get us out."

Samael glared at me. "I'm not taking that ring."

"Ma! Ma!"

"Stay back, Lux," I shouted, once more extending the ring toward Samael. "Take it. You stole it from Andvari. You're the one he cursed. You fucking deal with it. I'm not letting my kid spend his life fighting zombies because you fucked up two million years ago and stole from a dwarf."

A deep voice from behind me called out. "Andvari? That's Andvari's ring?"

"*You* put it on and take the curse." Samael stepped away from me. "I dealt with it for hundreds of years. I'm not going through that again."

"You'd let Lux be deprived of his mother? Or have him hounded by zombies his whole life? For something *you* did?" I was so angry at Samael right now, not so much because he'd been the idiot who'd stolen the ring originally, but because he wouldn't step up to protect Lux when he needed to. Spoiled, selfish, overindulged youngest archangel. If he didn't make this right, then there would be no ugly Maid of Honor dress for him, and no wrist corsage.

Samael snarled, shoved one of the zombies, turned and punched me. My head snapped to the side, pain blooming all along my jaw.

"Stubborn, selfish, cowardly, dickhead," I yelled at him.

Samael punched me again, but this blow lacked the force of the first one. Then he took the ring from my hand and swore.

"You really do make a good Satan. Almost as good as I was." He jammed the ring on his own finger. "All right fuckers. This ring is mine! Mine, mine, mine. Come and get me."

He pushed his way through the crowd of undead and out the front door, but nothing changed. Instead of following Samael, the zombies kept coming toward us—coming toward Lux. I started to panic, chopping away with my sword. For every zombie I cut down, three more came at me. It made me wonder exactly how many corpses there were buried in this town.

"Get back in here and help us fight," I shouted, reaching

across that link I shared with every infernal being and tugging the Fallen angel toward me. "It's not working. They're not following you."

Did he have to truly want the ring? Maybe he had to be unaware of the curse to actually transfer the magic away from Lux and toward himself. Either way, I was out of ideas, and out of options.

Samael appeared beside me once again, pulling the ring from his finger before he started ripping the heads off zombies.

A short powerful form pushed between the pair of us. A muscular arm extended upward and grabbed the ring from Samael's hand. I looked down and saw Andor, his mouth a tight line in a light golden-brown beard.

"It *is* Andvari's ring." He scowled at the band. "Idiots. You're both a pair of idiots. I'd leave the two of you to deal with this yourselves, but I won't allow that little angel to be an innocent victim of a greedy dwarf's misguided temper."

Andor closed his fist around the ring. My sword vanished right out of my hand. The gravity in the room felt as if it had tripled, and I struggled to stay on my feet. Without my sword, I tried to launch a bolt of lightning at the zombies, but nothing happened. There was a sudden squeeze of pressure that made me drop to my knees. Everything went white and my head pounded like it was in a vice.

And then, just like that, the pressure was gone, even though the headache remained.

I staggered to my feet and opened my eyes. One by one, the zombies collapsed, becoming nothing more than decaying bodies and skeletons littering the church floor. With my mouth hanging open, I turned to look at Andor.

He opened his hand. The ring was now a lump of gold.

"You're..." I gaped at him. "Are you some long lost descendant of Andvari or something?"

"No." He turned his hand over and the lump of gold dropped to the floor. "I like your son. He's Karrae's best friend, and a very good influence on her, I might add. He does not deserve such a thing to happen to him. And this"— he pointed what was once a cursed ring—"is an abomination."

"I owe you a favor. Anything. I'm completely in your debt," I told the dwarf.

He laughed. "I have no need for a demon's favor, even one who is the Iblis."

I nodded, looking past him to where Karrae and Lux stood, holding hands. "Well, just in case you need something from me in the future, you've got it."

The dwarf turned and walked away. Gregory came up to me and wrapped me tightly in his arms.

"I thought for a moment there we were rubber tubed."

"Hosed," I corrected. "Yeah, me too. Did you know dwarves were nulls? Like, serious nulls?"

"How about you owe *me* a favor?" Samael interrupted. "After all, I helped fight these corpses. I put that damned ring back on. I wasn't even invited to this wedding, but here I am, helping."

I laughed. "Fine. What exactly do you want? You're already the Maid of Honor for my wedding. I'm even getting you a wrist corsage like you wanted."

"I get to give the speech at your wedding reception."

I glanced over at Gregory and bit back a smile at his horrified expression.

"Done. And Samael?" I waited for his eyes to meet mine. "You need to be in *this* form for my wedding, not Gimlet. And commando. There better not be any underwear on under that satin dress."

He grinned. "You can count on it."

I was tanning by the pool, listening to Godsmack, drinking chilled vodka, and trying not to think about human weapons that could kill angels or about possible human plots to lure groups of angels to their deaths when I heard the French doors open.

"Got some of that for me?" Terrelle plopped down in the lounge chair beside me.

I eyed my bottle of vodka, debating whether I was in a sharing sort of mood or not. "I don't know. Depends on what *you've* got for *me*."

Terrelle reached out and snatched up the bottle. "I've got *her*, that's what I've got."

I pivoted around on my chair and saw a woman standing a few feet behind Terrelle. At first I thought she was an elf, then I realized that she wasn't. She was tall and willowy, with silvery-blonde hair that hung down past her waist. Ears rose into delicate points through the hair, their skin the same translucent white as her face. Light green eyes met mine. No, this woman was definitely a fae, but not an elf.

"My names is Gwylla," she said in a light, musical voice.

"I'm a Sidhe, and I need to speak to you about the ring you have."

"Ring?" Fuck. That other ring, the last one, the one I hadn't returned—well, besides the one from Aaru that was hidden in the back of my underwear drawer, that is. With the wedding, and the zombies, and all the other shit, I'd forgotten about it.

"The ring." Gwylla moved to stand beside me. "It's a sidhe artifact, and by bringing it across the gates, it has severed a contract that has been in place for nearly ten thousand years."

I grabbed the vodka back from Terrelle. "Okay, let me have it. What contract? What's going to happen?"

The sidhe's eyes glowed. "I don't know. All I know is that the queen is coming. She's coming, and so is the king. Those who have held themselves from this world are no longer constrained to do so. The fae are coming, and no one is safe."

I took a swig of the vodka then passed it over to Terrelle. So much for my lazy day by the pool. So much for my summer, or even my year. With a sigh, I picked up my phone and texted Gregory.

AUTHOR'S NOTE*

This isn't The End! Sam's adventures will continue in 2021 with Through The Mirror - Imp Series, Book 12.

ACKNOWLEDGMENTS

Thanks to my copyeditor Kimberly Cannon whose eagle eyes catch all the typos and keep my comma problem in line, and to Damonza for cover design.

ALSO BY DEBRA DUNBAR

Accidental Witches Series

Brimstone and Broomsticks

Warmongers and Wands

Death and Divination

Hell and Hexes

Minions and Magic

Fiends and Familiars (2020)

Devils and the Dead (2020)

White Lightning Series

Wooden Nickels

Bum's Rush

Clip Joint

Jake Walk

Trouble Boys

Packing Heat (2020)

The Templar Series

Dead Rising

Last Breath

Bare Bones

Famine's Feast

Royal Blood

Dark Crossroads

* * *

<u>IMP WORLD NOVELS</u>

<u>The Imp Series</u>
A Demon Bound
Satan's Sword
Elven Blood
Devil's Paw
Imp Forsaken
Angel of Chaos
Kingdom of Lies
Exodus
Queen of the Damned
The Morning Star
With This Ring (2020)

* * *

<u>Half-breed Series</u>
Demons of Desire
Sins of the Flesh
Cornucopia
Unholy Pleasures
City of Lust

* * *

<u>Imp World Novels</u>
No Man's Land
Stolen Souls
Three Wishes

Northern Lights

Far From Center

Penance

* * *

<u>Northern Wolves</u>

Juneau to Kenai

Rogue

Winter Fae

Bad Seed